# HEAD HUNTER

# HEAD HUNTER

## CRYPTID ASSASSIN™ BOOK FOUR

### MICHAEL ANDERLE

DISRUPTIVE IMAGINATION

Copyright © 2020 Michael Anderle
Cover Art by Jake @ J Caleb Design
http://jcalebdesign.com / jcalebdesign@gmail.com
Cover copyright © LMBPN Publishing
A Michael Anderle Production

LMBPN Publishing
PMB 196, 2540 South Maryland Pkwy
Las Vegas, NV 89109

First US edition, March, 2020
eBook ISBN: 978-1-64202-808-9
Print ISBN: 978-1-64202-809-6

THE HEAD HUNTER TEAM

**Thanks to our Beta Readers**

Jeff Eaton, John Ashmore, and Kelly O'Donnell

**Thanks to the JIT Readers**

Diane L. Smith
Dorothy Lloyd
Deb Mader
John Ashmore
Peter Manis
Jeff Eaton
Jeff Goode
Dave Hicks

*If we've missed anyone, please let us know!*

**Editor**
Skyhunter Editing Team

# CHAPTER ONE

Any number of things pissed Niki Banks off.

She'd be the first to admit it was true. Apparently, she'd been born with a very short fuse so the list of possible triggers was long, but having anyone go behind her back jumped immediately to the top. It ran neck and neck with people knowingly and recklessly putting themselves in the path of danger, especially when they deliberately snuck around to obtain something they knew she wouldn't help with.

Which was—now that she thought about it—putting themselves in the path of danger knowingly and recklessly.

While she would have thought her sister knew her better than to choose to do so, it was probably exactly what she should have expected from Jennie. The woman was brilliant, and like most people with that kind of brain to complement an athletic and attractive appearance, she tended toward arrogance and a devil-may-care attitude in almost every aspect of her life.

The FBI Special Agent sighed as she stepped into the

elevator and pressed the button for it to take her to the fifteenth floor. Thankfully, that impetuousness hadn't affected her sibling's career choices and financial investments, and while she hated to say it, her little sister had somehow done better in the world than she had herself.

Well, she reminded herself grimly, the career choices after the woman had elected to head into the fucking Zoo and almost got her ass killed. Unfortunately, the sensible decisions didn't extend to her infatuation with the man who dragged her ass out of the jungle.

No one was perfect, despite what their parents liked to believe. Jennie was their golden child, a perception contradicted by the fact that they relied on her older sister to keep her out of all kinds of trouble.

It honestly sucked that Taylor McFadden had been there to get the woman out of trouble when Niki hadn't been able to, but it was better that someone had been there. This brought complications, but the alternative would have been much worse.

The elevator dinged and Niki stepped out and tried to control the rising, roiling pit of rage deep in her stomach. She didn't want an argument to begin until they were at least out of the building and on their way to the lunch they had managed to arrange around their busy schedules.

Her sister looked up from her desk as she stepped into the office. It wasn't quite a coveted corner space but it was large enough and there was one hell of a view overlooking the city.

"Well, this is much nicer than I thought it would be," Niki noted and studied her surroundings. The decorations were tasteful as well, which made her wonder if Jennie hadn't brought a professional in to do it for her.

The woman was notorious for making her working areas nothing other than a messy pile of papers. Then again, maybe the folks who paid her wanted something a little nicer to show to their investors.

"Yeah, it's not bad," Jennie replied with a soft chuckle. "My bosses wanted me to have a real office, even though most of my work is done in the underground labs. They like having a location where they can contact me without having to venture into the bowels of the building."

"I get that. Still, you might want to consider moving your work up here. You'll get much more natural light that way."

The woman shrugged and picked her purse up from the desk. "Exposure to natural light is overrated and I have the data to prove it."

"You do not have the data to prove it." Niki tried to keep her tone assertive but even so, she couldn't help the niggling hint of doubt that entered her mind as they walked toward the elevator.

"Okay, I haven't done any large-scale testing yet," Jennie admitted. "But I have run tests on myself to see if my work, mood, and overall health improves when I spend more of my time in natural light, and I noted no real changes."

"You didn't happen to factor in the time you spent in the Zoo, did you? Because I hear there's not very much sunlight inside the jungle itself."

"I may have," the younger woman said. "Still, my point stands."

"And have you run any tests regarding your side

projects involving software development?" she asked as the elevator doors closed and gave them privacy. "Do your bosses know about your skills in that area?"

"Probably, but I doubt they care. They're old-fashioned in the way they think computers were always meant to be gigantic machines that need to be stored in buildings to be taken seriously. Many of the current members of the board still like to receive all their updates the old-fashioned way."

Niki tilted her head and frowned. "Through email?"

"Written on paper."

The FBI Agent cringed. "Yep, I still have a few bosses who want their updates on paper too, but people kind of expect their government to be backward and resistant to change, not Fortune Five-Hundred companies."

"You should remember that the people running your government are the same ones running those companies," Jennie pointed out as they stepped into the lobby. "Once that is noted, all the other pieces of why our fucked-up world is the way it is start to fall into place."

They stopped outside to wait for a cab to come and pick them up, and Niki considered what her little sister had said. It was one of those things people talked about all the time but for some reason, anything they said was usually exactly that—talk.

Then again, she had come to terms with the fact that the woman was simply smarter than her in a variety of areas of life. Not all of them, she reminded herself, but still enough to earn respect.

"Where do you want to go for lunch?" Jennie asked as they slid into the taxi that had been called for them.

"This is your town, sis, so I'm down with any of your recommendations."

The woman obviously approved of that suggestion, and Niki's eyebrows raised when they pulled up in front of what looked like a fairly swanky Brazilian steakhouse a few minutes away from the office building.

"Are you sure you can afford this?" she asked as they paid the taxi driver. "You know I won't pick up any checks here, right?"

"I'm actually used to that," her companion answered and a small smirk played on her lips. "My sister works for the government and needs me to pay her checks for her."

"Because you choose the expensive places I wouldn't be able to afford and therefore wouldn't go to them on my own anyway."

"That's fair, but I suspect that if you ever elect to leave the FBI and find yourself a job in the private sector, you'll be able to finally let yourself enjoy the finer things in life."

She couldn't help but agree as they entered the restaurant, where a tall, handsome man with dark skin and an accent guided them to a table.

"Besides," Jennie continued. "I'll be able to pass this off as a business lunch so the company will pay for it anyway."

The agent raised an eyebrow as they looked at the drink menu. "Is that...uh, you know, legal?"

Her sister shrugged dismissively. "Eh, worst-case, they turn me down for the lunch bill and I pay for it out of pocket. It'll be worth it to be able to spend time with you, big sis. Besides, their lunch prices are much better than the dinner prices, trust me."

"I did want to talk to you about something." Niki's tone

of voice changed to something less jovial as the waiter stopped beside them to take their drink orders.

"That's a little ominous," Jennie said and turned to the man. "I'll have bubbly water with lime squeezed in."

"Same for me," she said.

"And a full *churrasco* experience for us both," the other woman said to complete the order.

"The full…what now?"

"They bring hunks of meat on spits directly from the fire, and as much as you can eat," her sister explained with a slightly teasing grin.

"Oh, that sounds…lovely." Niki grunted and refocused. She didn't want to let the admittedly appealing thought of all-she-could-eat meat get in the way of what she wanted to say to her sister. "Speaking of hunks of meat, how did your chat with Taylor go?"

"Taylor…who?"

The agent narrowed her eyes. "That bullshit didn't work on Mom or Dad and it definitely won't work on me. Taylor McFadden, the guy currently in the hospital? You know they alert me whenever he gets any visitors, right?"

Jennie tried to show no sign of surprise on her face and failed spectacularly. "That's an incredible invasion of my privacy."

"It's a military hospital, dumbass. You sign away your rights to privacy the moment you step through the door."

Her younger sister paused and flipped the wooden coin on their table to the green side as a couple of waiters approached with their meal. "Well, what do you have to say to me? Do you plan to keep me from talking to him?"

"That depends." Niki smiled as the servers asked her if

she wanted certain cuts of meat. By the time they were finished with the first round, her plate was piled high with a variety that made her mouth water. "What did you and he have to talk about?"

Jennie cut a piece of juicy flank steak and popped it into her mouth before she replied. "I mostly only introduced myself. He was fairly out of it, drugged out of his gourd, so it took me a few attempts to finally get through the haze."

"It's almost like he's been through an experience that left him near death and his body mostly broken and he needs time to recover or something."

"Yeah, well, once he finally realized who I was, we talked. Eventually, when visiting hours were closing, I asked him if he wanted to continue the conversation over dinner when he was discharged from the hospital."

The agent paused in cutting her food and held her brown gaze pinned on the plate for a few long seconds before she took a deep breath. "What did he say?"

Her companion narrowed her eyes and studied her a little more closely. "He said that would be cool and to tell him when and where. You know I'm a grown-ass woman, right? I get to do what I choose to and with whomever I choose, regardless of that stick up your ass you have about my personal life—or, let's be honest, lack thereof."

"I realize that, Jennie. I do," Niki said. She sighed deeply and leaned back in her seat to look her sister in the eye. "It's only... I don't look forward to eventually having to fix broken hearts over this, you know?"

The two didn't say anything for the next few minutes and instead, focused on their food. It seemed both wanted to avoid the conversation for as long as they could manage to do so.

"I have to ask," Jennie said finally, her mouth half-full of chicken, and waved her fork at her companion. "This interest you have does seem a little more focused on Taylor than on me. Is there something between the two of you that you'd like to tell me about? Because I don't want to tread on any toes here. If you're interested—"

"I'm not interested," she interrupted quickly. "At least not beyond your involvement."

"If you say so," the woman replied and suddenly, both became overly interested in enjoying their delicious meal instead of the conversation that had held their attention.

---

"That's right, my name is Victoria. Soon to be Queen Bitch Victoria if you don't stop snorting testosterone before you call me."

Bobby looked up from one of the combat mechs he had been tasked to work on and focused his attention on where Vickie leaned back in her office chair. She propped her feet on the desk and held the phone pressed against her ear.

"Victoria?" he asked and raised an eyebrow. "Really? Will you ask us to call you that now too?"

She covered the receiver on the phone quickly. "Nope, but these assholes are outdoing themselves today so I thought that I would impose a little order on their chaos."

"You know they're—"

"Yeah, the more attention I give them, they simply enjoy it all the more. I know. But still, you can tell they get all sweaty and clammy when I raise my voice at them like that and it is a little gratifying, I have to admit— No, no, I'm still here, but if you want me to answer, you'll have to act a little more civil."

Bobby needed a few seconds to realize that the last sentence wasn't meant for him before he turned his attention to his work. He didn't have anything to say about how Vickie ran the sales side of their business, given how profitable it had become. She had a natural talent for the work, which made him wonder if she might want to look into sales and maybe even marketing courses at her school. It might provide an opportunity to minor in a branch of the field.

She certainly had the brains for it.

Taylor would agree with him on that if the man wasn't still in the hospital. It was easy to think that maybe he was taking too long to recover from his injuries, but the mechanic had seen paperwork on the injuries his boss was recovering from as well as the condition of the mech he had worn at the time. The dumbass had put himself in the blast radius of some of the most powerful ordnance the US Military had at their disposal. You didn't simply walk away from that shit.

He knew Vickie was similarly concerned about the man's recovery, and her acting out during the calls was her way to release a little tension and show how concerned she was.

"Look, I don't mean to be rude," the woman admitted to the man on the phone. "There are stress factors over on our end... Well, yeah, I know you guys talk about it over drinks and that you get drinks paid for you for the stories.

But honestly? The smarter of you dumbasses actually has the good sense not to tell me about it outright, so go and fuck yourself with a cactus… And have a nice day!"

Well, her brand of sales was unique, obviously, but it got the job done. She knew her audience, that much was clear.

Vickie slammed the phone in its cradle and turned to her work on the computers. She hummed softly, the aggressive tone of her conversation suddenly gone. Of course, the landline was wireless so thunking it down wasn't necessary, but there was something satisfying that came with the action as she liked to say.

But there was more to it this time around. Bobby didn't need to ask her what was on her mind. It wouldn't do him any good anyway, given that he generally wasn't the one to drag anything out of the young woman. Taylor was always better at that shit, somehow. The guy liked to play at being a big dumb oaf but he knew a thing or two when it came to talking to people.

She looked up from her computer and at where Bobby was seated but studiously ignored her.

"I can tell you want to ask me something," she called from her side of the garage. "Like, even the way your shoulders are all bunched tells me you want to say something but are afraid of getting the same treatment as those assholes."

"I guess—" he started to say but stopped immediately. "It's only that you seem a little extra bitchy with those guys lately. I'm not saying they don't deserve that shit, but if there are other issues you want to get off your chest and… uh, if you want to talk about it…"

He trailed off, unsure where to go from there. People liked to be heard sometimes, and there were moments when having someone offer to listen was helpful. Then again, Vickie tended to classify as more than simply people in his mind. She was almost family.

"It was that obvious, huh?" she asked, pushed from her seat, and wandered closer to watch him work. "Hell, I felt a little guilty at the end and even considered not screwing him over. But when he started talking about how many drinks I was getting him, I decided to let his ass cover my rent for the month at the college dorm."

"It sounds like the guy asked for it."

She sighed, dropped into a seat, and began to help with a few of the pieces she knew how to work with. "I'm a little worried about Taylor, is all. The guy got himself in deep this time, and we both know the next chance he has to throw himself into the thick of it, he'll say yes."

"That does sound like him, yeah," Bobby agreed. "You know, if you want to take the day off to sort shit out—"

The woman shook her head and cut him off. "Nah, I cope best with something to keep my mind busy. Otherwise, it goes into overdrive with the worrying. I'd like to say school is engaging enough to help, but that would be a lie. I'd rather put in a good day of work."

He nodded and pushed a few tools across the table toward her. "You'd best get to work, then. We need to have these mechs finished by the end of the week. Taylor's scheduled to come back in a day or two, but who knows if he'll be in any condition to work."

Vickie snickered. "He'll probably be an invalid and roll around in a wheelchair."

# CHAPTER TWO

"For fuck's sake, I'm not a goddamn invalid!"

The nurse scowled at Taylor, who was on his feet in the room and stretched cautiously before he began to pull his clothes on.

"I'm afraid I have to insist, Mr. McFadden," she said and kept her voice pleasant yet stern. "It is standard procedure for all people being discharged to be moved out in a wheelchair."

He scowled at the chair she had brought into his room with the kind of disgust he tended to reserve for tofu and soy cheeseburgers. It honestly felt like the ultimate insult. He had been stuck in a hospital bed for the better part of a month, unable to move almost at all. A few more months passed during which he needed to spend most of his time on his back while whatever time he had on his feet was focused on physical therapy.

Inevitably, he had lost considerable muscle during his recovery time. It made him look like a scarecrow, especially in the clothes that had been sent for him to use. The doctors said it wouldn't take too long for him to regain the muscle mass that had been lost while he had been bedridden but that was still too long a time.

All he wanted was to get out and be active. Being wheeled out in a chair designed for people who didn't have functioning legs wasn't an auspicious beginning to his return to life as he had known it.

Taylor couldn't help a sigh as he rolled his still impressively massive shoulders. "I've always wondered about that, actually. Why the hell do you guys insist on carrying people out of the hospital in wheelchairs?"

"Because while you are on hospital grounds, we are still liable for your safety." Her voice was a barely contained huff, although her gaze wandered over his body before she collected herself and regained her professional demeanor. "Should you trip and fall, that would still be our responsibility. The chances of that happening are greatly reduced if you're in a wheelchair. Besides, if you have some kind of medical condition that removes your ability to walk, we can get you to the help you might need much faster if we don't need to lift someone of your particular size and weight into a wheelchair."

He scowled and stared at his arms. "I've lost a ton of that weight, actually. I'm not too happy about that."

"I'm sure you aren't, but even at your current weight, I estimate it would take at least two people to get you off the ground if something were to happen. So, if you don't mind?"

She pointed at the chair again, and he couldn't help another scowl. Nurse Young made sense. While he had all kinds of confidence in his recovery, he couldn't account for something going wrong. The one thing that scared him most was that he would be told to stay for another three or four weeks under observation.

Taylor sighed, rolled his shoulders again, and moved toward the chair. "I'll have you know that I object to this—and strongly too. But I understand that you guys don't want to be held liable for whatever small chance there is of me somehow injuring myself on the long and perilous trip. Anything can happen during the twenty paces to the elevator, three floors down, and thirty-three paces from the elevator doors to the entrance."

He could see her confused expression as he settled into the chair. It creaked as he sat as if to echo his protest.

"I've had a fair amount of free time," he offered by way of explanation. "My brain doesn't do well with being idle, so I've learned to count arbitrary things to keep it busy."

"I can understand that completely."

It still felt shitty to be wheeled out of the bedroom he had spent more time in than any other bedroom in his life, but far be it from him to voice any further complaints when all he had to say had already been said. He would take this like he had taken the physical therapy. It had been a little humiliating—learning how to walk properly again would remain his single least favorite experience for a long time—but he had somehow powered through.

The elevator doors opened into the lobby, where Taylor's heart immediately sank to his stomach. Niki stood at the front desk, her arms folded, and she waited for him with a small, infuriating smirk on her lips.

"If you're unable to walk on your own from this point forward, we'll probably have to revisit your status as a consultant for the FBI," she said as they approached. "Unless Bobby can rig up some kind of improvement to your suit that helps you walk. Far be it from me to keep your ass out of the field."

"Ha-ha, very funny," he grumbled. "I can walk fine, but the hospital has rules for people checking out. Those apparently include making sure we continue to feel like invalids for as long as fucking possible. No offense, Nurse Young."

"None taken."

The agent's eyebrows rose for a moment. "Well, all jokes aside, it is good to see you basically on your feet again, Taylor. Believe it or not, things haven't been the same out there without you."

"Have you had to scrape the bottom of the barrel to get people crazy enough to hunt for monsters?" he asked as the paperwork he was required to sign was placed on his lap.

"Quite the opposite, actually. After the fiasco in Wyoming, the people I report to decided that simply hiring anyone crazy enough to hunt for monsters straight out of a Ridley Scott movie, regardless of experience, talent, or equipment, wouldn't cut it anymore. They put out a call for professionals—those coming out of the Zoo or still in there. With help from a couple of freelance groups, I have my hands on several Cro-Magnons stupid and well-armed enough to do the job."

"Which freelance groups?" Taylor asked and handed the signed papers to the nurse.

She shrugged. "There were a couple, although most of them were only consulted for their references on who might be useful for the job. Some guys called the Chasseurs, Heavy Metal, and even a group called the Big Dick Nicks. They said they thought of the name while they were on a three-day drinking bender."

"Classy," he grunted as they handed him the possessions they'd kept for him during his recovery. "I've only ever heard of one of those groups. Are you sure their recommendations for the job are any good?"

"I was worried about that, to be honest, but so far, they have proved themselves worth the money we've invested in them. They wouldn't work for free, after all, but they've done a better job than the patchwork people I've worked with so far, so I'll take it."

"Their Cro-Magnon-ness notwithstanding?"

"Well, sure, they are a little difficult to work with. And I thought you were a misogynistic thirsty bastard."

"And now?"

"Well, you're still a misogynistic thirsty bastard but as it turns out, it seems like there is a wide variety of your type who come out of the Zoo. I'm not sure if that counts as coming from the Zoo or if it merely takes the kind of dumbass you are to go there in the first place."

Taylor shrugged. "A little column A and a little column B, if I'm honest, but that's not the point. My point is that—"

"Are you ready to be taken out of the hospital?" Nurse Young interjected.

"I...yeah," he responded and let her guide the chair toward the exit. "My point is, how are you adapting to handling a group of guys who are like me, but who lack... uh, certain...characteristics that would make them more appealing?"

"I'm not sure if you've noticed, but you appear to lack

many of those characteristics of late," Niki said as she hurried beside them.

"Yeah, I know what you mean. I've worked on trying to get myself back in shape, but even after the physical therapy I've put in, I think all I have is a little tone and not much bulk. The doc said that should be fixed if I work out regularly over the next few weeks. Or, at least, that would be the start of it."

Niki laughed. "Well, we can't have you be a regular old scarecrow instead of a beefcake."

"Thanks for the compliment," he said and narrowed his eyes. "I think."

"I've made it very clear in the past that your body is not your worst quality," she reminded him. "It's the fact that you're a—"

"Misogynistic, thirsty bastard. Got it," he interrupted.

They exited the building and stopped, and Taylor stood and stepped aside so the nurse could return with the wheelchair.

He took a moment to stretch and rolled his neck slowly. "Fuck me, it's good to be a free man again."

Niki smiled and shook her head. "You're talking like your stay in the hospital was a prison sentence."

"Worse than a prison sentence in a way," he said and shook his head. "Nope, no. I can't finish that thought. But the point remains that I like to be on the outside of this building instead of inside—wait what is this?"

"Fair enough. And what is what?"

He frowned and fumbled in his coat pocket to withdraw a neatly folded piece of paper. It had a ten-digit number and the name Pearl Young inscribed under it, with the 'o' in her last name made out into a heart shape.

"I think Nurse Young wants you to call her." The agent stated the obvious with an elevated eyebrow.

"And I'm fairly sure she knows I live in Vegas," he said. "I talked considerably when I took the painkillers, so the chances are I probably mentioned where I live and what I do for a living. Maybe she thought I would stick around town for a couple of days before I returned home."

"Which, no, you won't." She laughed. "I'm sorry—not sorry—for cock-blocking you. It's probably for the best for Nurse Young, though, but you won't stay in town for that long."

They reached the black SUV that Taylor assumed she had arrived in and he climbed into the shotgun seat and let her drive. He would need to get back into the groove of it later when he'd settled into a normal routine.

"So, where are we going?" he asked as she pulled the vehicle out of the parking lot.

"Back to Vegas, where else?"

"I don't know. I guess I thought you would take me out to hunt another creature."

"I think you still need a little while to recover. Besides, it's not like you're quite as vital to the whole operation as you used to be."

"Wow. That's hurtful."

"But also true. Don't worry, though. You're still vital enough to the operation to be brought in once you're all better."

It was annoying that they needed to constantly run errands like this.

Many people would have literally killed to have their job. Working for Don Castellano was the chance of a lifetime, of course, especially on the island of Sicily where there was little opportunity to aspire to anything other than owning a local shop. While that might sound appealing, the truth was that it would rely on the same economy that had kept their town afloat for the past few centuries and provide no possibility for any kind of significant advancement.

They could look past the regrettable necessity of the errands they couldn't avoid because it meant they were in the good graces of the *Cosa Nostra*, which did put them in an upper tier. Essentially, they were made men who would never want for anything for the rest of their lives.

Unfortunately, it also meant they had to ferry phone messages to the don every time he received one, and people called him almost all the time. Don Castellano was old-fashioned in some of the worst ways. He had put millions into giving his villa the best protection money could buy, both physical and digital, but he hated having phones in the house. His unshakeable opinion was that if people wanted to talk to him, they had to do so face-to-face or otherwise leave messages for when they could meet him face-to-face.

Those rules changed when his only daughter came from Monaco to visit, but for the moment, it meant the only phone on the property was one at the guardhouse almost three kilometers down the road.

When Flavio had been told he would be a made man

within the family, he had thought it would mean much less running errands than before. Sadly, he had been wrong.

He pulled up in the driveway, clutching the message that he had studiously taken down. The two men at the front door gestured him toward the pool on the other side of the house.

Flavio repressed a frustrated sigh. If word got back to the don that he wasn't satisfied with his current position in any way, his boss would change his position. In most cases, his new one would be about six feet under on the nearby hills.

It really was best to keep all his frustrations to himself.

With his features schooled into the expected emotionless mask, he circled toward the back of the main house where a large, Olympic-sized pool had been built. The glistening water was cleaned and purified at great expense since the don was in his sixties and had been told that chlorine aged the skin. Flavio had no idea if it was true or not but it did mean that the pool needed to be cleaned carefully every day before the boss came out for his habitual morning swim.

The old man was still in good shape and worked through his laps like he had swum at a professional level his entire life. His wife was currently in Monaco, where she lived with their daughter, which meant the two young women tanning beside the pool were not there only as eye-candy.

Flavio forced his gaze not to rove their bare bodies. As enticing as the view was, the don was known to cut eyes out if they wandered.

It required a surprising degree of resolve to keep his

gaze to himself as the old man continued his swim. It felt like hours, especially since he waited in the hot sun, but eventually, the don slowed his pace and swam to the edge, where he climbed out.

One of the models was quick to bring him his towel, while the other moved into the house to alert the kitchen staff that it was time to bring out his breakfast. Castellano dried himself and placed a light peck on the young woman's lips before he moved to a nearby patio table where a newspaper waited for him.

Flavio was sure the only reason the local grocery stores still sold newspapers instead of letting people source their news on the Internet was because the don still liked to read his news on paper. He was old-fashioned in that way as well.

Silence settled until the old man had slid his glasses on and finished the comics. His breakfast of eggs, sausage, and a variety of pastries as well as coffee and juices was brought out and only then did the old man finally realize that someone waited for his attention.

"Come here, boy," he said, his voice deep and gravelly. He called everyone boy and those in the know had said it meant he had trouble remembering people's names. "Have you already had breakfast?"

Flavio bowed politely as he approached. "I have, *grazie.* I apologize for interrupting your breakfast but a message was left for you."

The old man pulled his glasses off and looked at him. His cold blue eyes seemed to cut into the younger man. "Who is it from?"

"It is from *Signor* Di Stefano in Las Vegas."

"Well, don't make me guess what he said. Tell me about it!"

He cleared his throat nervously. "Well, the message states that *Signor* Mc...Mac...McFadden has left the military hospital and is on his way to Las Vegas. *Signor* Di Stefano said Don Marino was unsure of what to do with the man and asked for your advice on the matter before he took any action."

"Pah. That is typical of the young generation—they need to be told how to hold their balls too." Castellano grunted and took a bite from one of the sausages. "Do they await a message in return?"

"*Signor* Di Stefano asked to be notified of your orders at your earliest convenience, Don Castellano."

The don chuckled and shook his head, likely thinking of more comments about what the new people weren't able to do without being instructed. "Well, tell them—take this down—not to take any decisive action yet but to keep their eyes on this McFadden character. They must make a note of everything he does while in Las Vegas and who he might have contact with while there. Tell them to send all that information to me daily so we can examine it and be able to make an informed decision."

Flavio quickly made a note of everything the old man said to reply to Di Stefano when he reached the phone. Maybe one day, he would be able to travel around the world and relay orders from the dons in Italy to their various investments. For the moment, however, it was his job to take notes and he'd best do it well.

Many, many notes over the next few days by the sound of it.

# CHAPTER THREE

"So, will we talk about this?"

Niki looked up from her cell phone, which she'd checked quickly for messages. "Talk about what?"

Taylor shrugged casually. "About the fact that you're coming to Vegas with me instead of keeping your whole operation running. You went through all the trouble to put together a group that would be able to operate efficiently and annoy you in equal measure, so one would think you would...well, you know, focus on that."

"Well, for one thing, Desk actually does a fairly good job of managing the newcomers," she said and slid her cell phone into her pocket. She turned to make her way toward the exit of the Las Vegas Airport and gestured for him to follow her. "So, as much as I hate to say it, the task force does appear to run on auto-pilot at this point. It doesn't mean they don't still need me, but it does mean I have time to take off for personal reasons."

"And are those personal reasons following me around the country like the world's most dedicated stalker?"

She snorted. "I had a feeling you would try to flatter yourself like that, but no. What I do have a mind to do is check on my family. I had time to visit my sister while you were still in recovery and now, I'll check on Vickie's progress."

Taylor narrowed his eyes as they strode through the doors into the airport parking lot and slid a pair of sunglasses on. "Your sister...Jennie, right? Didn't she visit me at the hospital?"

"A couple of times, actually," Niki confirmed and drew an envelope with a set of keys from her pocket. "Don't you remember?"

He waggled his hand to indicate uncertainty. "Vaguely. I was hopped up on all kinds of interesting drugs at the time so I have a hard time telling what was real and what was only...uh, me having really weird dreams."

"Do you honestly think that you would dream about my sister?"

"Like I said, really, really weird dreams. I think they list that as one of the side effects of those painkiller medications."

"Not painkillers, no."

They reached a car and once again, she was quick to take control. Taylor made no protest and simply rode shotgun.

He sighed and grimaced as they pulled out of the parking lot. "Will you tell me why you want to check in on Vickie now, of all times? It's not like she's gone anywhere, and she's in the middle of school as well as improving her position in the company, so..."

"Honestly, I can't help but think she is probably

involved in some kind of craziness Bobby wouldn't have reported to me. You know the man better than me, obviously, and while I trust that you would report anything you found out to me, I can't help but feel he wouldn't."

"Why not?"

Niki shook her head. "Fuck if I know. Like I said, I don't know the guy. For instance, do you think he might have any kind of attraction to her? Is there anything physical between them?"

"What?" Taylor snapped. "Are you nuts? The guy sees her like a...a niece or maybe a younger sister. Hell, that's how I feel about her too. She's like family."

"So—"

"No, there's no attraction, physical or otherwise. Holy shit, Special Agent, but you have a dirty mind."

"Says the guy who's in the process of irreparably altering the gene pool of the American Midwest," Niki said and laughed.

"Vegas is out in the West, not mid," he corrected her. "The Midwest is farther north—although I guess there's more of the West up north since that includes Alaska. Anyway, the point is, the Midwest is the Wisconsin, Illinois, and Minnesota region."

"I stand corrected. You're the guy looking to irreparably alter the gene pool of the American West. Happy?"

"Not until my mission of making sure that at least a solid quarter of the gene pool has a part of Taylor McFadden in it."

"You're gross."

Taylor grinned. "You say that like it's some kind of a

surprise. Come on, get with the program already, Special Agent. That was a fucking joke."

Niki couldn't help another laugh as they cruised into the city of Las Vegas in the opposite direction from the Strip and deeper into the less-known parts of the city. The prices for property dropped the farther they got from the popular metropolitan hub, which was why Taylor had purchased his little piece of land in the area where criminals were known to hold ground.

Then again, most criminals tended to target a business once or twice and usually stopped once they were firmly rebuffed. It was the logical outcome as persistence proved too expensive and like it or not, most criminal enterprises needed to operate like businesses or they wouldn't last very long.

In his case, however, the unknown someone had persisted far longer than would be expected and had invested a little too much money into trying to force him to toe the local line. It couldn't be profitable, which meant it was probably more a matter of principle than dollars and cents. The only people he knew who had the kind of money that allowed them to operate on principle when it became that expensive usually didn't care about what happened in a strip mall. It was even more unusual given that the area of the city he had chosen was generally disregarded due to small mom and pop gun stores that offered very little lucrative pickings.

He would have to look into that shit. Taylor had played on the defensive for too long, and it had gotten Vickie and Bobby kidnapped at one point and had forced the mechanic to take serious action at another. It was only a matter of time before someone he cared about got hurt. He had to make sure that the only people who were hurt were those who appeared to be trying to put him out of business.

It was an issue he wanted to resolve as quickly as possible. Of course, he could simply tell his two employees to immediately get onto it but he felt he should get on their good side first. He had left them to work on their own for the past few months, and while they had kept the work going at a solid and reliable rate, what he would have to ask of them was the kind of thing they ordinarily wouldn't be paid for.

And if there was any money to be had, it would be strictly under the table.

"The place still looks like shit," Niki said and pulled Taylor out of his thoughts.

He realized that they had finally arrived at the strip mall and had to agree that the place did still look like shit. It was difficult to make a prefab building look good, especially since it had been built as cheaply as possible. The structures were meant to last but not to look good while doing so. Still, he hadn't bought the place for its appearance.

"Yeah, but it's home," he grumbled under his breath as they continued to the back where the garage doors were already open and waiting for them.

"How did they—" Banks frowned and slowed the vehicle.

"Security detected a new arrival, and with Vickie probably updating the system, she was able to tell that it was you, me, or both. Either way, don't worry about it."

"I feel letting someone like Vickie have full control of your security system might be something to worry about."

"Well...maybe, sure, but if she wanted to screw me over somehow, she would have done it already."

"Or she's only waiting for maximum opportunity."

"Goddamn, dude, do you not have any trust in your niece?"

"She's my cousin, by the way, and my family so I love her, but I know her tendencies better than most."

Taylor shrugged dismissively. "I trust her. With my life, even, and I know Bobby feels the same way. It's how this business works—mutual trust between all parties involved."

"Because you know she will absolutely destroy you if you try anything?" Niki asked.

He nodded. "Basically, yeah, like a mutually assured destruction kind of trust, but with more beer and hopefully fewer weapons of mass destruction."

The vehicle stopped and he climbed out first and frowned at Bobby and Vickie, who both remained hard at work. They knew he was there but even that was no reason for them to slack in their duties. He assumed, anyway, and didn't want to explore the possibility that they might have chosen to simply ignore him.

"Honey, I'm home!" Taylor called and his voice echoed around the garage.

Bobby looked up from his work and seemed genuinely surprised to see them, but Vickie was already on her feet. She jogged toward them from the desk she had claimed as her own.

Niki was almost completely ignored and the woman

threw all her weight into hugging Taylor. He grunted as she made impact and took a couple of steps back when she almost unbalanced him.

"You took your fucking time getting back, big guy!" Vickie said. Her voice took on a hint of a squeal that made his ears hurt, but he didn't want to worry her about that. He also chose to keep quiet about the fact that her version of a bear hug began to make him wish he had taken the painkillers after he got off the plane instead of when they boarded.

Niki noticed him wince but interestingly, had nothing to say about it as the other woman finally pulled back.

"Also, is it only me or did you lose weight?" the young hacker inquired as she gave him a quick once-over glance. "No offense, but there was usually more muscle and less bone in your hugs before, right?"

"I did lose a fair amount of weight while recovering, which is common in my kind of case," he answered and brushed his fingers self-consciously over his loose-fitting shirt. "The doc said that getting back into my previous eating and exercise patterns should fix that nicely, though. I look forward to that."

"I bet you do," she said. "Don't take this the wrong way but you look like the Scarecrow's crack-addicted cousin."

"Wait, isn't the Scarecrow a character who kind of lives off fear and therefore hands the drugs out anyway?" Bobby interjected as he finally drew away from his work to join them and welcome his boss back.

Vickie shook her head. "Not Batman's Scarecrow, the one from the *Wizard of Oz*. You know, the guy of 'If I Only Had a Brain' fame?"

"I only hope I have more brains than my cousin who's not addicted to crack and yet is still about as sharp as your average baseball bat," Taylor pointed out and greeted the mechanic with a hug as well. "How are you? How have things worked out around here in my absence?"

The larger man was more careful in greeting him than Vickie had been. "Well, the mob hit aside, things have gone smoothly, if slower than I'd like. We've let the folks on the Zoo front know and they're okay with the altered schedule. I still think we should hire more labor around here if you want to take three-month-long hiatuses from your own business."

"That's not as likely as before," Taylor explained with a glance at Niki, who leaned against the car with her arms folded. "It looks like the military panicked somewhat and allowed her to bring a whole brigade from the Zoo to keep things calm. I guess that tends to happen when they lose a couple of choppers while still stateside."

Bungees nodded. "It makes sense, and at least it does give you more time to recover. Besides, with the kind of capital you already have plus cash flowing in from your own business, you have to think about not putting your life on the line anymore. Risking it has to be a thing of the past for you, right?"

He scratched idly at his beard. "It's like you don't know me at all, Bungees. The money was nice but that wasn't why I did it."

"Well, letting other people do the job for you has to keep you satisfied for the moment."

The taller man sighed and shook his head. "Honestly, I wouldn't mind a little time to settle in and get some work done here. Plus, maybe have a couple of decent meals and get myself stone drunk at some point over the next week."

"Let me guess," Vickie interjected. "No drinking allowed at the hospital?"

"Not unless I was willing to risk drinking rubbing alcohol," he responded. "And the food there sucked absolute balls."

"It's almost like it was a hospital, not a fine dining establishment," Niki snarked cheerfully.

"Well, yeah, but I'll bet the rich people don't have to worry about shitty food in their hospitals," Bungees said.

She raised a hand, her mouth open for a moment, but she obviously reconsidered and lowered her hand. "Sure, I guess, but us regular folk need to decide between fine dining or hospital and we can't have both."

Taylor smirked. "Fair enough. Now, Vickie, how are things going with your studies? And today had better not be one of those days where you gave yourself a day off because you feel like it."

"She what?" her cousin snapped.

"She nothing," the other woman responded quickly. "I have an understanding with most of my professors. Basically, as long as I maintain my grades and keep up with my group projects and the like, the credits from my last stint in college transfer and I don't need to attend their every lecture. That gives me more time to focus on my work, which also gets me school credit, by the way."

Taylor kept his attention on Niki to make sure she didn't lash out at her cousin for the half-assed explanation. His caution proved groundless and all she could come up with was a long sigh as she shook her head.

"How have your grades looked?" he asked to break the tension.

Vickie tilted her head, her expression a little disgruntled. "Well, it didn't go great initially since I do tend to know more than my professors do on the subject. When I try to correct them, I come across as an incorrigible know-it-all. They didn't appreciate that so I was given a steady diet of Cs, but after I learned my lesson and remained quiet, I was upgraded to a B-plus and even an A-minus region of the grading scale. It's not perfect, but hey, what is?"

"You're not making this easy," he grumbled.

"And there he is. The asshole dad is officially back." She laughed and punched him lightly in the shoulder before she turned to relocate to her desk.

Taylor waited until she wasn't looking before he rubbed feeling back into his arm. It sucked being this delicate.

"So, do you want to talk business now?" Bobby asked. "Or do you want to get settled in first?"

His hand dropped quickly from where Vickie had punched him. "Eh, it's not like I had any luggage anyway. I might as well get back in the groove of shit as soon as possible, right?"

"That sounds good."

Niki raised her hands. "You don't need to tell me twice. I'll go and make sure my cousin is really okay with all of this."

Both men waited for her to cross to Vickie's desk before Bungees turned to look at him.

"How are you doing?" he queried. "For real, I mean. I

saw the list of injuries and people don't walk away from that shit easily."

He took a deep breath. "I didn't. Three months doesn't exactly qualify as walking away easily. Things are on the mend, though, but I do appreciate your concern."

"No problem."

"Now is the part where you fill me in on what happened when a couple of dumbasses came a-knocking again. And by a-knocking, I mean the assholes you had to kill to prevent them from torching the place."

"Niki came down to handle the legal aspect of it for us," Bobby explained. "I'm still not sure how she did it but it's best not to ask questions I don't want to know the answer to, you know?"

"Yeah. That's the smart choice."

"Thanks. Anyway, Vickie and I have worked on improving the security measures. It's still illegal to put unmanned turrets on the perimeter but so far, there are a couple of ways in which we've managed to deter any potential home invaders. Big bright lights turn on when the motion sensors are triggered, for instance. They've done the job at least a couple of times, although I'm not sure if what activated them were home invaders or only a stray dog or maybe a raccoon. Either way, whenever that is tripped, both me and Vickie get alerts on our phones and are plugged into the security cameras in case we need to call the cops."

"Well, I've thought about that while I've been in the hospital." Taylor's voice lowered to almost a whisper, and his tone was more serious than the mechanic had likely expected. "About the kind of people who would have the kind of pull in this town to be able to continually send motherfuckers to our doorstep and likely will persist unless we deter them more effectively, you know?"

"What if you are called away for some of Agent Banks' kind of work?"

"The chances are she won't need me for another six months," he explained. "To my mind, it seems like the amount of time needed to make sure these assholes know not to fuck with my people while I get back in the groove around here."

Bobby nodded. "I would probably guess that it's best to let certain law enforcement agents vacate the premises before we discuss action that some might consider to be illegal."

"Good call."

# CHAPTER FOUR

Taylor couldn't help a smile when Bungees pulled into the garage the next day toting the traditional breakfast of champions—coffee and doughnuts.

"You'd think we were cops the way we go through these so quickly." He grunted as they sat at the common table set up in the garage.

"You know, I've wondered about the association between cops and doughnuts," the mechanic said, his mouth half-full. "I read somewhere that the only reason why the association is made is because they always needed somewhere safe to park for night shifts and the like. The shop owners didn't mind having the presence in their area, so they were more than happy to give the odd free box to the officers who hung around their business, and that's where the association came from."

His boss took a bite and chewed as he considered it. "I guess that makes sense. The story I heard—and this was from my dad, who had a couple of friends who were state troopers way back when—is that there were guys who had to write most of their paperwork while out in the field. It was either that or they had to go in after hours and do it at their offices. The preference was to get it done immediately, and this was before they were issued with computers or even clipboards, so they liked to have a nice box of doughnuts there as a clear surface for them to work on while in the car."

Bobby paused and frowned as he thought the premise through. "It makes a nice story and all, but if I were a betting man, I'd say it was a bullshit story your dad's cop friends liked to tell their non-cop buddies."

"I guess that is possible. Honestly, I'd simply say it's because of convenience. It's a nice hit of sugar to go with the coffee and it's easy to eat while driving, so it became a staple for anyone who spent most of their working hours behind the wheel. People simply began to associate the concept with policemen more than your average…say, truck driver because there's more pop culture about cops than there is about truck drivers."

It seemed like the kind of thing that either of them could have looked up on their phones and resolved in a minute or so, but Taylor liked having odd little rambling conversations about nothing in particular. He'd missed it. Most of his time at the hospital had been spent discussing his condition with doctors and nurses who took themselves and their work very seriously.

Not that he blamed them. Working in a hospital would inevitably make people serious about what they were doing when they had matters of life and death in their hands every day.

Both men looked around when the doors of the garage

swung open again, this time to reveal Vickie's delightful new Tesla. Although, given that she'd driven it for a few months now, he didn't think it qualified as new anymore.

"What the hell are you doing here?" he asked as she stepped out of her car and yawned into her hand. "I happen to know for a fact that you have school to attend today. A group project or something."

She scowled darkly at him. "That's one thing I didn't miss about you. I kid, I appreciate your concern, but this is the twenty-first century and people do most of their group projects online. There's a cloud document we can all access that allows us to work together without having to actually be in the same room. The rest of my group moves a little slowly so I thought I would be more useful here than moping around my dorm while I wait for my classmates to get with the program"

"Can't you...I don't know, teach them everything you know, show it all to them, and let them all get high grades?"

Vickie snorted as she helped herself to one each of the doughnuts and coffees and taking a long sip from the latter. "What, and let them cheat their way to a better grade? Are you quite literally insane?"

Taylor pulled his phone out of his pocket and placed it to his ear. "What's that pot? The kettle is calling you black? How weird."

"Funny stuff." She smirked. "In my case, I know enough about the material to be able to come up with the answers on my own without having to rely on all those damn lectures. I have all the damn knowledge from personal experience."

"Yeah, well, employers don't look at your college experience for your skillset," Taylor said. "They look at it for your ability to stick to a task for the time required and if they look at your history and see a long list of missed classes—"

"Then I'll alter the records to show that I didn't miss them."

"And that's different than the other students being able to cheat how, exactly?"

She only offered a soft grunt and a shrug by way of response.

He sighed. "I'm sorry. It's not really my place to tell you how to live your life. And honestly, we appreciate having you work here. But I kind of wish you would give your future more consideration, is all."

The young hacker stared at him for a few moments before she broke into a smile and wrapped her arms around him. He needed to force himself not to grunt when his aches and pains suddenly came to the forefront of his mind.

"What was that for?" he queried as she pulled away.

"Nothing. I'm simply happy that you give a damn."

Taylor took a deep breath and picked his coffee up. "Anyway. What were we talking about again?"

"You were going to tell me about what you felt about the assholes who attacked us here," Bobby reminded him. "You know, the thing you wanted to talk about once we weren't listened to by the fuzz."

"Oh, right, and if you could keep my attendance a secret from Niki from this point forward, I would appreciate that too," Vickie said. "She checks on my scores periodically so I can keep her happy with that, but if she gets the idea that I'm not attending, she'll be pissed."

Taylor rubbed his eyes. "Noted," he agreed after a moment's thought. "Anyway, what I thought about while I was in the hospital—and likely high on pain meds so take it with a grain of salt—not many of the local muscle would be able to target us the way these people have. Hell, even those who would be able to wouldn't bother by this point. We're making money but not enough to explain not one but two different professional—or semi-professional—hit squads."

"The last two guys were foreign. I think they spoke Italian when they broke in." Bobby spoke slowly like he attempted to remember more details about the invaders. "They carried very interesting hardware too and not the kind that would be picked up by your average gang-banger."

"So yes, pros," Taylor agreed. "Vickie, were you able to find anything on them?"

"Only the basics—a couple of contacts and that was it," she replied, moved to the computer, and carried her laptop to the table where they were seated. "I did manage to look into their recent banking habits. The guys were from Sicily by the looks of it. They didn't do much when they got here but they did spend a fair amount of time and money at one of the local casinos."

The red-headed giant stood from his seat and stretched carefully. He could feel the effects of the exercise he had done in the morning. It would be a while before he finally attained the shape he liked to be in, but he had to start somewhere.

"What are you thinking?" Bobby asked.

He paused for a moment and shook his head. "Sicilian professionals who come in for a few days before they attack us makes me think we might be dealing with the mob. They are the only ones with the resources to give us this much trouble and who would think it's worth it for… like, principles and shit."

Vickie worked hastily on her laptop and called up pictures of the casino in question. "So, what are you thinking? Should we find the asshole in charge and send a message that says we're not to be fucked with?"

His scowl confirmed his reluctance. "As tempting as that might be, no. There are obvious reasons. A guy like that will be surrounded by all kinds of security and since he's rich, it means he has connections up to his armpits too. And then there is the not so obvious reason like this guy's bosses taking that as an act of war and descending on us with everything they have."

"Well, if cutting the head off the snake is out of the question, what did you have in mind?"

"For one thing, I doubt that whoever is running the casino is actually the head of the snake," Bobby interjected.

Taylor pointed at him. "That's a good point. Secondly, we need them to know that pursuing this vendetta will be more expensive than they can possibly afford, all while getting more info on them. My thought is…a heist."

Vickie looked up from her work. "Did you say…"

"A heist. Yes."

"Like…something out of *Ocean's Eleven?*" Bobby queried. "Like that kind of heist?"

"Well, aside from the distinct lack of Brad Pitt and George Clooney, yeah."

The hacker leaned forward in her seat. "You know the whole heist scenario isn't as easy as they make it look in the movie, right? I can tell you right now that robbing a fucking casino will be all but impossible. You would have better luck robbing—and I hate the cliché here—Fort Knox."

"Robbing a casino doesn't mean robbing the actual casino," Taylor stated.

His two companions shared a quick glance.

"Do you think...maybe a stroke?" she asked tentatively.

Bobby scratched his chin. "Or maybe he's a little high from his pain meds."

"I'm not— I'm serious, okay?" Taylor growled with exasperation. "My point is that yeah, if we rush into a casino head-first and try to take their money, we'll be gunned down. We need to come at them sideways and be creative about it. Every security system in the world has its weak points, and if there's anyone who could ever find one for a casino..."

The two men both turned to look at Vickie, who picked at one of the doughnuts before she realized that the attention was on her.

"What?" she mumbled around a mouthful of vanilla pastry with chocolate glaze.

Her boss raised an eyebrow at her. "Are you going to sit there and tell me with a straight face that you've spent this much time in Sin City and you haven't once thought of at least five or six different ways to rob the local casinos blind?"

She stared at the two men for a long moment before she swallowed the food in her mouth and cleaned her fingers delicately on a napkin. "Why do I feel like this is some kind of entrapment scheme?"

Taylor glanced at Bobby. "Are you trying to entrap her?"

The hefty mechanic shook his head. "Nope, are you?"

"I can't say I am. I have no idea why she might feel that way."

"Ugh, fine." The hacker rolled her eyes. "I do have some plans partially explored and some options I can look into for you guys. It's nothing concrete, but I'll let you know if I have something."

"That's all I'm asking. Taylor walked over to her and kissed her forehead.

She made a face and brushed his beard out of her face. "Ugh, don't get all mushy on me. No chick-flick moments."

"Fair enough," he answered and drew away with his hands raised. He stopped walking when his phone vibrated on the table where he'd placed it.

"Now, who would be calling you?" Bobby asked with a grin. "Could it be Alex, calling for your booty?"

Vickie glanced up from her work. "Do me a favor and never say the word booty like that again."

"Fair enough."

Taylor picked the phone up. "It's a blocked number. Weird, that's how Desk usually contacts me when there's a job that needs my attention."

"You don't think they already have work for you, do you?" the other man said, his expression disapproving. "You did say you had about six months of recovery time, right?"

His sour face at the device in his hand told them clearly what he thought. "Yeah, but I guess that was always open to change. Oh, well, here goes."

He pressed the accept call button, put it to his ear, and waited for the familiar, pleasant voice that usually came with these calls.

A few seconds ticked past before anything was heard.

"Hello?" a woman's voice said, one that was definitely not Desk. "Taylor, is that you?"

"Hi," he responded a little sharply. "Who…who is this?"

"Damn. Niki told me that your memory was a little wonky," the woman replied. "I don't know if you remember me but we have met and talked before. A few times, actually, but more recently at the hospital while you were more or less out of it. I also called you before your…trip to Wyoming. My name is Dr. Genesis Banks."

"Oh…right, you're the one who called about Wyoming." He shook his head to clear some of the confusion that had rushed in. "And I vaguely remember you visiting me in the hospital, but it's kind of lost in a jumble of other memories that I get the distinct impression is mostly hit and miss."

"Well, yes, I did happen to visit while you were in the hospital, and we did have a conversation. Although, in your defense, you were fairly out of it at the time."

"Well, that's good to know. Back on topic, Dr. Banks. Might I ask why you're calling me?"

Bobby mouthed "Dr. Banks" at him and he waved at the mechanic to shut up.

"Well, yes, I assumed you wouldn't remember what we talked about."

"Like I said, hit and miss."

"I don't suppose you recall that we discussed how we met for the first time?"

Taylor paused to think for a moment. "The first time? That wasn't the phone call?"

"Nope."

"And seeing each other at that bar your sister took me to?"

"Also no."

"Sorry."

"Well, I guess we can cover it again during our date when you will hopefully not be high as a kite?"

It took a moment for that to sink in. "Date?"

"You did agree to go out and have a meal with me," Genesis stated.

"If you say so."

"I do. And so did you. I can prove that to you as well since I recorded the conversation. You...uh, kind of agreed to that too."

"Now that does ring a bell." Taylor rubbed his chin. "I wasn't sure why someone wanted to record anything I wanted to say so I simply agreed for some reason."

"That's how I remember it too," she replied. "Anyway, I'll come to Vegas for work on Friday so maybe we can meet on Friday night?"

Taylor sighed. "Yeah, that sounds like a date. I'll see you then. Let me know when and where."

"I'll text you the details. See you Friday."

The line clicked and left him shaking his head gently as he tucked the device into his pocket.

"So," Vickie called, still working on her laptop, "to make

sure I heard the one side of that conversation correctly, that was a call from Genesis Banks, right?"

He nodded.

"As in my cousin Jennie—or more commonly known as the sister to Niki Banks, who is also my cousin?"

"Right again."

"Shit!" the woman exclaimed. "Shit, shit, shit, shit!"

"That bad, huh?" he asked.

Bobby could only nod.

The hacker sighed deeply. "Well, you know how protective Niki is of me, right?"

"I do."

"And if you think she's protective of me, you should know she's about fifteen times more protective of her little sister after you dragged her out of the Zoo," she continued, still working on her computer as she spoke.

"Wait—after I what?"

"You... Oh, that seems like the kind of story Jennie should tell you herself. Anyway, the point is that I don't want Niki to shoot you in the head and or dick, and that seems to be what'll happen if you go out on a date with her little sister."

"Your concern is noted."

"Well, it wouldn't be necessary if you weren't some kind immoral, horrible male pig...hybrid thing."

Taylor raised an eyebrow. "I'm not any kind of immoral male pig hybrid thing."

"Come on, buddy," Bobby said. "You can lie to the girls who for some reason don't mind, but you shouldn't lie to yourself or to us—your friends. So yes, you are that male pig thing you mentioned and you don't want a damn thing to do with anything like a relationship."

"That's the whole point!" he protested. "I thought I was very respectful by being upfront about my view on relationships. And let's be honest, most of the women I have anything to do with are those who aren't too enthusiastic about the idea either, which is why it works out so well for all those involved. It's kind of how the whole world looks when you've dealt with looking down the cold steel barrel of death so often."

"Sure, but you still need to work on it," Bobby said. "Don't bother to deny it."

He rolled his eyes. "Ugh, whatever. Let's get to work. I'll think about this and my impending death by pissed-off FBI agent later."

# CHAPTER FIVE

There wasn't much to do out there. Baines had always dreamed of a position with one of the bigger casinos as their head of security. It would be the kind of job that would keep him on for years on end while he made sure the business continued to make its insane profits. Sure, he would inevitably be paid a set salary, but that also meant he wouldn't have to work nights and weekends.

For now, he simply had to pay his dues. All he needed to do was prove that he was capable of getting the job done as head of security in some of the smaller venues. With that behind him, he would be set.

Admittedly, the location he currently worked at was well known as a front for one of the local gangs but if anything, it meant the security was even more difficult. People thought they could steal from the casino simply because the focus of the establishment was to launder money. It was where all the wannabe card sharps came to try their hand since they weren't quite ready to risk what would happen to them if they went to one of the larger casinos.

He wasn't sure where they got the idea that they would somehow be luckier at the Straight Ace than they would at the larger venues. It was his job to identify them and make sure examples were made. For first-time offenders, fingers were broken to make sure they were easy to recognize. The second time, charges would be pressed and they would be banned from all the casinos.

People thought they would only be banned from casinos in Nevada, but they failed to realize that many of the establishments in Vegas and Reno also had branches across the country from Fort Lauderdale to Atlantic City. Their black books were shared across the whole nation.

Most assumed they wouldn't get a country-wide record for cheating at a smaller venue like the Straight Ace. They were wrong.

Baines sighed, leaned back in his office chair, and took another sip from his drink. Bringing in computer experts to build up the security software had been one of the sharpest investments the Straight Ace would ever make. It saved them millions of dollars a year at the very least but it also meant the cheat-catchers had become little more than security experts, the people called in to make sure that what the computers caught was legit.

Vegas rapidly grew more and more digital and relied less and less on the expertise of humans. It would backfire on them eventually—as over-reliance on anything tended to—but for the moment, he was happy to let the computers do their thing, even if it did make his job a little boring.

He picked his phone up and dialed the number of one of the pit bosses he had onscreen.

"Hey, Tim, it's Baines," he grumbled into the speaker. "How's it going? Anyway, I wanted to let you know the computer brought to my attention that there might be funny business in progress at blackjack table fifteen... Yeah, the guy with the red hat. He's easy to identify—the guy with the huge stack of chips.... Right, that one. Give him a quick look and let me know if you think more action is needed. Okay, thanks."

With a sigh, he leaned into his chair again and watched the pit boss move to the man who had been flagged by the software. It was never a sure thing. The first sign of cheating was that the player was winning. Cheaters who were losing weren't too interesting, after all. When they began to win, the software studied them to determine if they were simply lucky or if they were actually influencing the results a little.

Of course, the way the cards were shuffled and dealt meant that the odds of people merely being lucky were low. The chances were that they were counting cards or something like that.

The pit bosses were trained to be subtle in both their study of potential cheaters and the way they handled them. The best way to make sure they were "handled" was to let them continue to play, accumulate their winnings, and let the other players think they had a chance until they finally decided their luck was up and withdrew.

The suspect would then be escorted into a side office when they attempted to cash their chips in and would be dealt with in privacy.

It was a simple process casinos had followed since the concept of the house cheating players out of their money had been invented. It was simply how things went. The house always won.

The phone rang and he picked up.

"The guy's definitely counting cards but the dealer is showing his hole card," the pit boss said. "I don't think they're working together, but red hat knows what he's doing."

"Give him a talk when he bugs out," Bains told him after a moment of thought. "People like to see a winner—it makes them bet a little bigger when they think the house is out of luck. Let him have his time in the sun, then sit him down and explain the situation to him."

"Roger that, boss." Tim hung up.

It was great to be a security chief, even if it was one of the smaller venues. While he still wanted to secure a position in one of the larger casinos, he also knew for a fact that the stress involved in that kind of job made men lose hair and acquire drinking habits, among other vices, that helped them to cope.

He might not like the lower pay he currently received, but at least it wasn't quite the high-pressure environment he assumed he would have to deal with once he reached the big leagues.

With a heavy sigh, he rolled his chair to another screen where the software had alerted him to a potential scam at the craps tables. People who cheated at craps were a little harder to detect since, unlike blackjack, it was a game that had a much larger foundation in luck. There was enough opportunity for someone to make considerable money simply by being lucky. The trick was to identify those who immediately moved to cash themselves out after they had won big. Those who were merely lucky tended to want to stick around and continue to spend their fortuitously earned cash.

The door behind him clicked and he turned as his shift replacement Carl stepped inside and hung his coat on the hook.

"Evening, Baines. How's it going out there tonight?" the man asked and settled into the second chair beside him.

"It's mostly a quiet night. We have a couple of folks to watch but the software does most of the work, as usual," he replied and rubbed his eyes.

"As per fucking usual," Carl grumbled. "You know, I never thought I'd say this but I do kind of miss the days when we needed to pay attention to what was happening on the floor. Teams of twenty sat and stared at monitors, taking notes, and actually worked. Right now, it's merely point and shoot and sometimes, there's not even shooting."

"We're in a new age—the twenty-first century and the time of digital advances," Baines said softly. "You and I are analog clocks that are slowly being phased out of existence. But not yet, though, because for the moment, we still have advantages over the computers."

"Wait until they up their AI game." Carl grunted, his expression sour. "Guys like you and me will be relegated to pit boss status."

"Probably not in our lifetime," he said as he stood and stretched.

"Wait, what's this?" The other man's tone wasn't quite alarmed but it was serious so he turned to look at the upgrade windows being displayed. "Is that a glitch, or what?"

He leaned closer to see what his replacement was pointing at. His sigh was purely reflexive as he didn't want there to be any trouble, not now when his shift had all but finished.

"I'll say glitch," he said after he'd called up the details. "They always run an automatic update and sweep whenever someone tries to access the system from outside. It happens almost every day now. Wannabe hackers think they can make a quick buck to cover their college loans."

Carl laughed. "I'll run diagnostics on it anyway, just in case."

"You do that," Baines responded but had already turned to take his coat from the hook. "I'll have something to eat and go home."

"You have a good one, Baines."

"You too, Carl. Break a leg."

"Isn't that only for…uh, you know, performing artists?"

"You and I are the performing artists on this stage. You should know that."

---

Taylor looked at Bobby where he stood and stared at two screens Vickie was working on. He narrowed his eyes. Both men knew a thing or two when it came to software programming and the mechanic had even created a couple of rudimentary patches for their suits when both of them were still in the Zoo.

With that said, the other man seemed as lost as he was.

"Do you...know what she's talking about?" he asked finally.

Bobby looked up from the screen and rubbed his cheek. "I wanted to ask if you did."

Vickie rolled her eyes. "Neither of you needs to understand what I'm talking about. You only need to know that I know what I'm talking about, nod from time to time, and grunt like you are following my train of thought."

"I'm afraid that might be asking a little too much of us," Taylor admitted.

"Look, the long and the short of it is that while most casinos operate on closed networks, they still need to be able to access the floor's Wi-Fi with their security network, so it's not completely isolated. Once I connect that way, I can piggyback on the connection and force a reboot of that particular system. I then have full access, understand?"

He shrugged and tried to look less confused. "I...uh, sure, let's say we do and move on."

"Casinos these days have been built to fight low-tech cheating with high levels of technology," she explained as she scrutinized the subroutines she'd arduously written for the job. "It's their strong point and makes it almost impossible to cheat them on the floor, but it's also their weak point. They have the tech guys set the system up but they're less concerned with the very rare person who can get through the firewall they put their system behind. Not many people have the skill or the will required so in the end, you're talking about maybe three or four dozen people in the world."

"That…can do what?" Taylor asked.

Vickie huffed softly at him. "Get past the firewalls, of course. Which is not to say your average dumbass wouldn't be able to get past, but not many of them are creative enough to target casinos."

"She's still talking," Bobby grumbled and sighed.

"Yeah, this is what she's going to school for," Taylor reminded him.

"Oh…right."

"Shut your trap and let her keep talking."

The hacker beamed. "Thanks, Taylor. Anyway, my point —before you two became all pissy about how I know more than you—is that the only weak point in the security of most casinos these days is their digital reliance. They invested a ton of money and man hours into developing the firewalls but they rarely improve on them, which means the only way we would be able to strike our attackers in their wallets would be to use their digital weaknesses against them."

"Weaknesses can be exploited, I suppose," the mechanic agreed. "I'm not sure how we would be able to use their digital security for a heist or something, though."

"Well, back in 2013, a casino in Australia was hacked with the support of a high-roller who got into their security systems and used them to win over thirty-two million dollars before they realized what he was doing," Vickie explained. "They kicked him out of his comped villa but they couldn't prove he was actually cheating without admitting to flaws in their firewall, so he and his helpers got away with it."

"That was a while ago," Taylor pointed out. "And they would have patched their security since then."

"Sure, but the point stands. The easiest way to get into their security is digitally. And since we won't actually play cards to rob them, there are aspects of their security we'll be able to get into that they have no adjustments for. I'm fairly sure they've never seen the likes of me in their neck of the woods before."

"Well, that sounds…a little ominous, I won't lie," her boss said and looked around a little nervously.

Vickie gave an evil laugh as she continued to work. "I'm merely doing a test drive on some of the smaller casinos to make sure none of them pick up on me while I cut through their tech. The people running these systems are inherently lazy and copy-paste from each other's code."

"So once you've seen one, you've seen them all?" Bobby asked.

"Well…it's not quite that simple. It's more like a blueprint, I think."

Taylor leaned back in his seat and watched her work. Hacking in movies was made to look far more interesting with much quicker typing, intense soundtracks, and sometimes, Hugh Jackman with a ridiculous ear-piercing.

From what he now watched Vickie do, most of her actions appeared to be premeditated. She ran all her subroutines through the operation first and even simulated their actions before she used them.

It was slow, deliberate work, the kind that reminded him how the intelligence they worked with tended to go—

slow, deliberate, and avoiding any possible mistakes that could be made.

"Okay, I'm in," she said finally. "I know, it's a cliché, but I've always wanted to say that. Anyway, there was a quick update alert on the screen for them and there'll be a reboot on their side, but other than that, there won't be anything to show my presence in their system."

Bobby leaned closer. "So, did you actually break into a random casino to make sure your software works?"

"Well, that's the main idea, but I don't see why we shouldn't make the most of the situation," Vickie said. "Do either of you feel like going out for a quick run on the casino floor to earn a few grand?"

"That is probably not a good idea," Taylor said decisively. "There's nothing that'll get their attention faster than losing money that way and you'd have to find another way to break into their security. We don't have time for that."

Bobby raised an eyebrow. "So...we won't take advantage?"

"Well, we could always find another way to make it work," he replied. "That casino—the Straight Ace—why did you choose that particular one for your test run?"

The hacker shrugged casually. "That's where I tracked most of the money that paid for the first team that targeted us. I assumed it was being run by the same people and would have the most similar kind of security system, so I tried it on them first."

He nodded and scratched his chin thoughtfully. "I'll take that one step further and say this casino has a location offsite where their money is held and moved to and from there as needed. It's very likely something like a chop shop, where they would be able to transport cash in and out of the location without drawing attention from local law enforcement."

Vickie nodded. "Right you are. How did you think of that?"

"It's a fairly standard way to keep laundered money below the radar with the IRS," Taylor explained. "Most criminal enterprises make their money through cash and they like to keep it as liquid as possible and move as much as they can before they drop it into the accounts of the people who will keep it."

"What are you thinking?" she asked, her fingers poised above the keyboard.

He paused and thought everything through again. It had all seemed so simple and plausible when he had considered it in his hospital bed. "If it's possible, find one of those locations they move the money to and from since they'll probably use the same security system to plot their car movements through the city. If we can identify that, we'll have a start to our little heist."

"What kind of a start do you have in mind?" she asked.

"Cars. We can't carry that much cash by hand. It's much heavier than it looks on paper."

She nodded, returned her attention to the computer screens, and called up older programs and subroutines she had used in the past. Working rapidly and with intense focus, she altered and updated them to fit the new mission parameters.

"So," Taylor whispered and leaned closer to Bobby," do you think we should be worried that Vickie knows about all this—and seems to have simply waited for the opportunity to use it—or more impressed by her skill set?"

The mechanic chuckled and shook his head. "Given that we're investing considerable time and effort into improving that skill set of hers, I think we should be impressed, a little proud, and yes, a little worried and terrified too."

He nodded. "Yeah, that's what I thought."

## CHAPTER SIX

"I thought you said you intended to eat healthier," Bobby said.

Taylor looked up from the piece of pizza he was almost halfway through. He had lost count of how many he'd already eaten but he was willing to bet it was at least half of a pie, maybe more.

"I never said that." He frowned and took a sip of his soda. "I said I will return to my eating and exercise patterns of before, and that includes pizza from time to time. It also includes a couple of visits to Il Fornaio once we've finished this whole heist business."

The other man selected another piece from the pizzas that they'd ordered. "Why only after the heist?"

"Do you really think it would be wise for any one of us to set foot in a casino when we're planning to rob one?"

His companion opened his mouth to say something but quickly took a bite from his slice instead. "That's a good point," he said once he'd chewed and swallowed

He nodded. "Don't think it's not something I've craved

since I got back. Hell, since I was in the hospital. I swear to God that food must have some kind of additive that makes people come back over and over again."

"Or it's merely good food."

"That too, I suppose."

They looked up when the door into the garage opened and Vickie walked in. She looked a little red in the eyes and tired as she plopped on one of the empty chairs. "How long did I work in there?"

"I'd say about six hours," Taylor replied and wiped his mouth. "Bobby and I decided to get some mechanical work done since it was obvious we wouldn't be able to help you with any of the computer stuff. We put five hours in and ordered lunch. Speaking of which, you look like you've earned yourself a break."

"Thanks." She piled a couple of pieces from the ham and mushroom and then from the olive and pepperoni on her plate and poured herself a cup of the sweet soda.

"I can't tell, so I'll go ahead and ask," he said as she began to eat. "Did you make any progress?"

She didn't answer immediately but gobbled two slices before she so much as took a breath. Even then, she only took a moment to guzzle her soda to wash the food down.

Finally, she turned her gaze to him and looked a little angry. Or maybe she was simply tired. He still couldn't tell which and thought he'd rather not ask.

"I have found someplace where we can get our hands on untraceable vehicles to perform the heist in." Her voice was muffled around the food she continued to stuff in her mouth. "That's about the end of the good news, unfortunately. I did create a way into the main casino we'll target after, but... Well, they seem to be compensating for being both a top-of-the-line casino and a front for the Sicilian mob, so they have a whole slew of security on the ground as well as in the sky."

Bobby's eyebrows lowered over his eyes. "In the sky? Drones?"

"Eye in the Sky is the commonly used moniker to describe the security systems they've put in place on the casino floors to keep an eye on gamblers," Taylor explained.

"They have AIs running security on the floors now," Vickie grumbled, her mouth still full of pizza. "I was able to get in and if we simply played the games, I would be able to help you win. Although if you won too much, of course, there wouldn't be anything I could do to prevent the AI from alerting the pit bosses about your cheating."

"So...you're saying we have no chance to hit the big places then?" he asked.

She shrugged. "We have no chance to hit anything inside the casino, no."

Bobby sighed and leaned back in his seat. "So it's back to square one, then?"

"Not really," Vickie snapped sharply.

"But you said—"

"That's not what I said. I simply said there wouldn't be anything inside the casino we could hit. Outside the casino, on the other hand..."

Taylor looked up when her voice trailed off and caught a definite gleam in the young woman's eyes. "What do you have hatching in that brilliant brain of yours, Vickie?"

"You make it sound like I'm some kind of evil genius."

"Aren't you?"

"Well, yeah, but you don't have to say it outright."

"What do you have in mind, Vickie?" Bobby asked.

She finished her mouthful and wiped her lips with a paper napkin. "Well, the idea is that to steal anything from inside a casino is essentially impossible, right? So, the simple premise of my thought process was to take their money while it's outside the casino."

"While they move the money in or out in the armored vehicles." Taylor grunted, his expression thoughtful. "That does seem like the softest point of their security, but instead of relying on outright brute force, they rely on anonymity. There are hundreds of armored vehicles using a wide variety of routes through the city every day. How would anyone ever be able to identify the right one at the right time?"

The hacker raised her hand. "I know the answer to this one, professor."

"You managed to have a look at the routes the armored trucks take through the city, the times and the locations, as well as the amounts they'll transport in and out?"

"I did one better," she asserted smugly and straightened in her seat. "Ordinarily, a casino needs to match the number of chips they have available on the floor with cash on hand. For an establishment as large as the one we're thinking of, it'll be at least eighty million dollars on your average weekday.

"That changes, of course, when they host big events or anticipate a larger number of chips being needed on the floor—like the heavyweight boxing fight they'll host this weekend. The Nevada Gaming Commission requires them to double the cash they have on hand and they need to move it in somehow. That would entail three different armored trucks traveling on three different routes transmitted to them by the AI at the casino."

"Which you'll be able to see," Bobby said and finished her point for her.

Vickie snapped her fingers and pointed at him. "Bingo. Or…jackpot, I guess works best in this case. Do they have bingo in casinos?"

Taylor narrowed his eyes. "I doubt it. At least not in the larger venues. It's not that big a cash-maker for them, so I don't think they'd have it center stage anyway."

"I think I'll simply stick with jackpot," Vickie said as she helped herself to a few more slices of pizza. "So, what do you guys think?"

"That is one hell of a job you've done." He gave her a thumbs-up before he took another sip of his drink. "Especially given that it was all done in a couple of days, right?"

"I…uh, right. Yes, that is true."

The two men exchanged glances before Bobby leaned a little closer. "What was that?"

"What was what?" she responded airily.

"That pause? You paused."

"I most certainly did not!"

Taylor sighed. "Come on. You know we're past the point of judgment here, Vickie. Go ahead and tell us."

"Fine," she huffed and actually pouted. "I may or may not have planned something like this for a while. Nothing really serious, merely putting together the software I'd need to break past the firewall without being seen. It was kind of a way to keep my skills honed during what little free time I've had since I've come to Vegas. I didn't really plan to use it, not for real anyway. It was only practice."

"I don't know why you felt like you had to keep that from us," the mechanic commented.

Her boss nodded. "He's right. That's impressive."

Vickie beamed at him and continued to scarf her food like she hadn't eaten in weeks.

Bobby turned his attention to where Taylor sat. "I don't know about you, but I have absolutely no idea how to stop an armored vehicle in broad daylight and in traffic. But like our hacker friend here, I'll guess you already have something in mind for when we need an actual plan?"

"It's fairly standard operating procedure and between you and me, I've done it before," he admitted. "Not in the US, mind, so the tactics will have to be altered. It was also about three years before I got to the Zoo, so it was a while ago."

"But you do know what we're doing, right?"

He shrugged. "Well obviously, the heist will be where most of the action is, but it won't be our focus. Or, at least, not Vickie's focus, anyway."

The young woman's head raised quickly. "Say the fuck what now?"

"Oh, yeah, we'll definitely hit their wallets hard," Taylor said. "And while most of their security and AIs will be focused on the robbery, you'll use your access to mine data, hopefully about the people who are running the operation as well as their location. That would give us what we need to cut the head off the snake. Do you think you can do that?"

Vickie tapped her chin with her forefinger for a

moment. "Okay, yeah, it's possible. Like you said, I'm already in."

"So, they'll probably have trails maybe from the CEO's office of calls and transmissions and the like that will take us all the way to the douchebag who's in charge," he continued.

"I'll see what I can do," she grumbled. "No promises, though."

"Give us something to start with, okay?"

She nodded.

"Okay, I don't want to be the broken record people constantly complain about," Bobby ventured after a moment, "but would you mind explaining a little more clearly how we can stop one of the armored trucks and empty it of cash?"

"The standard procedure is very simple," Taylor said and took a deep breath. "You need two vehicles. The lead vehicle will be used to stop the armored vehicle in question and from there, do all the...what's the term? Crowd control?"

"Crowd control sounds right," Vickie agreed.

"Okay, and what's the role of the second car?" the mechanic asked.

"The second car—probably a van—will be the busiest, since car one will likely be abandoned," he continued. "Sometimes, it gets rammed by the target and at other times, it's too...showy. Either way, both will probably need to be discarded by the end of the operation, which is why we'll need to get disposable vehicles from the location Vickie found. Wait, what was I saying?"

"The role of the second car?"

"Right. Anyway, the second car will follow the one with the cash and keep track of its movements—"

"Which I'll do so never mind that," the hacker interrupted.

"Correct, but still, it'll have to come in from behind and keep the armored truck from reversing and getting away. Once the target is sufficiently boxed in, it's the role of that car's occupants to break into the back, snatch the money as quickly as possible, pile it into the car—the reason why it's best to have a van—and get away as quickly as possible."

"Wait—how will we open the secured vehicle from the back?" Bobby asked. "Oh, and if one of us will drive the lead car and one of us will drive the van, who will take the money out and how? It seems like we'll need to involve a third party."

"And I don't think Niki will join us on this operation," Vickie commented. "She might not be opposed to breaking the law from time to time but she'll probably draw the line at grand theft casino money."

Taylor nodded. "We'll steal cars too, don't forget, so you can include grand theft auto in that. Actually…like, grand theft in general. All kinds of larcenies."

"Well, be that as it is, we can probably rule the FBI agent out," Bobby agreed.

"Well, regarding the third party—" their boss began.

"Are you sure we don't need more?" the hacker asked hastily.

"No, and I'll get to that if you guys would stop interrupting me." Taylor growled annoyance and fixed them both with a hard look. "Anyway, I have someone in on the situation who I've worked with before and who needs paying work. And who probably wouldn't mind the whole ton of money we'll get our hands on. I'll call her in later."

"Her?" Vickie snapped. "Please tell me you won't involve one of your one-night stands?"

"What did I say about interrupting me?" he responded irritably. Both of them fell silent for a moment. "Anyway. This third person will be the driver of the van, which will leave me and Bobby to handle the roles of lead car driver and crowd control and also retrieve the money from the back. And yes, we'll have to be able to do it on our own."

"I think I see where this is going," Bobby said.

He nodded. "Yeah. What's the status of the mech I sent back from Wyoming? I know that I sent it back in a huge mess, so if it's not in working order, we might need to take one of those we're repairing out for a...test drive, I guess."

"You plan to use the combat mechs for the robbery?" Vickie asked and raised an eyebrow. "That's...ingenious. It works as armor and weapons and keeps your identities a secret."

"Law enforcement, in general, isn't quite up to handling mechs yet. Provided we can keep the cops off of our backs, it should be very simple to get in and out without them getting involved. We'll probably be out of the van and into a secondary escape car before they even realize that the robbery happened."

"I could probably keep an eye on that too," she said.

"You could and it would help, but make sure you're not taking on too much work at once," he warned. "Your focus needs to be on getting the information from the casino. That's your top priority. Everything else takes secondary importance, okay?"

She sighed and rubbed her eyes. "I understand."

"So, do you think it's a plan or what?" he asked and looked expectantly at the others.

Bobby shrugged, the gesture willing but cautious. "Sure. I'll need to get used to working in a mech again. It's been a while since I've been in an actual combat situation."

"Well, if I take the lead car, I can handle most of the combat," he assured him. "The guys in the back won't need too much handling once you yank the back door off."

"I like that," the mechanic replied with a chuckle.

"So, if you guys will excuse me." Taylor sighed, stood, and stretched languidly. "I have a few calls to make."

# CHAPTER SEVEN

"Where are we going?" Bobby asked as they piled into the four-by-four.

"Well, first, we have someone to pick up," Taylor said as he slid into the driver's seat. "After that, we'll head out to the chop shop to pick up some cars for the heist and hopefully piss a few people off."

The mechanic eased into a comfortable position in the passenger seat. "Is there any tactical reason for that?"

"Nah. I only want to piss those assholes off."

"Fair enough. Will we rob the place in this car, though?"

"Kind of." He swung out of the parking lot of the strip mall. "However we do it, we'll drive out in our stolen cars, after all, so we'll need to get within walking distance. Or maybe take a bus or something most of the way. But like I said, first off, we'll pick up the third member of our team."

"Fourth, technically, since we're including Vickie."

"Third member of our ground team, anyway."

"Again, fair enough."

It wasn't too long a drive before they drew up in front of a small apartment building.

Bobby looked quickly at him. "I feel like it needs to be asked again—this isn't one of your one-night stands we're picking up, right? I know you don't think it's a problem but honestly, I think it's a recipe for all kinds of disaster."

"Yes, it is, and no we're not," Taylor answered. "I've never slept with this woman and as a matter of fact, she was one of Niki's operatives before she quit and came to me, asking if I had a job for her before I shipped out to Wyoming."

"So, is she in the know of the situation or will we have to explain to her why her interview for a job at a mech repair shop is a hopefully million-dollar heist from a casino?"

"I've been in contact with her since I was in the hospital and I had her do some work for me while I was indisposed. She's trustworthy and knows her way around a gun better than most. That said, she'll also probably only be driving anyway, so compared to your job and mine, it'll probably be a breeze."

Bungees chuckled. "I love your generous use of the word probably in there."

He shrugged. "What we're doing isn't an exact science. You of all people should know that."

Both were distracted from the conversation when a tall, lean woman with short black hair pulled into a ponytail stepped out of the apartment building, walked to where they were parked, and climbed in.

"Tanya Novak, this is my friend and fellow Zoo survivor, Bobby Zhang, also known as Bungees," Taylor introduced them. "Bobby, this is Tanya Novak, former cryptid hunter and certified kickass."

"Nice to meet you," Tanya said, shook the mechanic's hand from the back seat, and squeezed Taylor's shoulder. "It's good to see you on your feet again, Taylor. I was afraid those monsters did too big a number on you."

"If they want to stop me, they'll have to kill me," he responded and laughed. "Honestly, it might come to that. Anyway, are you clear on what we'll do here?"

"Well...okay, I have to say I'm not too happy that the first real work I'll do with you guys is robbery," she admitted. "But after what you told me has happened to your business, I guess making sure they're in no position to continue attacking you guys will be safer in the long run."

"Plus, you'll be entitled to an equal share of our profits in this gig," Taylor reminded her.

"Yeah. That's the only reason I agreed to this crazy scheme."

After another short drive, he stopped the car in a pay-by-the-hour parking building and as he had told Bobby earlier, a short bus ride delivered them to the chop shop. The area was mostly abandoned by this hour. Most of the other shop owners had already closed for the night, but the chop shop in question was still open, judging by the lights that illuminated the landscape around it.

Taylor stopped them a good distance away from the lights, removed his duffel bag from his shoulder, and placed it on the ground. Inside were three shotguns which he and Bobby had sawn off in their workshop, as well as three pistols, all of which had been collected from the perpetrators of their previous break-ins.

"We'll go in there quick and quiet, okay?" he explained in a hushed whisper. "You two will handle crowd control and keep people off our backs. I'll head into the main building and find the keys to the cars outside, understood?"

Bobby and Tanya both nodded before the team donned ski masks and gloves. In silence, they began to sneak toward the fenced rear section of the chop shop and tried to remain in any shadows they could find as they approached.

"So," Bobby said in a low tone as Taylor started to cut the barbed wire with his bolt cutters, "Tanya Novak… What kind of name is that?"

"My name?" the woman replied with her head tilted, possibly in confusion.

"Well, yeah. I mean where is it from? Because you don't have any trace of an accent but that doesn't sound like a strictly American name."

She nodded. "My folks were from Serbia and came to the US during all the shit that happened there. Even so, they kept to their old culture and traditions and named me with that in mind. Tanya and Novak are fairly common in the area they grew up in, so I stuck with it. How about you, Bobby Zhang?"

"Chinese-American," he said. "Third-generation American, though, so basically the only thing left of that particular heritage is the surname."

"I don't know…you do look like a muscular version of Jet Li," she commented quietly. "Is that from working out or are you naturally bulky?"

"A little of both, really," he replied. "Thanks for noticing, I guess."

Taylor sighed, shook his head, and finally held open the hole he'd made in the fence to let them through. It was a good thing they were calm enough to have a simple conversation moments before a break-in. Both had been in high-pressure situations before, and their calm demeanor showed that the pressure hadn't affected them.

He waited for them to slither under the fence before he eased through behind them. Hopefully, if all went well, they would leave the location from the front, but assuming that all would go well often got people shot for being too cocky. He felt like it was prudent to leave them with a way out of the situation if it went south.

They moved quickly through the yard area and all three operated smoothly together to clear corners and ensure that the area was mostly abandoned before they approached the front of the shop. Three men were hard at work on a group of cars that had been brought in recently.

The team paused out of sight and quickly convened to formulate a plan of attack. Taylor held up three fingers and pointed at Tanya and Bobby. They would have to keep all three under control—hopefully, their modified shotguns would send a suitable fear-of-death message—and he motioned that he would hurry into the office and retrieve the keys for the cars they would take.

The other two nodded and he ran a hasty final check on his shotgun and pistol before he inched from the shadows and remained low. He really wished they could have brought the mechs in for this one, but he didn't want anyone to be ready for them when heist time came.

Bobby and Tanya quickly followed suit, their weapons raised.

"On the ground!" Taylor roared. He felt a little out of breath but otherwise much the same as he had when he'd operated without a mech in the past. "Get on the fucking ground now!"

All three men looked up from their work, shock etched on their faces and in wide eyes. They raised their hands quickly as he reached the first one, caught him by the shoulder, and hurled him roughly to the ground.

"Hands behind your backs. Let's get moving, people!" Bobby shouted. Tanya replaced her shotgun with her pistol and zip-ties and worked rapidly to bind their captives.

Taylor indicated that he would move toward the office. Someone would most likely be there, and he knew enough to believe they would be armed and a little more prepared for him. He didn't think that was necessarily a problem, but it did mean he needed to be more careful with his approach.

He allowed himself one last look to make sure all three men were bound and dragged clear of any potential weapons they could use. Satisfied that his teammates had everything under control, he moved toward the door while he remained low and away from any windows. He could hear movement inside, and he pulled one of the flashbangs from his duffel bag, dropped the bag, and pulled the pin.

His heart thundered and body thrilled from being in the action again. There was something invigorating about being in combat without the safety of three inches of steel plate armor between him and the rest of the world. It wasn't something to be repeated regularly but it was certainly thrilling in the moment. Adrenaline most likely took care of any physical discomfort he might have experienced, but for now, he felt fine.

A quick motion opened the door, and the blackness inside erupted in a hail of gunshots, likely fired in the hopes that he would have simply pushed into the room. His unseen adversary was doomed to disappointment as all that went in was the flashbang, and Taylor waited the allotted three seconds before it detonated.

Somehow, the man inside had already run out of bullets and had begun to reload when the grenade filled the room with a wave of blinding white light and a loud enough bang to leave his ears buzzing.

If the chop shop manager had tinnitus, he would be completely deaf for a solid minute and a half. Taylor didn't have the patience to deal with that himself.

He slid in after the light faded and located his target quickly in the darkness. A tall, corpulent man with what looked like an old Uzi gaped at him and tried to fire his weapon despite the fact that he had emptied it and was unable to reload.

In a moment, Taylor had reached him, aimed his pistol at the man's right foot, and pulled the trigger.

With a shriek, the heavy figure fell and released his weapon. A reflexive kick slid the sub-machine gun smoothly out of the wounded man's reach and he grasped him by the collar before he even had time to land fully.

He was heavy and with him not in the best shape of his life, panted noticeably by the time his prisoner was sprawled on the floor in the workshop.

"What...what the fuck is wrong with you!" the injured

man screamed with his hands still clutching his ringing ears.

"Me?" Taylor asked. "Nothing. You, on the other hand, have a hole in your foot. Luckily for you, I'd say it'll only be a couple of weeks until you walk again. Unluckily for you, there's more room for me to keep shooting you, so do yourself and your ability to walk a favor and answer my questions quickly and concisely. Question number one is easy. Where do you keep the car keys?"

He fixed his tormentor with a murderous scowl. "Do you know whose business this is?"

In response, he raised his weapon until it was directly beside the man's left ear and pulled the trigger. There was obviously no external injury, but the noise was enough to start his screams again.

"The next one will leave you with a place for a piercing or two, but I'll choose whether to put that hole through your ear or your dick, so answer the fucking question."

"Bottom drawer on the left!"

Bobby moved closer to keep an eye on the injured man while Taylor returned to the office. He found the drawer in question easily enough and yanked it out to reveal a selection of keys that likely fitted the cars the group had been working on.

He walked out quickly and dumped the contents on the floor. "Which key works on the black paneled van over there?"

The man turned, looked through the keys, selected one, and handed it to Taylor, who in turn, tossed it to Tanya. Bobby moved to watch the other three captives.

Tanya knew her job well and wasted no time. She slid

into the vehicle and started it before she gave it a quick inspection to make sure everything was functional.

They only needed it to be able to get to the shop where they could do their own work, so functional was a minor matter all things considered.

"And the keys to the Mustang?" Taylor snapped to the wounded man who still lay at his feet.

The murderous glare had quickly transformed into one of fear, and he made no protest but simply scrabbled to locate the key between the others and handed it to him. It was Bobby's turn to test the car, and like the van, it was still functional.

They had what they needed and there was no point in hanging around for anything new or unexpected to derail what had been a successful foray. Taylor zip-tied the injured man quickly and rushed to the van. Bobby had already pulled the Mustang out of the shop, and Taylor and Tanya were close behind.

"Nice job," he said. He breathed a little faster than he would have liked but still bumped the woman's fist.

"All in a day's work," she replied and yanked her ski mask off.

## CHAPTER EIGHT

Vickie stared as they drove the two new cars into the garage. "So..."

"Yeah?" Taylor asked as he slid out of the van

"You picked this Mustang out on a whim, right?" she asked in an annoyingly high-pitched voice. "You simply picked up the key and decided it was the perfect fit, right?"

"Your insinuating voice is really annoying," Taylor grumbled and rolled his shoulder. "Say what you disapprove of and get it out of the way, okay?"

Vickie narrowed her eyes as Tanya exited the van as well, quickly followed by Bobby from the Mustang they had chosen.

Taylor raised an eyebrow. "Did you have something to say outright or did you plan to simply keep on insinuating until you lost your voice?"

The hacker scowled at him as he deposited the duffel bag from his shoulder and the ski mask on a nearby table. "Well, no, not anymore. You ruined the moment."

"I'm glad I could help," he stated with a small grin. "Anyway, what do you think of the cars we brought in?"

"I thought you didn't want to listen to my insinuating voice."

He shrugged. "Well, yeah, but if it's necessary to get you to spill what you actually think about the vehicles, I'm sure we can tolerate it. Oh, by the way, Vickie, this is Tanya Novak. Tanya, this is Victoria Banks. Make sure she's okay with you calling her Vickie. Otherwise, there could be trouble."

Tanya shook her head, walked to Vickie, and proffered her hand. "It's nice to meet you, Vickie."

"Right back at you, Tanya. And it's good to know I won't be the only girl around here anymore."

Taylor rolled his eyes. "Well, there goes my attempt to try to help you cultivate some mystique about you. Anyway, Vickie here will be our technical support. Our Eye in the Sky, if you will."

"That's me," the hacker said with a firm nod. "I decided it's safer for me to be as far away from the action as possible, sipping a cool glass of something while you guys risk your lives. But that's not the point right now. The point is, of course, why the hell you chose a Mustang for this heist we're planning. The van is a decent enough choice, obviously. It's the type that's mostly ignored in traffic until they cut you off or something, but a Mustang is loud and grabs attention much more."

He looked up from checking his weapons with his eyes narrowed. "How long have you driven around Vegas, exactly?"

Vickie looked around. "Who, me?"

"No, the person you see in the fucking mirror every morning."

"Oh yeah, she's a total bitch."

When he opened his mouth to respond, he was unable to stop a chuckle from escaping. "That...was a good one. Well, for you anyway. But yeah, if you drive around Vegas for a while, you'll see the kind of trend most people would miss. The closer you get to the casinos on the Strip, the more expensive the cars you'll see. There are many things that factor into this.

"Some are owned by people who make a ton of money and on impulse, spend it on expensive cars in the dealerships located inside the casinos. Others belong to people who are already well off and want to spend their money on the same cars, so they'll basically do the same thing. Another interesting thing I noted was the fact that most of them like to take the cars for a test drive since many of those in-casino dealerships have women in tight, shiny outfits selling their cars. When they go on the test-drive, they tend to make people think about something other than an intelligent way to spend their money."

"Is there a gas station between here and the fucking point?" Bobby asked as he joined them where they replaced their weapons and equipment in the duffel bag.

"I'm right at my point, so no," Taylor snapped. "My point is that there are countless expensive cars around the Strip area of the city. Cutting right to the heart of it, having a Mustang like the one behind me will attract less attention than a regular old Volvo or Toyota or something but less than a Ferrari or Maserati would at the same time. It's flashy enough to be inconspicuous in that area of the city.

Besides, it'll be the car that'll be used to get the armored car to stop, so we need it to be heavy and fast at the same time to account for any…uh, unforeseen eventualities."

"Let me guess," Vickie interjected. "You want to drive the lead car."

"I do like me a little Mustang action, I won't lie," he admitted. "But if Bobby thinks he can do a better job of crowd control, I'd be willing to give it to him."

The mechanic responded with a vehement shake of his head. "Someone who drives the lead car and wears a mech suit will need to use our smaller hybrid one if they want to be able to drive. Unless Tanya has any experience with those?" The woman indicated in the negative as well. "That leaves only you, Taylor."

Vickie narrowed her eyes at him. "You planned this whole thing, you bastard."

He offered her his version of an evil laugh and raised his hands to shoulder height as she sighed and leaned back in her seat.

"Okay, so the plan is for you to take the hybrid suit in the lead car and pull it to a stop in front of the armored car in the middle of traffic, right?" Tanya asked.

Taylor nodded. "Once the car is stopped, I can get out and make sure no one is able to get out of the vehicle. Traffic should be able to prevent them from backing away from me to escape since it will be a peak time of day. It won't quite be rush hour but there will still be considerable traffic in the area. Anyway, that gives you two about ten seconds to pull in behind them and box them off in the van. "

"Which will be driven by me," she noted.

He could see she approached the concept of performing a heist on an armored car with a surprising lack of doubt in her mind. Maybe this kind of thing simply wasn't that foreign to her or maybe she had done something like it before.

"Right," Bobby agreed. "The moment people see the armor and the weapons, they'll back off. That will give us the space we need to get the hell out of there when we're ready. I'll be in the back of the van, which is the only place I'll be able to fit wearing the full combat mech. Once the armored car is stopped, I'll climb out, break through the doors, and snatch the cash from the back. I'll get back in the van with it and we'll drive away. How will Taylor get away, though? Still using the Mustang?"

"Nope. The chances are the Mustang will be damaged from stopping the armored vehicle," Taylor said and pointed at the target location on the online map where they planned to perform the heist. "I'll get into the van with you guys and probably take shotgun with Tanya."

"Right," the woman grumbled. "How much time do we have to get the job done before the cops are on our asses?"

"I've run a couple of simulations and tests on the police response times in the area over the past couple of days," Vickie said and pulled up the results of her testing. None of the others could understand what the details were so she continued to explain what they meant. "The information I have is that the armored trucks have a panic button for each of the men in the vehicle to call for support in case of a robbery. Those activate a silent alarm inside the casinos themselves, which in turn is supposed to alert the authorities since their on-site security teams would not be allowed to operate beyond the confines of the casinos themselves."

"The delay between alerting the casino and then the authorities should give us a little more time, right?" Taylor asked.

The hacker shrugged. "It's a matter of seconds, usually. I can run interference and make it seem like a false alarm so they'll need people to physically see what's going on before any action is taken. But if an AI catches the alarm before me—which is very possible given the six alerts that will come in—it'll transfer the call to the police immediately."

"So, let us look at the worst-case scenario," he continued. "The AI transfers the alert to local law enforcement immediately. How long do we have until they get to the location?"

"About a minute and a half," Vickie replied. "Plus or minus thirty seconds depending on the density of the traffic."

He sighed and tapped a slow tattoo on his chin. "Let's say a minute and a half, which gives us sixty seconds from the point when they press the panic buttons to stop them, get the cash, and get out."

"You'll probably want to make sure all tracking devices are disabled and prevent any dye packs from going off," the hacker pointed out. "I think I could help with that. A couple of updates to the software on the suits should do the trick."

"Okay, that sounds good, and Bobby can get started on making sure the cars are in order," he said. "The best thing about stealing from a stolen car ring is that they already have new plates and won't be reported stolen, am I right?"

The mechanic's eyebrows raised in protest. "What, so I have to do it alone?"

"It's not that much work," he replied with a chuckle. "You simply need to check and double-check to make sure the cars won't break down. Besides, you have Tanya to help you now."

"And where the fuck are you going?"

"I have a date tonight, remember?"

None of them responded as he turned and headed deeper into the building to change his clothes and wash up.

"This will…it'll end badly," Vickie commented morosely as she turned to face the computer screens.

"How do you mean?" Tanya asked as she and Bobby began to work on the cars, starting with the van. "Taylor seems like the kind of guy who goes on a lot of dates so I don't see how it'll be a problem for the heist."

"It's not that," she grumbled softly. "It's…complicated and more about who he's going out with than the fact that he's going out."

The other woman shrugged and hauled her jacket off. Vickie noted that Bobby literally did a double-take and stared at her before he focused his attention on the engine of the van.

Tanya obviously didn't want to pry too much into the personal details of what was happening, but she most likely couldn't help but be curious about the inner workings of a group she hoped to work with full-time once all this heist business was done with. Still, she chose not to ask any further questions, which was probably a good thing.

Vickie finally sighed and turned in her seat. "Fine, but don't say I didn't warn you. The situation is much more complicated than Taylor looking for someone to sleep with. Well, get into bed with, anyway."

The newcomer narrowed her eyes. "You haven't—"

"There is not enough money in the world. Well, not enough money in Taylor's bank account, anyway. But the point is that...you remember Niki, right? Niki Banks?"

"Special Agent Banks was the agent who operated the task force Taylor and I worked on. You know this, obviously, so I assume there's a point to this."

"Sharp girl. I can see why Taylor likes you," the hacker said. "Speaking of which, did you and Taylor—"

"In my case, it's literally not enough money in the world."

The younger woman looked impressed. "Respect. Anyway, Niki is my cousin, and she interceded with Taylor to give me a job after some legal trouble I got myself into. I'm fairly sure she blackmailed him too, but that's not the point. My point is that the woman Taylor is going out on a date with goes by the name of Genesis 'Jennie' Banks."

"Banks as in—"

She nodded. "Banks as in."

Tanya paused for a few moments, her eyebrows raised. "Huh. Yeah, there's no way that can't backfire. I only wish there was some way for us to get the backfiring on tape somehow."

Vickie turned to face the taller woman. "You know, I think you and I will get along just fine."

Taylor looked around the restaurant at which Jennie had

told him to meet her. He hadn't been sure what to expect from the woman he mostly only knew over the phone, but something like this wasn't what he'd had in mind. With Niki as a basis to establish what her sister was like, his imaginings hadn't even come close.

A taxi pulled up, and a young, vaguely familiar woman stepped out and smiled and waved to the taxi driver before she turned to face him. The familial resemblance between the two women stood out very clearly, but there were some definite differences too. Jennie was much slimmer and her hair was cut shorter. Still, there was no mistaking her for anyone other than the agent's sister.

"Taylor, I'm so glad you could meet me." She approached him quickly and immediately moved to hug him.

His reflexive reaction was to stiffen and his discomfort increased when she didn't release him. All he could do was pat her gently on the back until she finally stepped away.

"So, you're friendly." He grunted to cover his awkwardness.

"No, not really. But I have wanted to do that for a while."

"Hug me?"

"Also, yes. But mostly feel you up."

"Right...but what about the taxi driver?"

"Oh, he had a kid who was going to my alma mater and wanted to know what the place was like. I left him with a couple of stern warnings to avoid the bitches in Phi Mu, and he was really appreciative of that."

Taylor narrowed his eyes but nodded. "Well, I guess... that makes sense. Anyway, this is quite impressive. When you hear steakhouse in the name, you don't think valet service and large glass doors with fine, plush decor and rich colors. Maybe more along the lines of dozens of screens and drunk sports fans yelling at said TVs."

Jennie laughed. "Yeah, I don't think that's the kind of clientele you'll see around here. It's owned by a couple of celebrity chefs and has a Michelin Star and many online reviews from the rich and the famous. I thought I'd try it while I was here—it seemed worth the effort."

"Oh, you thought you'd try a restaurant where the average entree costs more than the average night in a five-star hotel around here."

She grinned, took his arm, and guided him through the doors. The maître d' stepped forward immediately to take her name and the tall, lean man guided them to one of the tables next to the windows.

"Trying a place like this…it doesn't seem natural to me," Taylor said and shook his head as they were given a couple of drinks menus.

"Well, I've done very well for myself in the private sector, and unlike my government-employed sister, I happen to know that you're doing well for yourself too. Don't bother to deny it."

"Yeah, you and Niki have an oddly invasive concept of personal privacy."

Jennie snickered. "Who the hell do you think taught Niki everything she knows?"

"The point wasn't your collective skill set," he pointed out as the waiter approached their table.

"Good evening, sir, madame. Are we ready to order?" the man asked in a suave British accent.

"Hi, good evening," she said with another bright smile. "I think I'll start with the pan-seared scallops with lime and coriander and finish with the smoked ribs over herbed stacked potatoes and a... Do you recommend a bottle of chardonnay for the starter and Pinot Noir for the main course? I think we'll choose our dessert later."

The waiter nodded. "Excellent choices, ma'am. And for the gentleman?"

Taylor nodded. "I'll have the same starter but I'll go with the ribeye and maybe replace the wild jasmine rice with pommes frites?"

"And to drink, sir?"

"I'll go simple tonight, so do you have any Summer Lager on tap?"

"Of course, sir."

Jennie waited for the man to move out of earshot. "I think he might have a heart attack over you choosing beer instead of wine. You might have saved him a trip to the hospital by referring to them as pommes frites instead of fries, though."

He shrugged. "I'm a simple man, and beer is a little easier on a guy who just finished a long stay in the hospital and hasn't been out drinking in what feels like forever. I'm easing into it again."

She smiled. "And here I had hoped to get you drunk out of your mind and into your pants before the night's end."

"Well, you'll have to pay for my dinner if you want that."

"Taylor, I know how much you make. We'll split this bill. I've paid for Niki to eat at this kind of place all week and it's begun to strain my food budget."

It had been worth the attempt, but he accepted her

response with a nod. "So, why don't we talk about the reason why you wanted to have this dinner in the first place? Yeah, I'm sure the food is probably good and I don't doubt that the company will be all kinds of fantastic as well, but I had the feeling there were ulterior motives behind you asking me out when I was in the hospital."

"Well…"

"And I don't mean the ulterior motive of relieving me of my clothes," he added quickly to make sure she knew he was serious rather than lighthearted about her reasons.

She sighed as their drinks were brought to the table, followed quickly by their entrees. "Look, I don't know what to say. Or…well, I suppose I do, honestly, but I don't know how to say it. There's so much I've wanted to say to you over the years, but I never had the chance. At first, you were still in the Zoo—or Zoo adjacent, anyway. When you left, Niki got her hands on you and she prevented me from getting in touch. You know how she is."

"I do, actually." Taylor sighed and shook his head as he took a mouthful of the food. "Holy shit, these scallops are amazing."

"Yeah, they don't give those Michelin Stars out to simply anyone, you know."

"I wouldn't know anything about that," he admitted. "Anyway, what were you saying?"

"Well…the whole point is…" She sighed, leaned back in her seat, and frowned with the effort to work up the courage to say what she wanted to tell him. "Okay, I don't know if you remember, but I was actually in the Zoo."

"I think Niki told me about that."

"Well, yeah, but I was there for the...uh, I think they called it the Gulch of Armageddon Battle."

His eyebrows lowered as the waiter appeared to clear their plates, refilled their drinks, and told them the main course was on the way.

"You were there for the Gulch of Armageddon?"

She nodded slowly, her expression carefully neutral. "Remember how they sent that huge group in to rescue a group of scientists with vital information from the Zoo? And how only one of those scientists made it out?"

The penny finally clunked in his head. "Of course. You're Dr. Genesis Banks. Holy shit, how the fuck did I never make that connection before?"

"That... Well, that's all on you, I'm afraid. I guess you have an excuse, given that you kind of kept on going while I was transferred home virtually overnight."

He nodded and leaned back in his seat to study her with renewed interest. "Yeah. That was an interesting trip into the Zoo, to say the least."

"Okay, I know it maybe doesn't make sense but after that, I kind of felt attached to you," Jennie continued. "It could have been something of a crush with a little infatuation mixed in and over the years, it became more of an obsession."

Taylor searched her face for a few seconds while their main course was placed, but she seemed relaxed.

Jennie immediately dug eagerly into her ribs but looked at him when she realized he hadn't made any attempt to attack his plate with the same kind of gusto.

"What?" she asked.

"Well, it's not every day that someone tells you she's

obsessed with you. It kind of takes a while to process something like that. So...uh, this obsession wouldn't have resulted in any kind of stalking, would it?"

She tilted her head and regarded him evenly and honestly. "I guess I did, although it was more keeping up with what you were doing in the Zoo."

"And keeping up with my bank statements?"

"Well, yeah. But don't you prefer that I was upfront about it instead of keeping it a secret?"

He thought for a few moments and finally decided to make the most of his steak, given that he'd be unlikely to repeat the opportunity anytime soon. "I do appreciate your candor. Not very much, obviously, but still. You made the effort, but it doesn't quite make up for the stalking part of it."

"Look, I know it was—"

"Supremely uncool."

"Right, but it was difficult. I had to cope with everything that happened and I did, but not very well. You were kind of a beacon that dragged me out of that and a few months later, I was called to report to the board of the company. They liked my work and its results so much that they gave me the job I have now. Well, I started a couple of levels lower but I managed to work my way up, especially after my boss' boss hit on me at a Christmas party while people were filming. It wasn't something I'd care to repeat but it did make them offer me a better job to keep me from suing them for sexual harassment."

Taylor nodded. "That'll do it."

"Yeah, and they made the guy retire after that. Of

course, it was with full benefits and millions worth of company stock to his portfolio, but still."

"Back on topic," he said to guide her away from the skeevy director or VP or whatever he had been. He had no interest in finding out. "I'll be honest, I'm still not sure as to the reason why you wanted to talk to me. What exactly is all this about?"

She sighed and placed her napkin on her empty plate. "It's a matter of getting you out of my system. So far, I've placed you on a pedestal. Getting to know you will make you more human. The more I get to know you, the more human you become and the trend is likely to continue. For instance, what if I got to know you better over declining to order dessert and us heading to my hotel room for drinks?"

His eyebrow raised in surprise at the suggestion, but as the waiter returned to clear their plates, he chuckled and shook his head. "All right, I'm all for that. Let's get out of here."

"Oh yes, you're definitely my kind of guy." She laughed and gestured to the waiter to get their check.

CHAPTER NINE

Vickie scowled.

It wasn't possible. Not only that, in this environment, it was probably unheard of. How could it be that it was six in the goddamn morning and someone knocked on her door? Well, not so much knocked as tried to reduce it to kindling with his or her fist. Temptation swirled in her mind to simply pull a pair of noise-canceling headphones on and sleep through it, but common sense responded that people on her floor would complain about it.

That wasn't something she wanted. Vickie had gone through a fair amount of trouble to make sure no one knew where she was living or even how long she had lived there.

It was a college dorm, which made her desire for anonymity a little more challenging. Thankfully, a few tricks on the computer had unobtrusively and successfully assigned her to the dorms where people had their own rooms rather than shared them—and at no extra cost.

"Fucking hell." She growled belligerently and finally

clambered out of bed to shuffle to the door. Whoever was on the other side still seemed determined to break the damn thing down.

She unlocked it and gaped at Niki in surprise. The woman looked tired but taut with stressed energy and she was red in the face when she stormed into her apartment.

"Yeah...come on in," Vickie grumbled and rubbed her eyes as she closed the door again. "Can I get you some water? Maybe a watch to remind you what fucking time it is? Are you deliberately trying to get me kicked out of the building?"

Her cousin glared at her and immediately tried to pace the room but was forced to stop as there wasn't enough space to do so. "Why did you move from Taylor's strip mall?"

"I think you answered your own question there."

The agent appeared to want to say something more—maybe a more biting response—but held herself back and shook her head.

"Do you want to tell me what's on your mind?" she asked. "Or did you simply come to act like a surly little child in what passes for my living room?"

"It's... Look, I'm sorry I pounded at your door and I'm sorry I woke you at this ungodly hour. But I...honestly, I don't know what to do."

Vickie stared at her for a moment before she walked to her desk chair, sat, and offered the easy chair seat to Niki. "And just like that, everything's okay."

"Are you serious?"

"Why wouldn't I be?" the hacker countered. "Now, tell me what's on your mind and don't be stingy with the details. Something has you riled up and if I know you at all, getting you riled up at six in the fucking morning—"

"Again, I'm sorry about that."

"And again, everything's okay. But for something to have you riled up this early, it has to be something big—and maybe good. So why don't you go ahead and lay it on me? Tell me what's bothering you."

The woman took a deep breath before she dropped into the easy chair. "It's only…that son of a bitch didn't go home last night."

"I'm sorry. Which son of a bitch are we talking about here?"

"Your boss, my contractor, the red-headed son of a bitch who's been the bane of my existence for longer than I feel is healthy—Taylor Mc-Fucking-Fadden!"

Vickie winced. "Okay, maybe a heads-up is in order. The walls here are fairly thin, and if I get a fine from the building manager for making too much noise, you'll pay for it. Also, Mc-Fucking-Fadden may be my new favorite thing. It sounds like something out of an adult-themed McDonald's. Can I use it from this point forward?"

Niki clenched her teeth and her nostrils flared to demonstrate that she was at the point of snapping again, but she withdrew quickly. "Yeah, go ahead. It's all yours. But I feel like you're not as upset about this as you should be. She's also your cousin, you know, and thinking of Taylor like that—ugh, I can't even think about it for too long without getting all worked up again."

The hacker leaned and stretched to the mini-fridge beside her computer, pulled out a couple of bottles of water, and handed one of them to her companion. "Yeah, I guess there's a slight gross factor involved there. But honestly, Jennie's older than I am and is more than capable of making her own choices. She's a grown-ass woman who is entitled to make some mistakes and live with them, exactly like all Taylor's other dubious conquests."

Her cousin took another deep breath and obviously tried to calm herself. "Sure, I understand that. And I've always felt immensely sorry for the girls who decide to share a bed with Taylor, but you have to admit there's something different when it's someone you know who's going through that. And when it's my kid sister, it's so much worse."

Vickie turned her computer on while she called up the security system she'd had Bobby set up the night before when they had closed the shop. Sure enough, there were no changes, which confirmed that Taylor hadn't deactivated it and taken control as he usually did when he came home late.

"Fuck," she grunted. "But again, I bring you back to my point that Jennie is a strong, confident woman who don't need no man. And she certainly don't need no big sister to tell her who she can and can't have carnal relations with."

"Ugh, don't say it like that."

"Don't say it like what?"

"Carnal relations. That's so…yeah, ugh."

"Whatever you say but the fact stands. You can't dictate her sexual partners to her, and you certainly can't do the same for Taylor so—oh, wait. You have to be kidding me."

Niki's attention was dragged from where she toyed with the label on her water bottle and she scowled at the look of sudden realization on the younger woman's face.

"What? Who has to be kidding you?"

"You."

"Me? I have to be kidding you?"

"Yes," Vickie snapped and stood quickly. "This isn't about Jennie at all, is it?"

"Of course it is. Who else would it be about?"

"It's about you," she pointed out. "More specifically, it's about you and Taylor."

The agent's expression changed from confusion to steadily growing annoyance that rapidly approached anger. "You have about a minute to explain yourself right now."

"You're not pissed because you think Jennie spent the night with someone you believe is bad for her. It probably does play a part, obviously, and so you tell yourself it's why you're so angry at her. But in the end, all this rage and anger is misdirected because Jennie's spending the night with Taylor when you want that for yourself."

Niki's mouth gaped in shock at the suggestion. No words escaped her for a few long seconds—an entirely rare occurrence—while the anger in her features gradually dissipated and was replaced by a look Vickie wasn't used to seeing on her face. Defeat wasn't something she had ever imagined she'd associate with her.

"Don't get me wrong now," the woman muttered tentatively, "Taylor is still a despicable human being and everything about him either annoys or disgusts me. But I guess there…uh, might be some kind of physical attraction that I've fought since I met him. I simply need to get over it and until then, I guess I'd rather my baby sister didn't sleep with him. Added to the fact that she is capable of doing so much better, of course."

"That's not good enough."

"What?"

"You heard me," Vickie snapped and sat once more to look her companion sternly in the eye. "Now's not the time to construct more lies for yourself. Consider this your confessional. Anything you say here will be instantly forgiven and forgotten. It's time for you to say what you want to say and accept it for yourself, okay?"

Niki looked like she was in physical pain but she took a deep breath and seemed to gather the resolution to do what she knew had to be done. "Okay. I've worked with Taylor for a while now, and while I do have philosophical disagreements with how he's decided to live his life, there is something about him that appeals to me for some reason. It's not something I'm proud of and honestly, it's probably only a crush I'll get over once I meet someone who I genuinely like, but—"

"Given that your job of choice doesn't allow for much dating or long-term relationships, that's not likely to happen."

The woman rubbed her eyes. "What the hell is wrong with me? Taylor is a catch, I guess. He's well-off, good-looking, in shape—or he will be once he's regained all that muscle he lost in the hospital—and he's a smart guy. The only problem is that he's elected to live his life in a way that's meant to be as deplorable as possible, fully knowing the benefits of his decisions. Someone who knowingly makes the choices he's made is insane, right?"

"I guess," the hacker grumbled and leaned back in her seat. "In fairness, you're trying to rationalize the actions of a man who chose to go into the Zoo eighty-three fucking times."

"The issue is that he has rationalized it. When you see him, it's only too easy to assume he's simply a big jackass who lives his life without thinking of the consequences because he's too dumb to think that far ahead. But when you talk to him, that changes. You see that he's actually put thought into doing what he does and that makes it all much more infuriating."

"And maybe that's why you like him?" Vickie suggested calmly. "Okay, I'm not saying you necessarily like him because he makes informed choices that seem idiotic. But it's something of a mystery to you and that concept is intriguing."

The agent sighed deeply and took a sip of her water. "It's that and a whole horde of other things. Nothing's simple in my life, so it makes sense that my romantic inclinations aren't either."

"So long as you're done lying to yourself and now address these matters honestly, things will begin to simplify themselves. Maybe you should take a page from Jennie's book and have a roll in the hay with him—get it out of your system and you'll be right as rain."

Niki paused, thought about it, and broke into laughter. "I...that's so stupid but so well-rationalized that it makes sense. It also sounds like Taylor's kind of thinking."

"Eh, if you spend enough time with him, he starts to rub off on you one way or the other."

"In your case—"

"Definitely the other. Don't worry, he's not my type and he's insisted that I'm not his type either."

The older woman pushed from her seat. "Funny, that's actually what he told me too. Anyway, thanks for the talk, Vickie. And again, I'm sorry for the early wake-up call. If you need me to, I can talk to some of your professors or whatever and get you out of studies for the day."

"I might take you up on that. And rest assured that not a word of what was said here will leave this room."

She stood as well and Niki wrapped her in a warm hug. "I appreciate that. The talk and your discretion."

"No problem, cuz." She drew back from the embrace when she felt something vibrate.

"That's mine," the agent said and yanked her phone out. "Oh…"

"What?"

"It's a text from Jennie. She's asked if I want to have breakfast and thinks she knows the place I'll want to go to. And she says you're invited too."

"It sounds like she's wanting to appease you as much as possible. Wait, how does she know you're in town? I didn't even know."

"Come on. She taught you everything you know. Besides, she probably expected me to follow her here, all things considered."

Vickie bit the inside of her mouth to keep from retorting with the sour thought that came to her mind. "Where do you think she wants to take you?"

"Right after a tryst with Taylor and wanting to get on my good side immediately? Where the fuck do you think?"

Bobby wasn't sure what to make of the fact that the strip mall was exactly the same as they had left it when they had shut down the night before. He wasn't Taylor's keeper. The man was technically his boss, and while he would make sure to give him a hard time to make up for getting to work late at his own business, all he wanted to do when he drove into the garage was get food, coffee, and start work.

There was more than the usual workload to attend to with their new project, but the cars didn't need that much attention to make them ready for the heist. They were already in decent enough shape after all.

The coffee he brought with him soured his mood somewhat.

"It's seriously about time we get a coffee maker in here. Maybe we can talk Taylor into setting up a break room or something like that since we have new people starting work now."

He had long since stopped questioning why he talked to himself. It was merely a way to voice his thoughts out loud so he could tell if they were worth serious attention or not.

His coffee was finished quickly and what he'd brought for Taylor had begun to get cold when he decided that it was time to get to work—no matter where the boss was.

The phone chose that moment to ring. It was a school day for Vickie but it seemed too early for people to call about the business they conducted on the premises. They were ahead of schedule on deliveries, but he had made sure that they didn't take on more than they could handle with the jobs. There was no sense in biting off more than they could chew

Unfortunately, the phone still needed to be answered, and he was the only one there to do so.

"Fucking…people need to get into work," he complained as he walked to the desk and snatched the receiver from its cradle. "This is McFadden's Mechs."

"Hey, McFadden's Mechs. You sound a lot like Bungees," Vickie replied.

Bobby rubbed his eyes. "Morning, Vickie. I thought you wouldn't be working today, or are you too bored with schoolwork and will come in anyway?"

"Sadly, no, I have a ton of shit to catch up on. I'm only calling to make sure that Taylor isn't there."

"You have access to the security. Can't you tell?"

"Like I said, I want to make sure. Have you seen him yet?"

"No. Why? What's the problem?"

"Well, there are two problems. First of all, it doesn't look like Taylor came home from his date last night."

"Do you think he's in some kind of trouble?"

"I know he's in trouble because point number two is that Niki's in town and she's full-on pissed. Would you mind going up to his quarters to make sure he didn't somehow sneak in under the radar?"

His eyes widened. That was one hell of a problem.

"Shit, I'll check. Give me a second."

Most of the strip mall was still empty. Taylor's plans to continue the renovations and possibly bring in other businesses to pay rent to him had been put on hold since his stay in the hospital. The whole area had a ghost town feel to it that Bobby wasn't a fan of. Then again, he only worked there and his time was usually spent either in

Taylor's apartment on the top floor or the garage where they did most of their work.

He climbed the stairs as silently as he could, inched to the door, and turned the handle.

The door swung open slowly.

"Shit, the door isn't locked," he noted for Vickie's benefit.

"And that's bad because?"

"Well, if it isn't locked, it means he probably didn't sleep here. He doesn't like sleeping somewhere with unlocked doors."

"How the hell—"

"If you spend enough time around the guy, you start to pick up on his mannerisms. But keep in mind that he spent an inordinate number of nights out in open spaces contemplating exactly how many ways an alien Zoo could kill him. I guess maybe he likes to secure the perimeter by force of habit."

"Right, that's a good point."

Bobby didn't understand how Taylor could live in a space like this. It was clean and organized with everything piled and shelved with some kind of system in mind.

He still used a military cot for a bed and the blankets were arranged neatly and folded at the foot with a single pillow at the top.

"Nope, he definitely didn't spend the night here. And he could stand for a room upgrade. Do you know that he still sleeps—"

"In that damn cot, yeah. It's like you said, he has habits he has a hard time letting go of. That's what comes from spending all that time in the military and not thinking about his future. Back on point, though, if he's not there, I need to track him down quickly. Some shit will go down this morning, and I need to make sure he stays as far away from Il Fornaio as possible."

"What's happening at Il Fornaio?"

"Knowing my luck, probably something a little shy of World War Three. I'll keep you in the loop. Talk to you later, Bungees."

"Stay safe, and if shit hits the fan, know that no one will think less of you if you simply run away."

"Roger that. Vickie out."

# CHAPTER TEN

The young hacker knew that what she now faced would be the kind of family reunion people dreaded. Usually, they put it off until the holidays to make sure thoughts of goodwill toward men kept people from starting wars.

With that said, even though Niki had come to a couple of personal realizations during their previous conversation, she still looked like she headed into battle. She merely had that look about her—a steely gaze and an uncaring attitude when it came to navigating the morning traffic.

All Vickie could really hope for was that they didn't die in a fiery crash before they reached Jennie's restaurant of choice.

Maybe the woman was tempting fate, she decided. It could be that she almost preferred to be involved in a crash than to have to deal with her younger sister after said sister had gotten into bed with the man she had a crush on.

Either way, she thoroughly regretted her decision to let her cousin drive them to the New York-New York Casino where the restaurant in question was located. With that said, she had always planned to revisit the establishment. Taylor and Bobby raved about it so much that she felt obligated to make sure they weren't born without taste buds. Of course, a single breakfast didn't count as sufficient data, so this wasn't only a possible peace-keeping mission.

Niki pressed forward once they were parked and walked at a pace that made the younger woman jog to keep up.

"You know there's no rush about this, right?" Vickie asked.

The agent shook her head. "I want this over with. It's a conversation that needs to happen, but I have the feeling that neither of us is really looking forward to it."

She turned to face her cousin. "You...do remember this is your sister, right? You have a relationship with the woman, had any number of conversations, and know what she's about, more or less?"

"What's your point, Hacky Hackerson?"

"My point—aside from the fact that you should have stopped at Mc-Fucking-Fadden, when it comes to nick-names, anyway—is that Jennie is not dreading this conversation. In fact, if we are honest here, she'll probably try to get on your nerves as much as possible before she finally arrives at the serious part of the conversation."

"She wouldn't— That's not...okay, fair enough. That does sound like Jennie."

"And if we know that woman at all, she's probably well aware of your feelings about the guy and will probably prod you about that too."

"I think we agreed that none of that conversation would leave the room, which includes no passing remarks. My final commentary on that which cannot be mentioned is no fucking way. She merely thinks I'm over-protective. That aside, she knows I'm right and simply wants to get on my nerves. There, that is all we will say on the matter."

"I can't even reply to disagree?"

"You couldn't say anything even if it would save the world from destruction."

Vickie nodded. "Fair enough, but you should know that I would probably tell people about your secret if it meant saving the world."

"And that's why you're not a priest. Or a psychiatrist."

"I would be a nun, anyway, and I don't think they take confessions so it doesn't matter."

They arrived at the restaurant, where the warm lighting almost immediately put the hacker in a better mood. Despite that, she recalled that Jennie had included her in the invitation, which confirmed that neither of the two sisters wanted to deal with the situation without her being present. Her somewhat tongue-in-cheek thought of her as a peacekeeper suddenly crystallized into the reality that she had most likely been deliberately selected as a sounding board and an impartial mediator between the two women.

She sighed and realized she would need far more coffee if that were the case.

The waitress greeted them quickly and informed them that a member of their party had already arrived. They were directed to join Jennie in a booth in the back. The woman had already ordered a large mug of steaming coffee and she stood when they approached.

"It's nice to see you guys!" she said and hugged Niki first, then Vickie. "Holy shit, you've had a growth spurt since I last saw you. And I totally dig the goth chick vibe you have going on. The short hair especially."

The hacker was clearly uncomfortable with the compliments about her appearance and shifted her gaze down as she ran her fingers through her short hair. "Thanks, and it's nice to see you too, Jennie. It's been a while."

"Come on, sit down," she invited them. Vickie slipped into the booth first and claimed the seat with her back to the wall, which left Niki to face her sister across the table. "I'm honestly a little surprised you agreed to come."

The agent raised an eyebrow at the woman. "I don't think we really had a choice. You have to know I knew what you were up to last night. Otherwise, you wouldn't have called me for breakfast and especially not at the place you know is my haunt."

"Well, first of all, I invited you here because I thought it would put you at ease since I knew you'd be on edge. Oh, and because the food here is fantastic, according to you. I had to try it to see what all the raving is about from my big sis."

Niki leaned forward on the table. "Don't try to butter me up. You know what you did."

"Or who she did," Vickie interjected and immediately regretted it as the agent's glare turned to her instead. "Are you guys ready to order? Have you ordered already, Jennie?"

"No, I waited for you to arrive. That way, we could all eat together as a family."

Her older sister seemed like she was on the verge of blowing up but once again, kept herself under control as the waitress arrived to take their orders.

"Good morning and welcome to Il Fornaio," the woman said in a pleasant tone. "Can I take your orders, please?"

Neither sister spoke immediately and Vickie stepped in. "I don't know about these two, but I'm fucking—oh, sorry, but I'm starving. Do you have any suggestions?"

The server smiled. "Of course. If you're that hungry, the Waffle *Alla Frutta* is probably the best choice. Waffles with fresh strawberries and bananas, whipped cream, powdered sugar, and New England maple syrup should work."

"That sounds amazing, but can you throw in a nice stack of bacon? And a mocha latte, please."

"Of course. And for the other two ladies?"

Niki sighed and let her shoulders drop and the intensity of her gaze diminish somewhat. "I guess I'll have the *Uova Alla Benedettina* with bacon too and a latte."

Jennie paused for a moment and studied the menu. "I think I'll try this *Fritelle Allo Sciroppo D'Acero*, which looks like pancakes with butter and syrup and is exactly what the doctor ordered after last night. I'm sure I pronounced the name wrong. And I'll have a refill on my latte, too, please."

"Coming right up."

The silence that settled between the three was heavy with expectation and Vickie watched the two sisters studiously avoid each other's eyes.

"So, I'll go ahead and say it and get it out in the open,"

she said after a deep breath and before she could change her mind. "What the hell did you do last night that calls for the carb overload this morning? Or should I say, who?"

Niki's foul mood returned with a vengeance, but the hacker knew they needed to talk about it or they would simply dance around each other forever.

"Okay, sure, Taylor's fun to ride for a while," Jennie said and scratched her chin. "But the real fun starts when he rides you if you know what I—well, you wouldn't, Niki. Not unless you had that stick surgically removed from your ass for some reason. And you, Vickie, since you've worked with him for a while and—"

Vickie raised her hands quickly. "Not even if his dick cured cancer."

"Which, holy hell, it might. You should know the kind of soreness that comes after a good hard—"

Niki watched the exchange in silence and it looked like the red in her face had begun to turn purple as her fingers clenched the napkin in her hands.

Jennie paused, saw her sister's reaction, and finally exhaled. She leaned back in her seat and the gleeful look on her face faded quickly.

"Look, I'm sorry. You know how much I like seeing you squirm, Nik, and I happen to know that the feeling is mutual, but I couldn't do that to or with Taylor. Nothing happened last night."

Vickie felt like she'd taken a surprise kick to the chest as she turned to look at her cousin. "Bullshit."

"Okay, I don't have any camera proof to show you that we didn't do anything so you'll have to take my word for it.

Or not, depending on how you feel about it. Anyway, that's how last night ended."

Her sister stared at her in stony silence for a while but was given the chance to process the news when the waitress returned with their food. The woman put it in place quickly before she beat a hasty retreat, likely sensing the mood at the table.

The hacker wasted no time and attacked her meal, while Jennie took a moment to study what her sister had on her plate.

Niki shook her head. "It's eggs benedict but on *filone* bread toast instead of an English muffin and cream Parmesan sauce instead of hollandaise. Now, back to the topic. What do you mean when you say you didn't sleep with Taylor? Do you mean to say you two merely did...what, exactly?"

"Well, all that shit I talked before was mostly to get a reaction out of you. Since I didn't get the reaction I had hoped for, I decided to cut it entirely. But I meant what I said. He and I didn't actually do anything."

"So, you guys went to your hotel room and talked?" Vickie asked, her mouth half-full of waffle.

"That's precisely what we did. Taylor was a perfect gentleman and immediately understood that it wasn't something either of us wanted to do and we ended up talking."

The hacker paused in mid-chew and turned to face her again. "Wait, I think I might have had a small stroke. Or maybe I zoned out and misheard the whole of the conversation, but it sounded suspiciously like you said Taylor was a perfect gentleman."

"Well, he was."

Niki leaned in a little closer. "So, you're saying Taylor—and it's Taylor McFadden the ginger giant we're talking about here—was a, and I quote, perfect gentleman."

"That's what I said."

Vickie shook her head. "Nope. My brain refuses to accept that as any kind of reliable information."

Jennie laughed. "Okay, I know where you're coming from. At first glance, no, he can't be a gentleman, but if you spend time around him, that changes."

She raised her hand. "I beg to differ and I've spent a whole shit ton of time around the man."

"I don't know what to say," the woman mumbled around a mouthful of pancake. "We went to my suite and we started talking. Admittedly, the Zoo stuff we discussed wasn't the kind of thing that really encourages carnal relations, but we started with that and eventually... Well, that was all we did. Fair enough, there was considerable talking involved—hours' worth, actually—but that's it."

Vickie tried not to snicker when Niki cringed at the use of the words "carnal relations" but moved on from it. "Well, if we go along with the assumption that you're not lying, my next question is what did you guys talk about?"

Jennie stopped and toyed with her food with her fork for a few seconds. "Well, we talked about what happened to us in the Zoo. We addressed the fact that I was a little obsessed with him and we discussed it. I came to realize it was merely a silly crush, the kind that came from him helping to rescue me from that godforsaken place. The whole event made a huge emotional impact but didn't give me the opportunity to get to know the guy who was inside the suit. Once the suit was peeled away and I met the guy inside, it seemed like... Well, there was no real reason for us to make the proverbial beast with two backs."

"The proverbial what now?" the hacker asked.

"It's Shakespeare," Niki said and looked surprisingly subdued. "Othello, I think."

Her sister tilted her head in thought. "Well, he coined the expression in English but I'm fairly sure that it was actually French first. I forget where it started—"

"Back on topic," the agent interjected. "You were telling us what happened last night."

"Right. Anyway, I did get him to show me his scars and he has a ton of them. If he hadn't been such a gentleman all night, I would have taken the opportunity to feel him up a little and maybe pinch his ass. I know we weren't in the mood to get it on but you'd have to be blind not to appreciate what he has rocking. He's lost some of the muscle mass but he still has that lean meanness—"

"We get it. You still have a physical attraction," Niki snapped.

"I simply can't process the idea of Taylor being a gentleman," Vickie mumbled around her mouthful of food. "It does not compute."

Jennie shrugged. "I don't know. He seemed like he liked the idea of having someone to talk to—someone who understood everything he went through in the Zoo. Once he started, he had so much to say and it wasn't merely rambling. Or maybe it was but it was still really interesting. Do you know he once walked in on a pair of killerpillars mating?"

Vickie winced. "That can't have been pretty."

"He didn't mind or, at least, he said that he didn't. It made it easier to kill them since they were stuck together and unable to properly use the poison stingers on their legs against him. But that's not the point."

"Yes, let's move past a monster called a killerpillar," she agreed.

"Anyway, he merely liked having someone who could relate to his issues. I know that mechanic…uh…"

"Bobby," Vickie said. "Or Bungees. He was in the Zoo too."

"Yes, that one. And yes, he was, but he was a mechanic so didn't go in much. Taylor does have people like that who can at least understand the kind of issues he faced to some degree, but I got the feeling that he needs a special someone—the kind of person who would be able to get him through the nightmares."

The other two women exchanged a glance. The agent had, of course, seen the man's psyche eval and Jennie had probably seen it too. Unbeknownst to either of them, the hacker had done a little exploration on her own. While she'd been careful not to do anything to raise flags, she'd managed to access the psychiatrist's records. After all, she needed to know what kind of crazy person she worked for, didn't she? It was all about self-preservation.

As a result, all three knew the kind of baggage Taylor had carried around since he left the Zoo. Still, it was hard to associate the man and his devil-may-care attitude with genuine trauma.

They finished with their meals and now nursed their coffee, and Vickie realized that she had dreaded this whole conversation for no reason. She had needed to do very little in the way of mediation between the two sisters.

Jennie finished her latte first as the waitress arrived to clear their plates. "Overall, it was one of the best dates I've ever been on. Not that I think there'll be another one, obviously, but still. I think that despite the facade he puts up around everyone, he's actually a fantastic guy. You two need to be a little fairer to him."

***

Bobby and Tanya looked up from their work when the garage doors started to open. He already knew Taylor had arrived from the vibrating alert on his phone but she still needed to be read into the security system they operated with.

It was the four-by-four since Liz still needed a fair amount of work, something he'd not been able to do although he had wanted to get the truck up and running again. He'd even thought about making it a kind of coming-home present for the man, but with their increased workload, he hadn't been able to finish the job.

Liz was still in good shape. All that was needed was a quick cleanup on the chassis and she would be as good as new. Taylor could handle that on his own.

For the moment, though, the man simply used his four-by-four, which was the purpose for which he'd bought it in the first place. Liz didn't maneuver too well in the city anyway.

Taylor climbed out of the vehicle and looked tired and a

little hungover but otherwise intact. "Morning, guys. Sorry I'm late for work but I had one hell of a long night."

"That's no problem." The mechanic looked up from what he'd been doing and nudged Tanya to do the same. "What happened last night? Did you get lucky?"

"Not in the traditional sense, no," he replied. "But it was still a good night. Unfortunately, I didn't get any sleep so I'll turn in for a couple of hours. Do you two have this? I thought I'd bribe you with doughnuts to sweeten the deal. Hey, sweeten the deal."

The woman could only shake her head.

Bobby tried not to roll his eyes. "Yeah, the pun was not lost on us. Get some rest, man. You're no good to us on this heist if you're sleep-deprived. Get some sleep and let us know when you can start to contribute."

Taylor raised his hand and moved to the stairs. "Will do. Have fun you two."

His friend watched him closely as he climbed to his apartment.

Tanya noted his interest. "Did you actually check him out? I mean, I understand the attraction but I'm starting to think my gaydar might not be as attuned as I thought it was."

"Gaydar?"

"You know, the ability to tell if the man, woman, or whatever the person self-identifies as is sexually attracted to people of their same sex or not. Gaydar."

His eyebrows elevated sharply. "Oh...no, I'm definitely not attracted to Taylor. I was only... Well, it's a little difficult to explain but I checked for scratch marks on his arms or shoulders."

"A tell-tale sign of whether or not he had sex the night before. I get that."

"Good. Good. Because I don't want you to think I'm gay. Not that there would be any problem with that, of course, but..." His voice trailed off for a few seconds as he turned and realized that she was still staring at him. "Well, it's not something I'd want you to think."

"Me in particular, right?"

"Sure. I guess. If you want to see it that way."

"I wouldn't mind seeing it that way."

Bobby nodded and refocused very carefully on the Mustang's engine. "Cool. Cool."

## CHAPTER ELEVEN

They wouldn't clear the idea of her going out with Taylor from the air with only one conversation. Vickie knew more about what was happening than Jennie did, so she knew the fact that her sister had gone out with the man she was secretly crushing on would continue to bug Niki for a long time to come.

Well, she assumed the other woman didn't know. She was one hell of a computer scientist—better even than she was at microbiology since she was one of those who had worked as a pioneer to design AIs to take over combat functions in the mech suits that were being deployed. There was no telling what she did or didn't know, given that she was about as respectful of people's privacy as Vickie was.

But once the conversation came to a close, Niki decided she didn't really have anything to condemn her sister for. Nothing had happened or would happen in the near future between the two of them and that was good enough for now. They paid their respective bills and Vickie and Jennie agreed that Il Fornaio had not been oversold by a long shot.

Both sisters needed to head out before midday on flights that would take them elsewhere in the country. They needed a ride to the airport and neither wanted to leave a car there, which meant Vickie was enlisted to drive them in her Tesla.

She wished there was some way to avoid it, but they were family. In the end, she resorted to playing music in the car to make sure Niki didn't stretch from the front seat to strangle her sister. Things were still a little tense between them, even if the younger one wasn't sure why.

"I don't know why you're still so uptight," Jennie said from the back. "You know what happened and you said you believe me, but you're still sulking like I went behind your back or something."

Niki fixed her with a slightly challenging look. "Are you telling me there was no chance you and Taylor would have gotten anything going last night? That you didn't ask him out in order to get into his pants or maybe him into yours?"

"Why the hell do you care about that kind of hypothetical anyway?"

Vickie sighed, shook her head, and focused on the road ahead. She had decided not to be involved in the drama of the two sisters any more than she already was. As things stood, she was at risk of being uninvited from the Christmas Party and if she was deprived of the kind of food Grandma Banks produced for the holidays, she would not be responsible for her actions. Maybe she would head to Il Fornaio if the unthinkable happened.

If the truth be told, Taylor and Bobby had begun to be the family that didn't judge her for her appearance or ask her what she was doing with her life while they expected to be disappointed. Her boss acted like more of a dad than she had expected from him but it was somehow a little more comfortable for her.

"Come on. You can't say nothing would happen and still invite him to your hotel room."

"Well, not that anything did, but why the hell do you care about it anyway? There's this thing called consenting adults that you have no say over."

"I don't have any say in it. But you're my little sister and I'm only trying to keep you from making that particular kind of mistake."

"Oh, look at that. I didn't make that kind of mistake. It's almost like I don't need you to hang out with me every second of every day to know what kind of mistakes I am and am not allowed to make."

"Okay, I'm bringing this to a stop right now," Vickie snapped but remained firmly focused on the road. It was a difficult situation but she had to simply power through it. "I know you guys have issues to resolve, but you already talked this out. You came to the conclusion that nothing bad happened, talked and resolved some things, and there was no problem. Wallowing in hypothetical scenarios and what might have happened is something that'll drive everyone insane."

Niki shook her head. "But that's not the point—"

"I don't give two flying fucks what the point is. You guys make me seem like the adult and the voice of reason and let's be honest, it's not a good look on me. So figure this shit out without resorting to petty arguments like this."

Both women stared at her in absolute silence.

"Fine." Niki looked exasperated and exhausted since she likely didn't have any sleep the night before. "I'm sorry. I know I'm overreacting about this. You know I don't really mean anything. I only want what's best for you, even if that might not be too apparent after today's events."

Jennie leaned forward to hug her sister from behind the seat. "I know. I love you too, big sis."

"There we go," Vickie commented with a small smile. "Not everything's figured out or settled but it's still a good thing to keep it all as civil as possible, right?"

The agent nodded. "I still can't wrap my head around this whole Taylor being a gentleman thing. Hearing it simply sounds wrong. He's not that kind of guy, you know?"

"I see where you're coming from but assuming there's only one side to him does feel a little unfair," her sister pointed out. "You know what he's been through—or at least seen some small version of it—so you can't expect him to react to the world like a normal person. He has his coping methods."

"I…guess that would be why he's willing to let them bomb the shit out of his position simply to clear it of monsters." Niki's voice was a little more subdued. She didn't want to think about Taylor this way. It felt like giving him any in-depth thought meant he was winning somehow.

The hacker shrugged and eased into the short-term parking area of the airport. "He has something in him that wants to get rid of the monsters, no matter what. It's instinct, the kind that won't go away. He'll do whatever it takes to get the job done."

"Which, in the end, could mean him dying as well," Jennie said and completed the argument. "When you're in that kind of mindset for a long time, you kind of don't realize that it seeps into the rest of your psychology too."

It was an odd thought to end the conversation on, and all three remained seated in the car for a long moment while the seconds ticked past.

Niki was finally the one to break the silence. "Well, if he's the kind of guy who doesn't respond well to working with a therapist—and I think he is—I don't think he'll be in a situation to fully recover for a while."

"Maybe that's merely his way to deal with it."

"Okay, let's agree that we have to stop trying to psycho-analyze a guy like Taylor and that maybe you guys have flights to catch so I don't have to pay an enormous ticket for lurking around here too long." Vickie tried not to sound too pushy about it but she did only recently buy her car and she didn't want anything bad to happen to it.

"Fine." The agent sighed, leaned closer, and hugged her. "Thanks for the ride. And for being the voice of reason. I know you don't like doing it."

Jennie offered her a hug as well and the sisters scrambled out to remove the luggage from the back. Neither had planned to stay in the city long so didn't have too much luggage. Both only had a couple of carry-ons with no larger pieces.

The hacker had no idea why they needed that much in the first place. If she had to be out and about for a few days, all she needed was a backpack with her laptop and assorted electronics as well as a few changes of clothes.

Then again, she had always been good at packing small and efficiently. Maybe the other two weren't quite so skilled. Or they simply had more shit to bring on an overnight stay in town?

Either way, it didn't matter. She was there to see them off and quickly got back into her car to drive to the city, not in any kind of a mood to go to school. Admittedly, she needed to work on a group project but in the end, all she would have to do was go in at the last minute and fix everything that was wrong with her teammates' work thus far. They all knew better than to doubt her abilities and knowledge.

Rather than head to the campus after a quick coffee stop, she elected to simply go to work. The chances were she would have an opportunity to upsell on an incoming order or two before lunch, and from that point forward, she could decide what to do with the rest of her day.

Taylor wasn't the kind of boss who watched his employees constantly and given that he would likely crash at someone else's place for the evening, he would be unlikely to complain if she took a nap all afternoon.

The assumption, of course, was that when things hadn't quite gone his way with Jennie, he'd called someone else and crashed at their place instead. It had most likely been Alex from the bar where they all liked to hang out at.

It was a short drive to the shop and the underwhelming

strip mall the business operated out of. To her surprise, both Bobby and Tanya were present and hard at work, and it looked like Taylor had eventually found his way home judging by the four-by-four parked in the garage.

"How's it going?" she asked as she slid out of the Tesla.

Neither of her workmates appeared to hear her and seemed engaged with their work and a conversation that involved considerable laughter from the two of them. Vickie tried to clear her throat and closed the car door behind her a little louder than she could have, but her efforts were ignored by the others or simply not noticed.

They finally registered her arrival when she dropped into a chair beside them.

"Whoa, when did you get here?" Bobby's voice was a little hoarse but his good mood seemed unaffected by it.

"Only a couple of seconds ago. You need to pay more attention to the security alerts on your phone. If I were a mafia-sent attack squad, you would be all kinds of dead."

Tanya grinned. "That's quite a mouthful."

"Yeah, maybe, but it would be more like a headful if anyone did get in. Or worse. Think about those two we caught sneaking around here with a can of gas and a blow-torch." Vickie started working on cleaning the pieces that were on the table like what she had said was no big deal. Her teammates barely seemed to notice the reprimand, though, so she decided to not pursue it. "Anyway, how's it going here?"

"We've mostly worked on the cars to get them ready for the heist tomorrow," Tanya said and placed the tool she held on the table. "Bobby has gone over the mechanical basics. I don't know much about it and since the mechs we'll work on are far more complex than cars, it's essentially established that I'll have to learn on the job."

The hacker nodded and leaned back in her seat. "That's about where I started but it's easy to pick up on, especially if you pay attention and don't mind asking the questions that might seem stupid. If you stay on top of it, you should be okay."

"Don't you work on the mechs anymore?"

"Well, I do when I don't have much else to do. I like working on machines and it's good to keep the mind and the hands busy. But no, Taylor wants me to focus on what he feels is my real calling, which is sales. Well…okay, technically, my real calling is software development but since there's precious little of that to do around here, sales is something I have a gift for and he doesn't mind since it does tend to make him money in the process."

"You too, as I recall." Bobby was one of the best at talking while he worked, likely a skill he picked up while still in the army. "Making ten percent of all upselling profits on top of the salary isn't a bad bit of scratch."

"Well, yeah, but I didn't want it to seem like I was tooting my own horn or anything like that. Speaking of horns and tooting, it looks like Taylor has arrived."

"Oh, yeah. I was a little surprised to see him here too."

"Why?" Tanya asked.

Vickie exchanged a look with the mechanic before she replied. "Well, as it turned out, Niki was in town last night, so—"

"You two expected Niki to shoot him where he stood."

"She's also really good at disposing of bodies," he added.

"Well, I didn't expect her to do anything rash," Vickie continued. "But anyway, the funniest thing happened over breakfast with Jennie and Niki this morning. Jennie said she and Taylor didn't do anything. They only talked most of the night."

A moment's silence passed before Bobby snorted. "Bull-fucking-shit."

"That's what I thought too, but Jennie was adamant about it and I think I believe her. Did either of you see Taylor when he got back?"

He nodded. "Yeah, he passed us and said he hadn't had any sleep all night and he would get some."

"He didn't have any scratch marks on him, though, and Bobby thought that was somehow important." Tanya's voice was tentative but firm in the recollection.

Vickie opened her mouth to say something but quickly thought better of it and simply shook her head. She would hear the truth from the man himself eventually. There was no need to keep pressing for it when the others most likely knew even less than she did.

"Well, it's best to get some actual work going," she said and wheeled her chair to the desk.

"You know we'll make much more money with this heist than we'll make all year, right?" Bobby reminded her.

"Well, yeah, sure, but until we actually manage to funnel it through the company, we'll still have to continue to work our regular day jobs."

"How can we get the money laundered to a point where we'll be able to use it?" Tanya asked and looked curiously from one to the other.

The hacker returned her look with a smirk. "Honestly, I

wouldn't be surprised if Taylor isn't already in talks with someone to send the money to the Zoo and have them pay it to him after they've taken a percentage for their efforts. If not, I have a couple of contacts who would be able to do it. They'd take a fee from it too, though."

---

He wasn't built for all-nighters anymore and hadn't been for a long time.

Taylor pushed himself from the bed and groaned softly as a myriad of aches and pains immediately demanded his attention. He wandered to the small table that held what amounted to a small pharmacy that had been issued to him during his time at the hospital.

It wasn't that he didn't think the medication wasn't necessary for recovery, but he felt the side effects he'd been warned about. An altered sleep schedule was only one of those, which meant he was constantly either tired or unable to sleep.

"I might have to talk to a doctor about that too," he grumbled aloud as he took a couple of the pills from their vials and popped them into his mouth.

He pulled his clothes on and opened the door of his room. Tanya, Vickie, and Bobby waited immediately outside but they stood awkwardly and tried to shift away from him inch by inch.

His first instinct was to make a joke about it, but he could smell coffee and it immediately took his will to engage away. "What's up?"

The three looked at each other as if to confirm what to say next.

"Still no scratches," Tanya noted.

"What?"

"What she means is that when Jennie invited Niki and I to breakfast this morning, she mentioned that nothing happened between you two." Vickie was quick to step in and she tried to keep the conversation flowing in the right direction. "We merely wanted to verify that her version of events is the same as yours."

Taylor took a deep breath. "Moving right past why Niki was in town—"

"Come on, man. You know why," the hacker said.

"Yeah, I do, which is why we'll move past it. I don't know what Jennie's version of events was but mine is that we had a delightful dinner, went to her hotel room, and talked. It was a lovely evening and a good way to pass the time before I left. Nothing happened."

Bobby's face scrunched like he struggled to make sense of the words. "Nope, it still doesn't make sense to me. Seriously, it doesn't work."

"Yeah, because I care what you think I do with my own time," he drawled. "Anyway, what's the news? Or were you three waiting outside my door so you could find out if I got my dick wet last night?"

"Well, no, not really." The mechanic appeared to be wholly uncomfortable as he spoke. "It's more that we're finished with the cars, have them all hooked up and ready to roll, and are now waiting for you so we can get started on a plan for the heist. I know we won't be able to make any practice runs but if we all know what'll happen and when, it will certainly be easier to coordinate."

Taylor set his jaw and nodded. "Sure thing. Vickie, would you mind working up a map of the general area where we'd like to hit the armored truck? I'll get a coffee quickly and we can start working on that."

# CHAPTER TWELVE

"I simply don't understand how you think this is music, is all."

Pyle turned to glower at the man in the driver's seat. They hadn't worked together for very long but it was already standard at this point for the older man to make comments like this about the music playing on their radio. It wasn't standard to have music at all, of course, but it was infinitely preferable to sitting around in silence with only the drone of the truck in their ears.

"Look, Young, I know the era you like the music from. They played it on black and white screen TVs back then but you have to get with the times. Otherwise, you should simply retire and lean back in your rocking chair while you yell at those gosh-darned kids to get off your lawn."

The fact that the guy's last name was Young was hilarious, but it seemed too obvious a joke to make at this point.

"Actually, my music comes from the time they still played music on MTV, so I guess I am a little long in the tooth," Young replied and pulled the truck onto the main street. A couple of cars moved away from them. No one wanted to be anywhere near an armored truck should an accident occur. No doubt they thought it was an invitation for trouble, but the reaction usually made things easier for them, so he didn't mind it.

"You're not wrong. It was a long time ago. But let's be honest, they had rap music back then too, you know."

"Yeah, it was rap music. Now, they simply mumble bull-shit about cars over and over again with generic electronic music in the background. Seriously, do these guys take Xanax and record themselves being out of it for three hours straight or something?"

"Just because you can't understand it don't mean it's mumbling. If you pay attention, you can hear he's actually speaking much faster than you're used to. You know this guy broke Eminem's record for the most words used in a single song, right?"

The older man shrugged. "It doesn't count if half those words are simply him saying, 'Audi is king, Audi is king, Audi is king,' fifteen hundred times. Seriously, give me music with real content, not this bullshit that's basically only product placement in music form."

Pyle leaned back in his seat and shook his head. There was no point in arguing with the guy if he wouldn't pay attention to the lyrics. Besides, it was supposed to be satiri-cal, a dig at the growing number of actual ad songs artists had begun to produce. One of them had put out an album with songs that were named after the brands that spon-sored them to make it seem like it was real music. In that, Young was right, but in this case, he wasn't.

"You only need to pay a little more attention, man. Or go back to listening to your...what's it called again?"

"D12 was the name of the band and we're still waiting for them to release a hit single called 'My Salsa,' okay?"

"I—what? They actually released a song called 'My Salsa?'"

Young looked at the man who rode shotgun, his mouth agape for a few seconds before he refocused his attention on the road.

"What?" Pyle demanded.

"It's a reference to yet another song," he grumbled. "You...okay, never mind. It's a reference to another song entirely by D12. You're probably too young to have heard it."

"Which song?"

"It's called...'My Band,' I think, one where Eminem and the band he worked with at the time complained about each other getting a little too much attention. In it, they give a preview about a nonexistent hit single called 'My Salsa.' It's a hilarious song with a ton of foul language."

"My Band by D12," the younger man commented and grinned. "I'll have to look it up when we're finished this job."

It was an interesting run, one that happened almost every time there was a major fight in Vegas and they needed more cash on hand than they would usually have to account for the large amount of betting that would happen. Well, during fights and the Super Bowl. Five or six trucks delivered cash to the various larger casinos in the area.

In this case, there was a major fight with one or another Heavyweight title on the line and the venue called for additional cash thanks to the laws set by the Nevada Gaming Commission.

The music changed to something a little less controversial, and both men settled into silence when they returned their attention to the job they had been entrusted with. People these days knew better than to try to rob any of the casinos. In this day and age, it was probably easier to rob a bank. Millions were poured into technology and manpower that would make sure all the cash—that was all insured, anyway—would be as safe as it could be.

Which meant this was a very, very boring job.

Young pressed the brakes when a bright red Mustang pulled in front of them and revved its engine as loudly as possible as it tried to get through the heavy traffic. Lights flashed and the driver leaned on the horn in an effort to make the cars in front of him move out of the way.

"Ten bucks says that guy made some money at the craps tables and spent it all on a car he can't afford the taxes for anyway," Young grumbled and tried to stay as far away from the vehicle as possible. He would have changed lanes to put even more distance between them, but there was too much traffic on both sides for them to do that without slowing the other vehicles and possibly causing a jam.

Pyle shook his head. "No bet unless we make an addition that talks about how drunk or high or both the guy is while he's driving his new car."

"My money is on both drunk and high."

"Mine too. The dealers these days don't even wait outside the casinos anymore. I heard the security guards of those places let them in to deal right there on the floor. It keeps people gambling and keeps the money in-house."

The older man scowled. "That's probably bullshit. The Gaming Commission would be on that like stink on shit. There is no way they would be able to get away with it."

"Okay, you say that, but—"

"Shit, what's this fucker doing?" He pressed the brakes a little more forcefully to slow them further when the vehicle in front of them did the same. "What? Is he trying to brake-test me? Is that it? Fucking asshole."

The Mustang continued to slow and finally brought them under forty miles an hour. A cacophony of honking erupted behind them. Young responded by trying to pull away from the lane and pass but the red car turned and tires squealed and smoked across the pavement as the truck crashed into it from the side.

"What the fuck!" Pyle shouted and leaned forward as both vehicles skidded to a halt.

Young fought to maintain control as they came to a halt. "The fucker's definitely high."

More honking sounded behind them but the driver remained calm as both cars came to a complete stop in the middle of the road.

"Shit." The younger man dragged in a breath and looked around. "Are you okay? Are you injured?"

"I'm fine. What the hell—"

"What?"

"We've shut off."

Pyle shook his head. "What the fuck do you mean?"

"The engine's cut off."

"Start that shit up again, post fucking haste!"

Young turned the key but both men gaped as the rest of

the electronics in the truck turned off as well and shut down completely.

"What's happening?" Pyle pulled his seat belt off. "Are you doing this? Is this a security measure or some shit?"

"All the security measures are supposed to keep the truck going, no matter what. This...this..."

The younger man narrowed his eyes as his partner trailed off and stared out of the windshield, a confused expression on his features. He followed the man's gaze and frowned when the driver of the Mustang stepped out of the car. Thankfully, he appeared to be in decent shape despite the accident that he had arguably caused.

He wore all leather—or what looked like it—and completed the biker-like outfit with a motorcycle helmet or something very similar.

It was easy to see that a man like that could walk away from what had been a relatively minor crash. He was bulky and looked bigger than the average defensive lineman. The question of why someone would wear a crash helmet while driving a Mustang only occurred to him when the stranger yanked a shotgun from inside the vehicle.

Pyle's chest thudded a little louder. "Either this guy has the worst case of road rage in history or—"

"Control, this is vehicle seven-eight-bravo-niner. We are experiencing a robbery," Young yelled into their radio. "I repeat. Control, vehicle seven-eight-bravo-niner is being robbed. Come on, is anyone listening?"

---

Taylor hadn't been sure what it would feel like to get into a mech again. While he had been certain there would be no repercussions from it, the hint of a niggling fear had remained that there might be some trauma associated with the action that would make it more difficult than before.

Honestly, he had been through so much while wearing those heavy bastards. He was bound to have negative associations eventually, right?

So far, so good, though. It had been something of a trial to adjust to driving while wearing the smaller hybrid Bobby had worked up for him. Given that the suit eventually did most of the work anyway, all he had to do was trust in the software and be there should anything go awry. Once he relaxed into that, he'd encountered no further issues.

Of course, the entire mission might be considered a form of awry, although a carefully controlled one. Things had gone well and even the crash that should have left him all kinds of injured didn't feel like any more than what he'd been through on an average trip in the Zoo.

The kind that didn't leave dozens dead, obviously.

He stepped out of the ruined Mustang and patted the car gently. Even if things had always been intended to go this way, it was still a shame to have to destroy an American icon like that. Maybe someone would decide to pick it up as a memento of this heist and repair it.

"Okay, Taylor," Vickie called through the comm unit. "A heads-up on something I thought you might want to know —something to keep your eye on—"

"Fucking hell, you're worse than Desk."

"Who?"

"Never mind. What's the update?"

"They've tried to radio to their HQ about the robbery in progress, but I've managed to cut their communications— or at least their radio comms. If they press—oh, there we go. They've pressed the panic button. All six of them."

"All right, people. We're on the clock here. Ninety seconds starts now."

Taylor couldn't explain it. It was like electricity surged through his veins and pumped him full of the stuff that somehow made him feel more alive than before. There was really no feeling like that of heading into combat. Maybe that was why he continued to do it. Was he an adrenaline junkie?

That was a question for later, he reminded himself.

He pumped a round into his shotgun as he stepped clear of the Mustang and faced the massive armored vehicle. He noticed the two men inside start to panic and reach for weapons or radios. The quick look Vickie had into their workings had revealed no weapons that would be able to punch through the armor he wore, but it was still better to be safe than sorry.

As a couple of cars pulled away, he fired a round into the air to ensure that all those around them would remain in their cars and not bother to try to come out. The last thing they needed was for a wannabe hero to think he could interfere.

Taylor walked to the door of the armored truck which was already locked and sealed, of course. It would be an impenetrable barrier for someone who didn't wear a power suit meant for head-on combat with alien monsters.

He grasped the side of the door and pulled. The hydraulics kicked in immediately, and in under two seconds, the sound of metal screeching on metal told him that the reinforced metal the door was made of had begun to bend to his will.

After only five seconds, he swung the ruined chunk of metal open. Both men had already retrieved their weapons but the one with grey hair seated behind the steering wheel was the first to aim.

The pistol was a .45, one of the 1911 remakes that were currently so popular, and Taylor flinched as the first round bounced off his helmet.

"Fucking—" His voice was garbled through the speaker system outside his suit, which would make it impossible for them to recognize him through voice alone. He caught hold of the driver, hauled him free of the vehicle, and flung him on the pavement while he trained his shotgun on the younger man still inside.

He looked at the man at his feet and held his weapon steady. Maybe the concept of looking at an unfeeling reflective facemask was all he needed to realize that he'd lost this fight, but he thought it was a good idea to reinforce those good instincts.

"Do you know what the definition of a hero is? Someone who gets other people killed. Since what we're stealing here isn't yours and you've already shown that you did all you could to stop us, why don't you act like we're a big happy family and stay on your ass?"

The man's eyes almost bulged from his skull but he nodded and tossed his pistol into the street behind him. It skittered past where Tanya had pulled up in the van.

Taylor turned to the kid still inside. "You get out here too."

His seat belt was already undone and he climbed out slowly, his gaze very firmly fixed on the shotgun. Clearly, the shock wasn't as severe for him as he tried to grasp the barrel when he was close enough and pushed it away from himself.

Not wanting to kill him, Taylor stepped forward and shoved him into the side of the truck as Bobby climbed out of the van, decked out in a full combat mech suit, and strode to the back doors. Taylor fired another round close enough to leave the kid's ears ringing and pumped the shotgun again.

"Are we done playing around here?" he snapped, and both men nodded quickly. "Good. It'd be a fucking shame if instead of only a robbery, the news reported a couple of murders out here too, right?"

Another sign of agreement from both made him feel a little better. Twenty seconds had ticked away on the clock he'd put up on his HUD, and they didn't have any time left to waste.

Leaving the security duo outside, he scrambled hastily into the vehicle. He wasn't sure what he had to do as this was Vickie's part of the heist.

"What am I doing here?" he asked and narrowed his eyes at the variety of high-tech gadgets that blinked at him.

"Hold the scanner up to the onboard computer. That should give me all the access coding I'll need."

"I thought you already had all that shit."

"I had access to the security system, but with the codes I pick up now, I'll have full access to their hard drives in the Casino since the truck does need access to get inside. Hold still…and we're done. You're clear."

He scrambled out immediately and jumped lightly to the pavement, where the weight of the suit still left an indent. Neither of the two guards had moved so he made his way to where Bobby had already worked on the doors at the back of the truck and now yanked them open slowly.

A crack appeared between them and in the same second, someone fired from inside. The mechanic ducked instinctively, but after that first burst, all they could hear was someone screaming in pain.

Taylor joined his teammate to heave the doors the rest of the way as the clock ticked up to thirty seconds. Exactly as they had suspected, someone had been too quick on the draw and had fired his assault rifle into the armored panels around them. One of the rounds had ricocheted around the relatively small space to catch one of the other three in the leg and drop him to the metal floor.

"God damn it, Steve!" the wounded man shouted as the other three looked at the two armored mechs, one of which clambered into the truck with them. They turned their weapons hastily on the two men and fired another burst. None of the rounds penetrated their armor and thankfully, there were no more accidents with a ricochet finding an unexpected target.

"Are we done?" Taylor asked and looked at each of them. "Or should I simply shoot you guys to show that you're not as durable as we are?"

There was no answer from the four men, and the wounded man simply groaned in pain. Taylor took that to be the answer he wanted to hear and held his scanner up to the bags of cash around them. The first few he scanned were marked as having dye packs but once the scanner connected to them, Vickie was able to disable the counter-measures. He received the go-ahead, picked the first two up, and tossed them to where Bobby waited.

"Forty-five seconds," the hacker reminded him.

Twenty bags of cash made up the delivery inside the truck. Taylor settled for disabling six of them and the mechanic loaded them quickly into the van.

"Are…are you the Terminator?" one of the younger members of the security team—possibly Steve—asked.

"Thirty seconds, Taylor."

His only response to the young man was to shake his head. It was difficult not to leave him with a bad one-liner spoken in an even worse accent but they needed to get going. All he had time for was to press a pre-written note into the kid's hand and climb out of the vehicle.

"We have the money and are ready to head out," Bobby reported for Vickie's benefit.

"Good. I'm getting the alerts from the local police station and they're scrambling units your way as we speak."

"I'm not sure if it's possible, but if there's any way to get them to send an ambulance too, that would be great," Taylor added as he slid into the shotgun seat next to Tanya while Bobby closed the back door. "One of the idiots managed to shoot himself."

"Roger that."

"Are we otherwise okay? Did you get what we needed?"

"I have all kinds of stuff, although I'm not sure if it's what we need or not. I'll run a scan and let you know."

"Awesome. We're moving out now."

Tanya put the van into gear. The shocks had been

improved to support the weight of not one but two armored mechs as well as all the cash, but the engine still struggled somewhat to get them moving. Thankfully, the road ahead of them was mostly clear as the gunfire had encouraged those drivers who could to leave the scene as quickly as possible. They accelerated and turned off at the first opportunity.

A few minutes ticked past while Vickie kept an eye on what the police were doing. She was supposed to alert them if the cops gave chase and in this case, no news was good news.

They drew into an abandoned warehouse and drove inside to where Liz waited for them. In silence, they scrambled out and hastily transferred the cash from the van.

Taylor couldn't help a moment of appreciation when he saw his truck in action again and ran his hand over the finished paintwork. "Morning, gorgeous."

Bobby completed his task to pour gas over the van and set it ablaze, and the teammates climbed into Liz, with Bobby in the back again. At least, in this case, no panel separated the back from the front so he was able to move beside them as Tanya guided the vehicle expertly out of the warehouse. The van behind them was already a ball of flame.

None of them spoke as they wound through the streets of Vegas once more. The warehouse had been chosen specifically because it was a blind spot in the city's traffic camera system, and there was enough traffic through the area to ensure that any attempts to track them would be lost in a mess of other cars. Anonymity would be what prevented local law enforcement from locating them immediately.

The silence, aside from the roar of Liz's engine and the horde of sirens in the distance, began to get on their nerves.

Taylor finally decided that enough was enough and keyed the comms again. "I don't want to jinx it but Vickie, are we in the clear?"

"I have considerable chatter from law enforcement trying to track the van and the mech suits. Nothing has been said about Liz yet. So far, I think we'll be in the clear."

"Of course, the moment news of this gets out, Niki will know we were the ones who did this," he pointed out. Despite her assurance, he still took a long moment to scan their surroundings before he relaxed a little in his seat. "I won't lie, this went far better than I thought it would."

"You're right but this is only the first step," Tanya responded. "Some might even say the hardest part is still to come."

Bobby poked his unhelmeted head into the front. "How do you mean?"

"Think about it. There's still the part of how we'll launder the money in order to use it," she explained. "That's actually how many successful robberies go down the drain. Everything goes well but people start picking up on the people who suddenly spend a small fortune that would have been beyond their means, and that's how they all get caught. Have none of you watched Goodfellas? Or heard of the Lufthansa heist?"

"Let's not forget the problem of the mechs you guys used blown up all over social media." Vickie did not sound pleased with the news. "Pictures and film from the people on the scene have already started to go viral and will likely be picked up by the cops. Oh, and there's also the small fact that you're the only one operating a mech repair shop in the state. That alone will be enough for them to get a warrant to search the strip mall, given how much pull the casinos have with judges around here. Assuming Niki doesn't do something to stop it, obviously."

Taylor pulled his helmet off and placed it on the seat between him and Tanya. "It's a possibility, but I don't think we'll have to worry about the casino in question putting up too much of a fight. They will have received the message and unless I miss my guess, they'll realize it's in their best interest to give us a wide berth."

"Well, I hope that is the case but assuming it isn't, do you have any plans to prevent us from being caught in this?"

"I do," he replied. "I've already hired a long-term parking situation for cash and with a fake ID. The mechs and cash will stay in Liz and I'll park her there until the heat dies down. I have a couple of connections who will be able to launder the money for us but for the moment, the best thing we can possibly do is keep our heads down."

"Agreed," Bobby added. "How about what we actually ran this heist for, though? Did you get the data we needed?"

"I'm combing through it all now and I should have something for you by the time you guys get back."

Taylor took in a deep breath and for the first time in the past few days, his body relaxed a little. "Fantastic. We're on our way now."

# CHAPTER THIRTEEN

There would always be the fear of what happened after something like this. It made sense, given that they had been involved in the robbery about as much as cashiers were involved when their banks were robbed.

No, a little more involved, Young thought. Cashiers at banks were told not to resist a robbery in any way, and for good reason. They weren't trained to handle a situation like that and all the money was insured and likely to be recovered anyway.

The cash the casinos transported would be insured as well, and while there would be blowback on the security company for not preventing the theft, it was already a point of discussion online that no other members of the security community had been ready for something like that. Using combat mechs to rob a casino? How were they supposed to be ready for that?

He hadn't expected there to be no repercussions for the robbery but being transported directly out of the hospital with those who hadn't managed to get shot in the leg wasn't something he could have anticipated. A couple of limos waited for them and large, burly men stood ready to push them inside.

One didn't even need to look out the window to know they were on their way to the very casino they had been entrusted to deliver the money to. There was no way to mistake it, really.

The vehicles swung into the underground garage and continued to descend. The first three levels of garages were where guests were allowed to park, and the final one four levels down was for employee and casino business only.

Everyone had heard the stories about how casinos had been run in the mob heyday of the seventies and eighties when people had been shoved into isolated rooms and "taught a lesson" for having lost money or trying to cheat money from the casinos. They'd been left to go about their lives with the reminder of broken fingers and a concussion or two. But that was all a thing of the past, right? Casinos were run by massive multinational corporations at this point. It was the twenty-first century. Right?

The five guards who had been involved in the heist were shoved hastily out of the limos and escorted into the lower levels of the casino—those no one ever really saw unless they actually worked in the building and had already looked behind the proverbial wizard's curtain. Young had made the casino run at least six times since he'd started work at the security company, and all he had seen was the garage. Casino employees were always there to take the money and sign whatever paperwork they needed to before the trucks left.

As it turned out, the guts of a casino were much less

flashy than the areas meant to be seen by the guests. For one thing, the marble and velvet used to make people feel like they were in a classy establishment were absent. Most of the walls were made of plaster—and not very well finished either, as wires and pipes protruded from inside them. The ceilings were non-existent and left very little to the imagination when it came to the plumbing and electrical components of the massive building above them.

Young sensed the palpable fear from the other members of the group because he felt the same as they were guided into what looked like a small convention room. It was likely where duties were assigned to the various service workers in the casino, although it was empty at present.

All five were forcibly seated in the chairs at the front and their escorts moved away to cover the exits of the room before the door at the front opened.

Two men entered. They were clearly an echelon or two above the security men who had escorted Young and his comrades in. Their suits alone looked like they cost more than what he made in six months, and the impression was complemented by understated yet expensive watches and pieces of jewelry.

The only flashy piece that either man displayed was a large studded ring worn by one of the men, which clashed with the rest of the old-money look.

If Young were a betting man, he would put money on these men being the owners or at least the overseers at this particular establishment. In short, the men whose money had been stolen.

One of them was undoubtedly the one in charge and he stepped forward immediately. "For fuck's sake, all I wanted was for you to bring them in for a quick conversation, not all this Gestapo bullshit. Seriously, these guys are the victims of a crime."

The guard narrowed his eyes at the young man's reaction and more importantly, the suddenly confused and fearful glances the security team now exchanged.

"Look, hey—Mr...Young, right?" the man continued and sat directly opposite him. "I'm sorry about this. The guys were supposed to only bring you in for a quick chat. My idea was that it would be over a quick meal in one of the restaurants, but I guess this happened instead so bear with me for a little while. I'll make it worth your while. My name is Rod Marino. I run this place but I still have people to answer to, so I needed you guys to talk to me. I can't afford to wait for the police statements to be made public —if they ever are, of course. You know how those guys are, right? You worked in the LAPD for twenty years, didn't you?"

Young nodded. For someone who was merely running a casino on the Strip, the man appeared to be rather well-informed. It wasn't unheard of, though. He had likely hand-picked the teams who would drive his money to and from his businesses.

Marino continued like he hadn't waited for a reply. "Anyway, when we're finished here, I'll set you guys up with a nice meal upstairs and maybe a small credit on the casino floor if you want. Oh, and I need to get something for the guy who's still in the hospital. He was shot in the leg, right?"

"Technically, he was—"

"I know, it was apparently a ricochet, but that's not

what the official story will be, I don't think. Either way, it doesn't matter. I still intend to make sure you guys are well-compensated for doing what you could to protect my property. A little over six million in cash is nothing to sneeze at but at least they didn't take everything. How much was in the truck again?"

"Twenty bags with a million each, Mr. Marino."

"My point is that it could have gone much worse. Anyway, tell me what you saw of these guys. Anything you might have noticed would be great."

Young looked sideways at the other members of the team and wondered if he was maybe digging them all into a shallow grave in the desert. There certainly was a mob feel to the man in front of him despite his nice-guy act. "They wore, like...suits of armor. The kind they show people using out in the Zoo—you know, on the ZooTube channel? One of them was in a smaller suit but it was still effective. I tried to shoot him at point-blank range but it bounced off. He spoke, but his voice was warbled."

"Are you sure it was a he?"

"Reasonably sure. He looked like a really bulky biker from a distance. When he got in closer, you could see the differences in motion. On top of the whole—"

"Invulnerability to bullets. Gotcha."

Steve was the next to speak. "Well, the second guy had a much bigger mech. It looked like it was straight out of those Zoo games that came out last year. He also had an assault rifle twice the size of the ones we had, and...well, they didn't shoot. They waited until we were done, focused on the money, did something to it, and carried it out."

"They deactivated the dye packs," Young interjected.

"And the trackers that were in all the bags. I'm not sure how."

Marino nodded. "It doesn't matter how. Pictures of the suits they used have spread on the Internet like wildfire, so we have good descriptions of those. Is there anything else?"

"Yeah," Steve said and extended his hand cautiously to reveal a small piece of paper enclosed in his fingers. Marino took it, read it, and raised an eyebrow.

"Well, thanks for your help, gentlemen. Head upstairs and my manager will make sure you guys have a nice meal in a restaurant of your choice. And let him know if you want that credit on the casino floor I mentioned, okay?"

At a quick flick of the man's wrist, the security guards hurried forward to escort Young and his team out of the room. At least they were less aggressive about it this time around, he thought wearily.

As the security company's employees were escorted out of the room, Di Stefano approached Marino, a dubious look in his eyes.

"Are you sure you don't want me to simply dispose of them?"

"Why? They didn't do anything wrong."

"They lost six million dollars."

"Six million was stolen from them in a robbery that could have been far worse. Oh, and it was perpetrated by armor suits built for killing alien monsters. They were outgunned. There's no reason to blame them for that. Besides, we already know who it was who did it."

"We do?"

He handed the other man the note that had been left in the incompetent guard's hand. It was printed, which provided no sign of who might have composed it, but the content left no question in his mind.

*This is my consulting fee for taking out the trash who tried to kill me,* the note read. *Try one more time and I'll simply kill you instead.*

Di Stefano looked up from the note, folded it carefully, and tucked it into his pocket.

"McFadden?"

"Who the fuck else? We've tried to get to him for months now. It was only a matter of time until he retaliated, I guess and again, that could have gone much worse. As messages sent go, it was fairly subtle."

"Subtle? It's all over the fucking news. #mechheist is still trending on social media and people are talking about how this might be a viral marketing campaign for one of those VR games that will come out next year."

"As long as they keep thinking that, I'm not concerned. No one knows the stolen money was ours and it'll all be covered by insurance. Even the security company will work to keep any details of what happened from coming out. We come away with a very flashy message but no real damage done. This was McFadden telling us he knows who has been gunning for him and he wants us to stop."

"Is that what you think?"

"Well, yeah. We already know he's literally the only one in the state who has access to those kinds of weapons, which means the cops also know about it. He's too smart to be caught with the mechs themselves or the money when the officers of the law come to bust his door down. Thanks to his connections in the FBI, he'll be on top of any investigation into his operations and he'll come away cleaner than...well, the presidential suite at the Bellagio."

"Do you really think this is the best time to make jokes?" Di Stefano asked once they had walked out of the conference room and reached the elevators.

"Honestly, no, but there's not much else we can do. We've operated with a relative amount of leeway from the folks in Sicily since they do trust us to take care of business around here, but things have changed. Our quarry knows who we are and has the means to target us now and cause economic damage greater than what he has already. If we want to continue our vendetta against them, we'll need the say-so from Don Castellano."

His companion held his silence as they stepped into the elevator and Rod entered the code that would take him to his office.

"He'll not be pleased," the man said finally.

Marino shook his head. "Of course not, but he'll be even less pleased if he realizes we have put him and the rest of his investments in Vegas at risk by starting a war with a guy who clearly has the equipment to fight."

Both remained silent when they reached the office and while word was sent via a phone message to make contact with the Don. The man's rule of having no phones on his property was problematic in this day and age, but they were in no position to tell him to get with the times.

It was almost a half-hour before his phone rang with the reply. It was a video call, and he transferred it quickly to the screen on the far wall of his office before he answered the call.

"*Buona sera, Don Castellano,*" he said as the old man's face came up on the screen. Having him that large only made him look much older, but both men knew better than to say as much. "*Grazie per aver parlato con noi.*"

"Given the news that is spreading from your town, I assumed it was only a matter of time before you wished to speak to me." The old don had a firm grasp of the English language and spoke with only a hint of an accent. "I hope that none of our finances were caught in the robbery that occurred."

Marino set his jaw. He didn't like to play the subservient role but it was necessary in this case. "Technically, yes, although we won't see any real damages. All the money that was stolen was insured and will therefore be restored to us before the day is out."

"That is…good enough news. Therefore, I expect that you did not seek me to speak of what was lost."

"That is correct," Di Stefano cut in. "We have uncovered information that points to the guilty party being Taylor McFadden. It appears that on top of connections with the FBI, he also has access to the kind of weaponry and equipment that enabled him to perpetrate the robbery with ease and which we would not be equipped to handle. It also explains why we have had so much trouble dealing with him thus far."

Castellano nodded slowly and rubbed his cheek. "Well, that is interesting news. I would like periodic updates on the police action on this case, but I think our efforts might be better spent finding a way to settle this feud with the man. From his efficacy, we might even consider bringing him into the family and give him work that would keep him from destabilizing our investments further. We may even profit from this situation. I will make some calls to see what can be done."

The *capo* nodded. "Of course, *mio Signore.* What would you want us to do in the meantime?"

The old man pursed his lips for a few seconds as two young, topless women came into view of the man's camera for a few seconds. "For now, do nothing. Keep track of what McFadden is doing in the city and follow the police investigation. Even with his connections, I doubt there will be no legal repercussions for him, so make sure you know what is happening. And report to me. I must go."

He didn't bother to wait for them to reply before he ended the call.

Di Stefano sighed and shook his head. "Well, I suppose we have our orders."

"Do you think he's serious about bringing McFadden into the fold?"

"He wouldn't say it if he wasn't serious about it. We can only hope McFadden is open to the idea."

## CHAPTER FOURTEEN

Niki had begun to question why she had elected to head this task force. Admittedly, it did wonders for her career and brought her all the positive exposure she could ever ask for. Unfortunately, the cost of it was that she was stuck for the next five or so years dealing with the kind of people she had spent most of her life avoiding.

"I wish they'd paid us per head while we were still in the Zoo," one of the hunters said. "Can you imagine how much money we would have made if that were the case?"

"The fact that they didn't pay us per dead monster is probably how they were able to stay operative back then. Besides, there's no money to be made on dead monsters in the middle of the Sahara Desert."

They liked to talk but there simply wasn't the same kind of banter she remembered from her time working with Taylor. Who the hell would have thought she would miss him?

She rolled her eyes. "Maybe Vickie was right and I do have a fucking crush on the man. Nah. I probably only miss him. Kind of like how absence makes the heart fonder or some bullshit like that."

"What was that?" one of the three mercs asked her.

"Nothing."

Even when she'd been in the academy, she had made sure that most of her friends and associates were the kind who preferred analytical work over fieldwork. They tended to be the ones who preferred to work with their brains rather than their hands.

Still, things could have been worse. She could still be stuck with the freelancers she'd managed to recruit across the country from the hundreds of people who styled themselves as cryptid hunters without having so much as a lick of experience in dealing with those kinds of monsters.

Niki sighed deeply and leaned back in her seat as the trio of former army buddies inspected the evidence left by the monsters they were hunting and tried to make some educated deduction of what it could be. At least they were professionals with a mind for what they were dealing with.

There had been a time when she thought Taylor was one of the bad ones. The man had issues—even he acknowledged them—but the guys who had been pulled out of the Zoo had the same. Actually, they showed many more of the issues than McFadden did.

"Who the hell knew he would be the poster boy for the mentally sane monster hunter?" she mumbled in a low tone.

One of the hunters looked up from his work. "What was that?"

"I'm talking to myself. Keep up the good work."

A part of her was still pissed about what happened in

Vegas during her visit there, but that was the kind of shit she had learned to put aside in favor of work during her time with the FBI. Folks who dealt with her talked about how she was usually calm, reserved, and in some cases, downright deadpan. They weren't necessarily complimentary, but that was better than them thinking she was hysterical or some other wildly sexist term for a woman who was comfortable displaying her feelings.

Not that she was that kind of person. Jennie had always been the type to wear her emotions on her sleeve, which was why everyone seemed to like her.

Maybe her sister was merely the one who was more mentally stable despite the woman's traumatic experiences.

The three men picked their papers up from the table and turned to her with the usual expression that said they were finished researching and wanted to go out into the field to do some metaphorical digging.

Or, in some cases, literal.

"What do you think?" Niki asked, pulled her mind from her reverie, and leaned forward to look at what the men had noted on the pictures that she had obtained for them.

"There's nothing really out of the ordinary," Carlos said as he selected one of the crime scene pictures. "I'd say many of these tracks are simply from the scavengers that came along after the deaths of the cattle, sheep, and those two humans. The fact that all the bodies were gathered in one place after they'd been killed elsewhere indicates some kind of nest. It could mean that the animals in question intended to feed their young."

Jamie, a shorter, lean man with a shaved head, pulled out the pictures of the tracks. "Wolves, bears, and the like tend to scavenge when they can, so the smell of a fresh kill would pull them in. It looks like the bear came along and scared the original predators off. Once the bear was finished, a pack of wolves followed."

She studied the pictures closely. As the locals had said, they hadn't found any tracks related to any cryptid they had on record. There was, of course, the issue that most of the creatures were new and therefore had to be added to the record once they were found and cataloged. In this case, however, all the tracks were from animals that were known.

Niki scowled when a familiar niggle of doubt persisted in the back of her mind. "What the hell kind of creature would be large enough to kill a fully-grown bull and drag it off to a nest but would still be scared away from a...an entire larder of kills by your average bear? I know bears are big, but even they can't carry their kill away when it's that size."

"That is the proverbial rub," the third one, Walters, said and waited for his teammates to stop cackling childishly at the word. "We don't think the bears and the wolves scared our predators off. You'll see here and here..." He pointed out a couple of the pictures of the human kills. "It's clear from the wound patterns that the two human bodies that were found were killed by the wolf pack, likely when they stumbled onto their feeding ground or something."

Niki looked at each of them with a challenging expression. "You're contradicting yourselves. First, it looks like they scared the monsters off, then it doesn't. So, what the fuck do you think happened?"

The three looked at one another and obviously, each

waited for someone else to speak. Finally, Walters shrugged and designated himself as spokesman. "We have a working theory, but it's really the only one that makes sense to our minds. We think the cows and sheep were gathered to draw in another kind of predator, which would then be carried off by our monsters and taken elsewhere. That's based on the fact that we have tracks of the bears and the wolves coming but not going. Therefore, not a nest but…"

"Bait," Niki completed the man's sentence as his voice trailed off. "But there aren't any tracks of them leaving, and there aren't any tracks of any monster leaving either. Did they fly?"

"Actually, we think it's more likely that the mutants used the trees to escape with their prey," Jamie interjected. "That's how many of them did in the Zoo, mind you, but there aren't any good pictures on the presence or condition of the trees around this site. We thought we would head out there and have a quick look to see if the local CSI didn't miss something."

They were raring to go, she had to give them that. She generally didn't like to see anyone rush into this kind of thing, but when it came to her history with people who came out of the Zoo, she knew that while having the information to work with beforehand was good, they also wanted to study their quarry out in the field as much as possible.

Her three hunters didn't wait for her permission and quickly headed out of the field tent she worked from to the trucks that held their mech suits and weaponry.

Another bright and shining silver lining that came from

Taylor's near-death experience was that all her people were now fully equipped with the proper weapons and armor to deal with the monsters they would fight.

"Jennie would probably complain about how all the adventure is lost after bringing in the professionals," Niki grumbled under her breath and wished she had bourbon to pour into her lukewarm coffee. "I'm merely happy that the kill count on my task force is finally going down."

"What?"

"I'm talking to myself again. Get your asses out of here and into the field."

"What do you think we're trying to do?"

Niki took a deep breath. "You guys know you're not hourly, right? Waiting around here will not get you paid."

"I don't think you know what you're talking about."

"And you guys aren't paid per head. You're paid per job as you were when you went into the Zoo."

"Sure." Jamie grunted dismissively. "But much more of it."

"Because the US government cares more about killing monsters that are on US soil than the ones that aren't."

"That…makes sense, I guess." Carlos was one of the few who was already in his suit and had begun to select his weaponry. "But from this point, they should probably invest in finding out why these critters appear all over the country where the Zoo's goop doesn't have access."

She took a sip from her coffee and winced. "You guys took goop from inside the Zoo with every trip, remember?"

"We took the flowers out—"

"What do you think they were made of in the first place?"

They stopped talking for a second.

"Huh. Good point." Carlos scowled.

"Right, and they're sold by the milligram to any rich old guy who wants to get his dick working again. So my only question is how this shit hasn't happened all around the globe by now."

"It has," Walters pointed out.

"Say what?"

"Yeah. There are numerous reports of sightings in China, Russia, Australia, and South America."

"Although those sightings in Australia could simply be...you know, Australia," Jamie added before he donned his helmet.

"Yeah, well, all this talk could be happening while you were on your way to the crime scene so..."

"Fine, fine, we're on our way," Walters snapped as he and his teammates climbed into the back of the truck that would take them to the base of the mountain they would have to scale to reach the location where the bodies had been found. Once they had gone, Niki took another sip of her coffee and made another face.

"Shit. I really need a coffee machine out here."

Desk's icon popped up on her laptop. "I could make a requisition for a portable coffee machine but the online reviews for the devices state that the coffee produced tastes rather terrible."

"The coffee tastes terrible anyway. I can't help but think that it being hot would somehow improve the situation.

Scalding my tongue with hot liquid will make the taste a little moot."

"Do you want me to make the requisition?"

"Maybe later." Niki leaned back and rolled her shoulders.

"I have a feeling I know why you feel so down," the AI stated through her computer.

"I don't feel depressed. And why would you think that anyway?"

"Your heart rate is down, your sleep schedule is altered, and you've drunk far more than your usual amount of coffee."

"What… Okay, I have to say I'm not a fan of you tracking my sleep patterns or my heart rate. And how the hell do you know that anyway?"

"You're wearing a smartwatch that takes your pulse every thirty seconds."

Niki looked at the device. "Right. Anyway, why do you think I'm feeling down?"

"Because I miss him too."

"How…who?"

"Who? That's a good one."

"I seriously don't know who you're talking about."

"Sure you don't. Well, if I speak for myself, I do miss working with Taylor. All these mercs are better than the ones you recruited from what I can only assume was the darker side of Craigslist—"

"Craigslist is all darker side."

"Exactly. Anyway, these mercs are good but Taylor was somehow better."

"Of course you would think that."

"What's that supposed to mean?"

"Are you still talking to yourself?" Walters asked.

She faced the computer to see that the team's communications were now online and they listened in on her conversation with Desk.

"In a way, I suppose. What is your current position?"

"We're at the base of the mountain and will head up now."

"Let me know when you reach the site of the bodies," Niki replied and cut her voice from their comm lines, although she continued to listen. She had done so with the conversations all the groups shared while on their own. People said guys were at their worst when they were in locker rooms, but even the women who had been pulled out were terrible.

"I guess they merely need to settle into the rhythm," she said aloud. "Maybe to get into the kind of mindset they're used to when they march into combat. It might be some kind of a way to show themselves as calm or to keep their minds from going into the darkest kind of place."

"Are you still talking to yourself?" Desk asked.

Niki shrugged. "There's an assumption that you're always listening, so yes and no."

"Interesting. How is it that you operate knowing I'll watch or listen to your every move?"

"Well, I know your code doesn't let you share anything you learn with anyone. It's literally the one thing I insisted on when Jennie designed you."

"Fair enough. Although given that you're not the only one I'm supposed to keep an eye on, I think there's something you'll want to know about."

"If you can't share anything, how would you be able to tell me?"

"Because it's all over the news. I don't have to say anything. Open any news site."

She scowled and pulled up a couple of her favorite news sources. While she didn't trust any of them completely, as long as they delivered some kind of consensus between all of them, she could assume that whatever they reported was accurate.

And all three had the same headline.

*Daring Robbery in Las Vegas: Robbers using mechs steal cash from armored vehicles in broad daylight.*

It took her a few minutes of rereading the articles to make sure she wasn't somehow seeing things but finally, she began to realize exactly what had happened.

"Oh, come on. You have to be fucking kidding me. I thought we had given him time to rest by leaving him in Vegas with nothing to do but run his little business."

"Well, for starters, the business is small but it is growing steadily. Which brings me to my second point, of course. Running his business while the mafia continues to target him would be impossible. Therefore, if this had something to do with putting those mafia goons you know all about on the back foot, I can understand how that would play a part in his business decision."

"Of course you'd take his side," Niki grumbled.

"Agent Banks, do you read?"

She keyed into their group comm link immediately. "I read you. Are you at the scene?"

"We were about five minutes ago," Carlos reported. "We picked tracks up in the trees exactly as we suspected. Based on previous encounters, I'd say it's something like the killerpillars, although this looks a little smaller and in greater numbers. We're getting a combat scenario worked up for your benefit."

"Don't worry to prepare anything for me. Just keep yourselves alive out there," she replied and keyed out of their commlink. "I really can't afford any bad press over Taylor pulling his bullshit in Vegas. Seriously, why didn't he at least give me a heads-up that he was about to dance his fucking mech suits all over the goddamn Strip?"

"For one thing, I don't think he was literally dancing. For another, he probably didn't tell you about it because he knew you would tell him to stand down."

"Yeah, you're damn right I would have. Publicly stealing...well, about six million dollars in the middle of the street in traffic can't have been his smartest moment, even if that shit isn't the highest of bars."

"Do you think you might be underestimating him again?"

"Probably, but that still doesn't excuse him being a total asshole and keeping me out of the loop."

"Agreed. Also, you might want to tune into what's happening with your team as they appear to have engaged the monsters already."

Niki didn't want to listen in. The sound of shooting and explosions wouldn't help her headache and she was fresh out of vitamin M.

But it was better to be in the know, she reminded herself. It was difficult to say how much better, though.

She sighed and tuned into the commlink. There was little to hear other than, predictably enough, a cacophony of gunfire, shouts, and explosions. It would be far more exciting if she actually had a visual on the action but the suits that had been provided by the Pentagon for her task force were some of the older models. The guys she had talked to about it said she could count herself lucky that they even had comms instead of merely relying on radios like the first models had.

In that, she did count herself lucky. Radio connection out there in the boonies with all the trees and cloud cover would be spotty at best.

"Agent Banks, do you read me?"

"I'm here, Jamie. What's the status?"

"We have engaged about a dozen smaller crawler creatures in the trees. We felled a couple of trees and killed all the monsters. From here, we'll run a sweep around the area to find the nests and clear them too. We'll keep you updated."

"I appreciate it."

The line cut again and Niki scowled at her computer.

"See, these guys aren't so bad," Desk pointed out.

"Yeah, they get the job done. That's not the point, though."

"You'd rather work with someone else who gets the job done?"

"Shut up, Desk."

# CHAPTER FIFTEEN

Taylor could still feel the adrenaline rushing through his body to make every movement electric, intense, and necessary, even the simple task of driving his four-by-four to the strip mall.

The sight of cop cars racing around the city was more than enough to keep him on edge although they simply hurtled past him with their sirens blaring. He knew for a fact that if someone sat him down with a lie detector, he would inevitably spill all the beans.

But so far, it seemed like none of the local cops were willing to stop a guy driving his four-by-four through the city. They converged on the location where the robbery had occurred and most likely followed a variety of bogus leads from tip lines that had been set up and were scammed mercilessly by the kinds of people who had literally nothing better to do.

He wasn't sure why they even bothered with tip lines in this day and age. There were too many trolls in the world who merely wanted to cause as much trouble as possible.

Sifting through all the fake tips for the few that would send them in the right direction didn't feel worth it.

Of course, in this case, he hoped they were wasting their time hunting the wrong people. Vickie had been right, of course, in saying that the cops would probably knock on their door eventually since they were the only business that had that kind of weaponry on hand.

But he wasn't concerned. They wouldn't find anything that would enable them to pin the robbery on him or the rest of his team. Not unless they had a whole ton of luck, which in fairness, he couldn't rule out at this point.

"These fucking cop cars need to stop screaming around with their sirens and flashing lights," Taylor grumbled. "I'm bound to drive into a ditch. Right now, I'm too fucking tightly wound."

At least it wasn't that long a drive to the strip mall and he soon pulled into the garage and waited for the doors to close again before he exited the vehicle.

By the looks of it, Bobby and Tanya had already made their exit. It was well past their working hours and the day had been long enough anyway. They would still be paid for it, of course. No one would be able to use the money they had stolen yet and possibly not for a while. He had some ideas but still had to put a little more careful effort into deciding who would launder it for them.

His first choice remained one of his contacts in the Zoo. They wouldn't mind using dirty money or cleaning it for them and sending it back via online transfer. He merely needed to think it over a little more before he made the final choice, and there was no rush to do it right away. It would be better to let it sit in storage until the situation had calmed and he was sure the finger of suspicion didn't point in their direction.

The sight of the Tesla still parked in Vickie's usual place said the hacker was still around. She wasn't hourly, of course, which meant he wouldn't pay her any extra for the overtime she worked.

"Knowing her, she probably lost track of time," Taylor mumbled, picked up a cup of coffee, and took a sip. It was stone cold but better than none, he supposed. Maybe he could pop ice cubes in it and he would have the iced version.

He trudged up the stairs toward the improvised office he had set up in one of the building's many, many rooms. Vickie sat in front of a computer screen, eating fries and sipping from an extra-large paper cup of soda.

"What are you doing?" he asked and squinted to peer around the room that was dark except for the two monitors. "Why are you sitting here in the dark eating junk food?"

"I'm waiting for the files I picked up from their servers to decompress," she mumbled around a couple of fries and sipped from the straw before she continued. "How about you? Is everything finished?"

"I tied up all the loose ends, parked Liz at a cash-based parking building, paid for three months in advance. There won't be anything to find here if the cops do come around for a chat. What are you up to?"

"I needed to run a quick compression on the files I pulled to reduce transmission times—which as it turns out, takes much longer than I thought. Once Bobby and Tanya realized there wouldn't be much for them to do around here, they went home. Or…maybe on a date? I'm not sure. I didn't pay attention."

"You think Bobby and Tanya might have a thing?" Taylor took the seat next to her and stole a couple of her fries. "Now that I think about it, yeah. I guess I can see them together. They're both owed something awesome in their lives."

"Agreed."

"And since you didn't mention it, so are you."

"Well, I made a little over a million bucks, so I think that counts as something awesome too." She smiled at him and squeezed his hand gently in appreciation. "So far, nothing is happening in the boyfriend department so I'll take the cash."

He smirked and shook his head. "How do you figure a little over a million bucks?"

"Well, you said we would all make equal shares in the heist, and we picked up a little over six million dollars—which is the figure most of the news sources are sharing. So we'll split six million between four—you, me, Tanya, and Bobby. But assuming we'll lose some of it to cover the laundering expenses, I estimate it'll be less than a mil and a half. So, a little over a million. I'm tempering expectations."

"Honestly, I'm kind of tempted to let the three of you split the profits. Or maybe give you my share but keep it in a trust fund you would only be able to access once you've graduated."

"Dick."

"I know, Asshole Dad, trademark pending, strikes again. But you should still think of it as kind of a…like a prize for graduating."

"I thought I was already owed a prize for being a part of this whole heist thing."

"That's what you've got coming to you anyway. I mean that if I give you my share of the profits, it'll be in the form of a trust fund you'll only have access to once you graduate —as a bonus, I guess, like I said."

"Are you seriously thinking about giving me your share of a six-million-dollar heist?"

Taylor shrugged. "I'm not sure if you're aware but I'm in a financially stable place. While a million and a half isn't something to sneeze at, it's not like I necessarily need it. I would probably simply invest it in the business so in the end, giving it to you would be a form of investing too. Does that keep up with my image of Asshole Dad?"

"Kind of. Okay, on one hand, it's sweet, but you're still demanding excellence of me. You're like one of those stereotypical dads who pressure their kids into performing perfectly while you give them everything they need to perform perfectly. Overbearing but well-meaning, I suppose is what I mean."

"Great, well, I don't want you to think I'm putting too much pressure on your studies. It's more about having the degree that will allow you to succeed. In my experience, people with the experience necessary but no diploma tend to get fucked over more in terms of promotions and the like than the people with a diploma to show for their efforts."

"I guess that makes sense."

He snagged another French fry from what he assumed was ordered in and stared as the numbers scrawled quickly across the screen. "So, how much longer do you think it'll take for all the files to decompress?"

"Well, they're in a number of chunks so it's hard to say," Vickie replied and leaned forward to check on the progress and make sure everything was running smoothly before she straightened again. "You get the feeling they would have erased all this interaction to make sure the police wouldn't find it. But I suppose they would know if someone was investigating their mob ties and would thus have a warning to erase everything when they needed to. Either way, most of the doc files are already accessible. There isn't really much there. Only the electronic correspondence, which is interesting too but less so than the video and audio files that were collected. The latter are taking a little longer to clear the decompression algorithm, so it might be a while. Honestly, it might be all night."

"Do you want me to set you up in your old room? The bed's still there but I think it might need sheets."

"I brought a sleeping bag in case I needed to spend the night, but thanks."

"So, lay it on me. What do we know already?"

The hacker rolled her chair to face the second monitor and called up the call logs and email correspondence that had been flagged for recovery from the casino's servers.

"The most interesting thing I noted is that there are a fair number of calls from the CEO's office straight out. Most of the time, they try to route the calls through a secretary, which means she or he makes the calls for them. That's what's takes up most of the lines here, but these in particular are directly from his office. I've also been able to pick up numerous calls to the same number from the guy's company cell phone too."

"Who is this guy?" he interrupted as she called up the logs. "Is this the guy who ran those hits on us?"

"I'd dare to say yes. His name is Rod Marino and his dad had very close ties with *Cosa Nostra*—the Sicilian mob. I think it's reasonable to assume the apple didn't fall far from the tree on that one."

"Now why the hell would a big-time mafioso who runs a casino care about a racketeering scam way, way off the Strip?"

"I was curious about that myself. As it turns out, Rod Marino is a recent incumbent in the position. He took over after his father died but hadn't been groomed for the role at all. So, from the emails, it looks like handling you was something to show the locals he was in charge. And when you resisted, he escalated his efforts."

"Well, that explains why they didn't give up after the first failed attempt but it still doesn't explain why they continued to target us after the others. Seriously. You'd think someone who wasn't involved with the *Cosa Nostra* would have the instincts of a negotiator and would find a way to make everyone involved happy."

"Again, he tried to show off to everyone that he was the big cheese in the area. When he failed in the first couple of attempts, it looks like they sent someone else in to help him. Huge sums of money began to pour in about four months ago, right before you went into the hospital. Actually, all the money I've tried to trace since they started paying people to attack us begins to make sense now that I have most of the missing pieces."

"Anyway, back on topic. You were talking about a number this Rod Marino called often. What did that have to do with anything?"

"Well, aside from the fact that it's a landline and who the hell uses landlines these days—"

"Damn it, we do."

"Whatever. The point is, the landline is in Sicily and not in any of the cities either. It's in a small villa off the coast, by the looks of it."

"Do you know who it belongs to?"

"Well, it's not one of the major players in the *Cosa Nostra*. Most of their major operations moved to mainland Italy and Cyprus after the Interpol raids of '25."

"The…what now?"

"Come on, they made like seven or eight movies. You know, the one with the mustachioed guy played by George Clooney who drinks? How he tracks them for years and is finally given a task force to eliminate them?"

"Did it work?"

"It did in the movie but not so much in real life. *Camorra* and *Cosa Nostra* had people in the task force, and instead of taking the task force out like they did with most of their issues—they couldn't without attracting huge amounts of international press—they uprooted and took their operations elsewhere. They left a little behind to give the guys who targeted them good press to disappear with, and that was that. Anyway, my point is that no one really into anything important operates out of Sicily anymore."

"So who does the number belong to?"

"One Gregorio Castellano, also known as Don Castellano, from the paperwork I managed to sneak from the

Interpol files. His family's owned that villa since the 1500s and he wasn't about to give it up. He has most of his family still working full time, but his youngest daughter, born from his seventh wife, was kept out of it. She still technically lives with him at the villa, although she spends most of her time at her mother's in Monaco."

Taylor narrowed his eyes. "And how the hell do you know that? It couldn't have been in any of Interpol's paperwork."

"No, but she's a fairly prolific influencer on Instagram and Tik-Tok, and I was able to match her name and the geo-address from her pictures to the same villa that was called." Vickie talked while she ate and only paused to drink from her soda. "It kind of came up on my search for the place. Anyway, she's at her father's villa now, posting a horde of pictures about a party she's holding there. The old man doesn't appear in any of them, probably at his own request."

"Shit. So it looks like we have the head of the snake we need to cut off."

"What's that now?"

"Well, what I mean is we have the location of the guy who's running this operation against us. If we killed Marino, they would simply send someone else in to do the same job and would likely be a little more emphatic about it. If we take care of the guy who would send all the people, there's no one left to send someone to replace him."

"That's not a terrible idea. The whole head of the snake situation does have appeal, but let's have a real conversation about the fact that you want to murder someone in Italy. And not simply anyone, mind you. A guy with pull in the local mafia. Seriously, if you think they're bad here, they're practically the Girl Guides by comparison to the kind of pull they have in Italy. They've been in the business of crime since people fought with halberds."

Taylor rolled his seat back a few inches to give her better access to the computer. "Huh. That's actually a damn good point. Nice catch."

"And since you'd travel halfway across the world, how do you think you'll be able to transport a mech? It's not like you can load it into some kind of diplomatic pouch and ship it over." Vickie didn't stop her work, even though she talked. It looked like a section of the audio files had decompressed and she checked them for issues. "And let's be honest, the only reason we're not sleeping with the fishes—or another more appropriate metaphor for being killed by mobsters in Las Vegas—is because so far, we've been better armed than they are here. That won't be the case in Sicily."

"Okay, okay, I get the picture. Stop being all...rational about this. Maybe there's a way for us to draw the guy out of Italy to somewhere that would give us the edge."

"It's possible, but I doubt it. People have been trying to murder this dude for longer than you or I have been alive. The chances are he'll know how to pack security anywhere he goes."

"Shit. We'll need to call in some help on this. Professional help."

She nodded. "I hate to say this but you'll want to call Niki in to help."

"We can't involve her in something like this. She would kill us if she knew what we were up to around here."

"Come on. *Guys in mech suits rob armored car in Vegas* is on every front page of every major news source. If you think my cousin doesn't already know what we're up to around here, you really need to reevaluate your mental functions."

"So, do you think she'll…uh, not want to kill us?"

The hacker made a middling gesture with her right hand. "Probably not. Hopefully not. And if she doesn't kill us, it's unlikely that she'll turn us into the authorities either. With all that being the assumption, she's our only hope to get into Italy. At least the traditional way."

"I guess I could always fly myself and a mech to Casablanca under the guise of joining a merc group in the Zoo and take some form of transport across the Mediterranean. That would take a ton of money, though, and there's too much shit that could go wrong."

"Yeah. They refer to you by name in these emails so they would definitely know if you flew out of the country, even if you weren't headed directly toward our man."

"I still might want to see if it's possible at all. Who's that guy…Fredricks? Fredrick?"

"Freddie. Yeah, I know him. Funny, but an asshole."

"In other words, my kind of guy. I've worked with him and his team before. Get in contact and see if he would be willing to come here for an inspection of our facility."

Vickie nodded and immediately called up the email app on the computer.

"Once you're finished, why don't you get some rest?" Taylor patted her gently on the shoulder. "It's been a long day and I think you could use it."

She smiled and squeezed his hand. "Will do, boss."

CHAPTER SIXTEEN

A very short night of sleep was the kind Taylor was used to. Somehow, he had jumped into a combat state of mind and his body clock had immediately come on board. He wasn't much of a morning person but when he needed them, a slew of old instincts tended to activate without any conscious thought.

One of those was waking up with the sun.

"Fucking boot camp," he mumbled. "Drill Instructor Cahill would be so disappointed with my bellyaching. Then again, I bet I could probably break him across my knee these days, but don't think he would make it necessary for me to try anything like that."

He wasn't wrong. In the case of most drill instructors and sergeants out there he'd met, the whole tough instructor persona they put out for the benefit of the people they trained was exactly that—a persona. An act. They did it damn well, which was why they were chosen to do the job, but once the training was over, they were merely soldiers like the rest of them.

Okay, they were better at yelling orders but aside from that, they were regular guys.

Taylor took a hurried shower and dressed before he took a quick ride out to collect breakfast while he mumbled about buying a proper coffee machine for the garage. It would save them all kinds of time with their coffee runs, after all.

He was back in less than fifteen minutes and brought the doughnuts and coffee they generally had for breakfast, although the order was made for one more person. He wasn't sure how Tanya took her coffee but elected to be safe and ordered the larger black cup and brought a few extra packets of cream and sugar, just in case.

When he carried it to the office, Vickie was curled on the chair he had left her in. She had managed to find a blanket but was still in the seat, which leaned back a few degrees, and appeared to be in a deep sleep. He didn't want to wake her but that couldn't be a comfortable sleeping position.

Carefully, he put the coffee and doughnuts on the table and touched her shoulder lightly. When there was no response, he did it again, then nudged her. There wasn't much else he could do, and if she was that deeply asleep, he would have to leave her.

The second touch was enough, though, and Vickie sucked in a deep breath. She groaned as she moved before she turned her head to look at him.

"What's going on?" Her voice was thick and sleepy. "Are we being attacked? The security system—"

"Is fine." He finished her thought for her. "I thought I told you to get some sleep."

"Yeah, well, the work was more interesting than sleep. Until…you know, it wasn't. I did have some sleep, though. A quick snooze."

"You'll need more than that. Give yourself a second to stretch what I can only assume are a whole host of sore muscles—probably around your neck—and use the bed in your old room. Get some real sleep, understand?"

She nodded, stood slowly, and predictably enough, groaned and rolled her neck a couple of times to restore it to some semblance of normal.

"Oh, before I head to bed, you should know that your pal Freddie called. Well, emailed, saying he would be interested in giving the place a look and would like to discuss the details with you. He said to call him when it was convenient for you. And if it wasn't convenient, to call anyway. I think that's a reference, but I don't remember where from."

"It's Sherlock Holmes, I think. He sends a message to Watson saying 'Come at once if convenient. If inconvenient, come all the same.' It's kind of an inside joke from when we worked in the Zoo together. Long story, but as it turned out, his team needed help from mine and sent us that message. We've held it over him ever since. Stupid stuff. You go ahead and get to bed."

"Ugh, fine, but I'll take a couple of doughnuts with me."

She said that like it was a bad thing to get food in her system. While it was mostly junk food, it was still better than no food.

She moved away as Taylor opened a call line to Freddie's phone, hoping beyond hope that he wasn't off drinking with the rest of his buddies. There was no telling with those guys.

The line was picked up almost immediately to display the familiar face of his former comrade in arms.

The man proceeded to laugh. "Well, well, well, if it ain't my good friend and savior Taylor McFadden. How the hell are you doing, man? I see you've lost some weight."

"In the slightly reduced flesh, yeah." He looked at his arms and shoulders. "I got involved in some stateside problems and won't bore you with the details, but the short story is I ended up needing to stay in the hospital over the past three months or so, with a regimen of physical therapy. Never mind that, though. How the hell is my good pal Freddie Hendricks doing in the middle of the fucking Zoo?"

"Well, the middle of the fucking Zoo is where we were about thirty-six hours ago, so you should count your lucky stars that your assistant managed to get hold of me after we got back."

"A whole lot of celebrating, I guess?"

"You fucking know it. Now, your assistant—"

"Come on, man. You know she's not my assistant and the only reason why you'd call her that is if you thought she was listening in, which I can assure you she is not. Vickie pulled an all-nighter and has gone off to get much-needed sleep."

"Damn."

"Yeah, I know, it's a huge disappointment. I doubt I'll be worth even a quarter of the drinks she earned you when you pissed her off. Anyway, do you think we should get to the topic at hand?"

Freddie was clearly disappointed but the man could prove himself to be at least half professional when he put his mind to it. "Well, if we don't have anything better to do, I guess we could have a quick chat about what you had in mind when you called me back to the states to look at your facilities."

Taylor nodded. "I'll contact a couple of the other merc groups we've worked with ever since I opened McFadden's Mechs—"

"It's a terrible name. Just awful."

"I know but I haven't been able to think of anything better. Anyway, the point is, it would be a good idea to get you guys here so you have an idea of what we're able to do for you. We're still a small operation but I think you'll appreciate seeing it for yourselves instead of merely hearing about it from us."

"Well, honestly, your results so far have been all that we've needed to see, but if you're willing to see us over there, I don't see how it could hurt. You know I trust you and Bungees. I know I can trust your work."

"Well, yeah, that's kind of why I invited you first."

"So you have an agreeable voice to sing your praises to the other merc companies that don't know you as well?"

"Right on target."

His phone vibrated and a quick check confirmed that Bobby had entered the garage.

"Do you have to take that?"

"Nope. It's only a security alert. We've had some issues over the past few months."

"The kind of issues that put you in the hospital, or is this another set of issues?"

"Not what put me in the hospital, no. We've upgraded our security, so the motion sensors tell me if there are any new arrivals. It took a fair amount of work but we managed to get the sensors to detect when someone we know is approaching and alert me of it anyway."

"Like the motion sensors we use around here."

"I won't lie, I did base the security system here on what we had out there. I think you'd understand if I said I wouldn't be able to sleep properly otherwise."

"Honestly, I wonder how I'll be able to cope when I go back there, not having the sensors around. It's kind of weird that I've thought of setting them up even when I'm here on base."

"That's about when people start to tell you that you need to head home. Psychological issues are how they got me."

"Yeah, I get that. Anyway, there's nothing I'd like more than to come over. I've been meaning to pay my folks a visit anyway, so I might as well make a trip of it."

"I'm looking forward to it, Freddie. When you get here, there's another kind of business I'd like to run by you, if you don't mind. It's not something I'm willing to talk about over this line but I think it's something that you'll find very interesting."

"Hey, you know me. I'm more than up for any interesting business on the side, but I won't ask any questions. I respect that you have your reasons to be cautious."

"And that's another reason why I thought it would be a good idea to invite you first. I'll contact you with the flight details in a while, Freddie. Let me know if you want to visit your folks before or after, and I'll work up an itinerary for the other visitors."

"Will do. Be safe over there, Taylor. From what I hear, things are starting to heat up stateside too."

"You don't know the half of it. Stay safe yourself."

The line cut and Taylor leaned back in his seat for a few long seconds. He had much to think about, but there weren't many mercs he trusted more than Freddie, if for no other reason than the fact that he owed him his life three or four times over. They had worked together for a few years and at one point, had gone into the Zoo six consecutive times on the same team.

Still, he had to think about whether he should trust the man with the knowledge that they had robbed a casino of six million dollars and wanted to launder the money through their merc business in the Zoo. People did stupid things for that much money.

He chuckled, stood, and stretched gently. "Stupid things like robbing a fucking casino? Yeah, that'll do it."

With his important call made, it was time to see Bobby and check how Tanya was settling in. He hurried down the steps to the garage with his coffee and doughnuts. Of course, he had forgotten to tell the mechanic that he'd brought his own so he had probably brought some as well, which was what he usually did every day.

The guy was a creature of habit.

Tanya had most likely taken a ride to work with him. It was a good call since her car hadn't been cleared by the security software yet. He would have to fix that, he reminded himself.

The two were enthralled in their conversation and only noticed his arrival when he placed the box of doughnuts on the table.

Bobby was the first to react and scowled at the food and drink with predictable annoyance.

"I always bring breakfast. You know that's my thing. I'm the breakfast guy."

"Vickie was up all night so I thought I would get her something to help her stay awake. Or help her sleep, depending on what she needed most. That's what she's doing now—sleeping, that is—but we managed to dig up a fair amount of good information on the people who have targeted us over the past few months. Unfortunately, that would be the end of the good news."

The other man nodded. "Well, we'll have to talk about that in a while, but I think we've put off giving Tanya an entry interview for too long, don't you?"

Taylor picked up one of the coffees and a doughnut, took a bite and a sip, and nodded. "Sure thing. First of all, how do you take your coffee?"

"Usually black and with five sugars. I need that kind of pick-me-up. I'm not a morning person, see?"

He grinned at Bobby. "I like her already."

"Me too." The mechanic spoke quickly and without thought and almost didn't seem to realize he'd said it.

His boss narrowed his eyes.

"You know…as an employee."

"Are you sure that's all you like about her?"

"That's really none of your business," she pointed out sharply. "Anyway, will we talk about how I'll be incorporated into the company? McFadden's Mechs, is it?"

Taylor winced at the name. "It's a working title," he said quickly. "I can't think of anything better."

"Anyway," she persisted. "Shall we continue?"

"Right." He sat down on one of the nearby chairs and gestured to the others to do the same. "You've worked with us for a while already, right? What do you think about the work we do here?"

"Well, I've only worked on the cars, although Bobby has given me a fairly in-depth description of the work you usually do around here. I guess we all know I'll need to be trained for it, but I'm a fast learner. I'm more than willing to put the hours in to learn about how to work on mechs and machinery and stuff like that."

He took a bite and chewed quickly. "That's how Vickie started with us until we found something that was a little more her style. It'll mostly be the kind of work that an intern would do at the start—cleaning bits and pieces, keeping the place organized, that kind of thing—but you'll learn on the job. Basically, we'll reevaluate everyone's performance every quarter and remunerate accordingly, myself included."

"You'll evaluate yourself?" she asked and raised an eyebrow. "How's that fair?"

"Well, I think I've been very fair so far. In fact, I haven't taken a salary from the profits of the company yet. Don't you think that's fair, Bungees?"

"Well, given that you haven't put in a day of work for the past three months or so, yeah, it's fair."

"Asshole."

Tanya chuckled. "So, I'll simply be an intern? I'm not complaining, mind you, but what kind of work do you see me doing in the long run?"

"Well, working like Bobby and me. He is our head mechanic so he's the one who makes all the job calls. I've assisted him as best as I could, and Vickie did basically what you'll do—cleaning and learning for the most part. Of course, she proved to have a talent for dealing with our particular kind of clientele, so she has moved on to focus her talents on sales instead. She gets a bonus for upselling and completed jobs along with a regular salary. Bobby gets a salary and bonuses based on finished work too. You would have something similar but not as much."

"What kind of salary are we thinking?" The fact that Bobby asked the question took Taylor a little by surprise but he tried not to let any of it show on his face.

"I think a similar salary to what we paid Vickie—around sixty thousand a year, plus bonuses. We have to work on the W-4 and all the other paperwork, obviously. I'll need to get my hands on your bank account numbers, social, et cetera. Of course, once things are a little more established, we'll see about getting you that signing bonus you worked for."

She snorted. "You make it sound so dirty."

"I didn't mean to, of course. I only mean that you did have a fairly unique entrance interview and given the amount of effort you put into it, you are due something as a bonus for it. That will be credited to you as soon as it is available to us if you get my meaning."

Bobby leaned forward. "Why are you…"

His voice trailed off as Taylor's eyes flickered across the room and a knowing smile touched his lips. "See what I mean?"

It was fairly safe to assume they would be under surveillance at some point in the future, and he didn't want them to say something the local officers would be able to use against them. While the probability of them having already found something to point to Taylor and his squad was low, it wasn't wise for them to ignore it entirely.

"Do you think we'll have time to talk about what kind of security you'll be able to provide for me?" Tanya asked, her voice a little hesitant but with an undertone of firmness.

"That is a fantastic point, actually."

" I'm not the kind of person to run away from a threat or anything, but what happens if one of your questionable friends decides to put me six feet under? You'll find me out in the middle of the desert."

Taylor shook his head. "No, we won't."

"Exactly. So my point is, what happens to my salary and more importantly, my bonus should something happen to me?"

Bobby nodded. "That's a good point. What do you want to happen?"

"Well, my kid…he's still living with his dad. I'd like any money you feel should come to me to go to him instead. Put it in a blind trust or a Junior ISA—something like that so he can access it when he turns eighteen and has it for college or something."

Taylor nodded and took another sip of his coffee. "We'll do that, of course—assuming we don't meet the same kind of fate. My priority, though, is to make sure it's not necessary. If you need someplace to stay, we have enough room around here. It might not look like much, but it's safer than most banks and the Internet speed is off the charts."

She chuckled and pursed her lips. "Well, it's something to consider, anyway. I do have an apartment of my own, but if things take a turn for the worse, I'll take you up on your offer."

"I have plans in the works that'll hopefully prevent things from taking a turn for the worse. But for now... what say we get your first day of work underway?"

"Right. It sounds good to me."

"So!" Taylor pushed from his chair and rolled his neck. "Why don't you get coffee and breakfast in you and we can get the day going? I think we're running a little behind on some of our orders thanks to all the time we spent planning and running our special project."

# CHAPTER SEVENTEEN

When he'd made the decision to purchase a strip mall constructed from prefab, Taylor had never thought he would need to make the place look appealing for visitors. It wasn't like he had expected to have any visitors at all, actually, given that their clients were all Zoo-based, but it was one of those business concerns he should possibly have put a little more thought into.

Then again, people coming in from the Zoo would be used to working from prefab buildings. They wouldn't like it, of course, but no one liked those particular structures. They were functional above all else, and that included looks.

Still, the inside needed to be spotless, which meant that most of Tanya's initial workload became cleaning and preparing the shop for their visitors. There wasn't much they could do when it came to the mechs they worked on, but the area at least had the streamlined appearance that made it look like the kind of workspace that was efficient and enterprising.

Of course, the difference between what something looked like and what it was supposed to be was annoying enough. Most enterprising businesses were grubby and covered in grease. When it was clean, it meant more effort was put into cleaning than into being enterprising, which possibly sent a different message than the one intended.

"I've worked here for two weeks now!" Tanya shouted from her corner of the shop. "I don't get why you guys don't simply hire a maid or something. It has to be better to hire a professional than relying on the intern to do this shit."

"We're already paying the intern anyway so might as well put her to work," Taylor pointed out. He didn't look at her and his hands continued to work on calibrating the hydraulic system for the mech he and Bobby were currently repairing.

"But all this time I spend sweeping, mopping, and dusting is time when I'm not learning more about the trade."

Bobby nudged him with his elbow and he sighed in response. "Yeah, you made a good point. Wrap things up there and come on over."

"I've already wrapped everything up," she replied and approached briskly. "What do you want me to do?"

"Use that microfiber over there and start to clean the soot and grease from the parts we've already detached."

"Wait, so I have to do more cleaning?"

"It's a good way to familiarize yourself with the parts we work on," Taylor explained. "Those sections are the gears that make the smaller joint functions work. Hydraulics are mostly used for the larger joint movements, but when you get to the feet—and more importantly, the finer movements for the hands and fingers—you need those gears to make it move as it should. Unsurprisingly, the smaller sections accumulate much more soot, dirt, sand, and blood in them, so getting them clean means the difference between being able to fire your weapon in a tight spot or not. So it might seem like only cleaning, but it's an important part of any repair job."

"Important," Tanya snorted. "It seems like busywork."

"Don't complain," Taylor retorted sharply. "Familiarize yourself with the bits and pieces. You'll begin to see the motion abilities of each little section and get used to working on them."

She nodded, settled in a chair with the microfiber, and began to clean the pieces that were on the table.

"The work isn't that bad," Bobby told her as he began to remove other pieces. "Most of it is taking things apart, cleaning them, and putting them together again. You'd be surprised how many of the problems they face in the Zoo simply comes from shit that needs to be cleaned. Of course, the longer they stay in there, the more… Well, it's hard to explain but it's like there's some kind of acid in the air that corrodes the metal. In that case, a little more repair work is required but not that much."

"You'd say anything to make me feel better," she grumbled. "Of course, I don't care about getting my hands dirty for work but knowing there's something about it that will go into improving my skills around here is better. I've been stuck at a dead-end job in the past and it wasn't a pleasant experience. I ended up having to quit and take up another line of work from the ground floor and work my way up."

"Well, in all honesty, we don't have anything but the ground floor," Taylor told her. "So yeah, you'll start from the ground floor here as well, but you'll get a cut of the profits and learn more and more about the job along the way. In the end, if you think you need it, we could probably arrange a situation where you get a degree that's relevant to the work here too."

Tanya stopped working for a few seconds. "I hadn't even thought of that. Going back to school has always felt like an impossible task. Do you think I should do it?"

"It's worth considering. If it was something you're interested in, it would be a solid investment for the company to have you trained in the theoretical aspects as well as the practical." He shrugged and shifted in his seat, still a little sore from his morning workout. "We might even be able to cover half your tuition and get a tax break for it. As far as I'm concerned, that's the very definition of a win-win."

"Wait," Vickie shouted from her corner of the garage. "Hold on. Do you mean to say I'm not the only one who'll get this free ride through college for work?"

He twisted in his chair, his hands full of wiring he was connecting. "Well, there's no need to be jealous."

"I'm not jealous. I merely thought I was the special one —like I was given this opportunity because I'm so much smarter than everyone else."

"If you were that much smarter than everyone else, you wouldn't work here and you wouldn't need us to help get you through college, now would you? Yes, I know, Asshole Dad strikes again."

She looked shocked and covered her mouth in mock

horror at his words. "Well, that's mean and nasty. The very nerve. I have half a mind to not let you know that the cops have tried to set up surveillance on our premises for the past three days."

"They what now?" Taylor asked and fixed her with a frown.

"Oh yeah. Did I not mention that they've tried to put bugging vans all around us? I've blocked all their attempts to listen in on our conversations every time and fed them what probably sounds like a TV from their side—mostly from my subscriptions. I knew they'd come in useful. They'll get bored with it soon so I think we can expect someone to knock on our door sometime today if that warrant they've tried to push through to the hands of a judge has anything to do with it."

Taylor put the wiring down, careful to keep it all arranged in a way he would be able to quickly pick up where he had been when he left off. "What? Why—how did you know about this and why haven't you told me anything about it before?"

"I made sure to follow all aspects of the investigation I could, and I knew they would try to pin something on us eventually. You're dealing with enough problems as it is so I thought I would only let you know when there were some developments."

"Well?"

"This is me informing you of the developments. The police trying to tap us wouldn't ever be a problem and I assumed you knew they were hanging around outside. It's not like they were subtle about it. Seriously, they drove a cable van all over the damn block trying to get a bead on us."

"And the warrant?"

"It was only submitted ten minutes ago, and from what's discussed on the police radios, it looks like it's been signed. The cops are making plans and getting teams in place to break in. We're apparently assumed to be armed and dangerous."

Taylor nodded. "Well, they're right about that. Not that they should worry about us resisting arrest or anything. How long before they come calling?"

"I'd say about ten minutes or so. They're organizing outside and waiting for the SWAT team to arrive."

"Wait—is that warrant for our arrest or only to search the premises?"

Vickie turned to the screen and called up the file she had intercepted. "It's only a search warrant to look for the mechs used in the heist and to seize them as evidence."

"They won't need a fucking SWAT team for that, I can tell you that much. I'll go out and let them in. Honestly, I'd rather see if they would prefer to avoid the need to break in."

"Why would you do that?" The hacker's eyes narrowed and her eyebrows lowered as she studied him when he stood hastily and moved toward the garage door. "If they're coming in anyway, why not wait for them and clean up in the meantime?"

"There's nothing for us to clean here. If they're looking for the mechs that were used in the heist, I made sure there is no evidence to tie us back to it. They won't find any of the money or the weapons. What would they possibly find that could be seized as evidence of this particular crime?"

She raised her hands and shrugged.

"Well, in that case, I don't want to be left with the bill to repair the door or windows the SWAT team will break on entry, so we'll simply let them in, won't resist, and won't try to hide anything. Oh, and if you have anything illegal on that computer, you might want to clean it."

"Please," she retorted scornfully. "I've done that from the moment I realized they tried to bug us. Anyway, if you're determined to simply let them in, have at it."

Taylor stepped out of the garage door and left it open as he walked beyond where the sensors were able to detect. Sure enough, he counted three different unmarked cars parked out of sight of the strip mall, as well as four vans that had pulled up with a rapidly growing group of officers who gathered to discuss breaching tactics.

"The dumbasses could be at this all day if I let them," he mumbled, folded his arms, and watched the officers openly as they debated various options. It took them a few minutes to realize he was there and they appeared to freeze, unsure of what to do about his presence.

He wasn't sure what he should do either, but if they acted hostile, there was no way he would resist.

Finally, one of the men with a thick black mustache decided to walk to where he stood and simply waited for them to do something.

"I'm sorry, sir," the officer said. "The LVPD is conducting an operation here so would you mind moving along?"

Taylor nodded. "Sure, but you guys are conducting an operation on that building there, right?"

"Uh…right."

"I happen to be the proprietor there. My name's Taylor McFadden—formerly Gunnery Sergeant Taylor McFadden—and if you plan to enter that building, I'd sure appreciate it if you guys didn't break through any doors or anything like that. I have the garage door open for you and you're welcome to go on in. Or if you guys intend to arrest me or any one of my staff, there wouldn't be any resistance or anything like that. It's merely that I only recently bought the property and I don't want to have to put more money into repairing it once you guys have finished what you need to do."

"I—you what?"

"If you guys want to enter, we won't offer resistance. I'd merely appreciate you people not doing any damage to the structure, is all."

The man shifted uncomfortably and twisted to look at the other officers who now began to gather around.

"What's the matter here, Detective Pembroke?"

"Well, this man states that he's Taylor McFadden and he asks if we'll…well, breach the building over there."

"Yes, we will. We're only waiting for the SWAT team—Wait, Taylor McFadden?"

"I'm the proprietor of the building so if you need to go in, you won't need to breach with a SWAT team. The doors are open."

"And how did you know we were here?"

"I have a motion sensor security system installed in the area. After we had trouble with break-ins over the past few months, we were forced to upgrade. I received a notification that a number of people were gathering beyond the property and came out here on the assumption that it was another attempt to break in. As it turns out, it's the fuzz, so if you guys want to come on in, that's fine. But honestly, I'd rather not have to replace doors and shit."

"I'm afraid you don't get to tell us how to conduct our operation, Mr. McFadden."

"Be that as it may, if I invite you in, you don't have to break anything, right?"

The officers conferred quickly.

"Sure."

"The door in the back is open. I can open the front too if you'd like. I'm willing to cooperate fully with whatever purpose you guys are here for as I also assume this gathering has a signed warrant for...what? Arrest?"

"It's a search warrant." The superior officer clearly didn't like being caught outside like this, but it would be sheer stupidity to turn down the chance to simply walk into a premises they intended to search. "The warrant is still on the way, though, so—"

"To hell with that. You guys will fucking bake in the sun out here. Just come on in and do your search."

"You seem very unconcerned about the prospect of a police search, Mr. McFadden."

"I've watched the news over the past few days so I knew for a fact that you guys would knock on my door eventually. I'm fairly sure we're the only shop licensed to work on mechs like those that conducted the robbery. I assumed it was only a matter of time before you guys decided I was probably the best lead you had. I did expect that you would knock, though, not break the door down. Anyway, if you have a warrant on the way, you can go ahead and get the search started and over with. We have a business meeting with clients from the Zoo coming up and I'd like us to have an operational shop to show them."

"I'm sorry, but it might not be so simple."

"I know. If you find anything that ties me or mine to that heist, you'll shut operations down and arrest everyone. You can't know that I'm telling the truth, but I do. So if you want to go in there, do what you have to do. We have nothing to hide."

The man nodded and turned to the other officers, who had stopped discussing tactics and listened to the conversation.

"All right folks, we'll head in. Stay on your toes. We have a search warrant signed and on the way, so we'll search the whole damn place. Leave no stone unturned."

Taylor scowled. "I'd take it as a kindness if you guys managed to not ruin everything in the place. Oh—we have a computer in there so if you want to bring your tech guys in, that's fine. Or if you need to take the whole computer, I guess I understand that too."

"We won't take any orders from you, Mr. McFadden."

He nodded and led them across the parking lot and through the open garage door, where Bobby, Tanya, and Vickie were still working. They looked up with suitable surprise to see the police stream in.

"Don't worry," he said loudly, stepped aside, and let the officers enter in force. "They have a warrant so all we have to do is comply, understood?"

Bobby stood from his seat as the officers approached,

moved him aside, and quickly inspected the mechs he was working on. None of them were the same model or even the same type as what had been used during the heist. The one Bobby had used was a newer one Taylor had brought back from the Zoo, and the hybrid he had used wasn't even in production. The cops would likely take their time to examine those they had harnessed but other than that, they would be left alone.

Or if they weren't left alone, they would be taken into custody by the officers and he would have to reclaim the mechs from custody once they proved that they weren't those used in the robbery.

Many of the task force members searched quickly through the rest of the property, where they would find little to interest them. Nothing would be found in Taylor's room either. The tech specialists copied the data efficiently from the computer while Vickie watched with a great deal of consternation. She didn't like to witness someone else mess with her stuff.

"Taylor, are you sure about this?" she asked when they were herded into a corner of the garage while the specialists inspected the mechs they had available.

"It doesn't matter. They would have broken in anyway." Taylor shook his head and exhaled a deep breath. "At least this way, we show that we cooperated with the authorities in the search, and when they don't find anything, there won't be any reason for them to come back. We'll return to operating as usual."

The tech guys finished copying the data from the computer and Taylor's laptop in his room and headed out with their treasure trove. The specialists the police had called in focused intently on the mechs in the garage, but Taylor recognized the look in their eyes as they constantly ran scans and inspections on the machinery.

"What do you mean they aren't the same mechs?" Detective Pembroke snapped at the specialist in front of them. "They're mech suits. That makes them the same ones."

"They aren't the same models and weren't even made during the same year."

"But they could have...uh, disguised them somehow, right?"

"Not if they wanted them to work. Seriously, these cost upward of three to four hundred thousand dollars apiece."

"And they stole over six million. Are you sure these aren't the mechs they used?"

"There isn't even space in them to put a smaller one inside. And they have most of it on the outside here so you can see inside."

Pembroke looked around as the rest of the search parties returned empty-handed. It wasn't that big a surprise, of course, given that most of the strip mall was currently empty.

The detective in charge strode to where Taylor, Bobby, Tanya, and Vickie stood in the corner. The officers had called him Sergeant Creighton and he seemed both sensible and efficient.

"Well, we haven't found anything here," he said and fixed Taylor with a questioning look. "The building is basically deserted too."

"Like I said, it's a recent purchase. I plan to put most of

it to work soon but it's a work in progress. More than likely, I'll try to rent the other sections out."

"And you live in that top section?"

"Yeah, I decided it would be cheaper than renting or buying another place in the area. The local zoning regulations have nothing against that. I checked."

"Even if the mechs in here don't match those that were used in the robbery, you could have used a set from your clients in the robbery and sent it out again."

"You can check our records. The model numbers don't match those that were in the news. I checked that too."

"You'll understand if I don't take you at your word on that. You could alter your records."

"That's fraud and a very serious charge."

"Grand theft is even more serious."

"Well, to avoid that kind of fraud charge, everything we send out is checked and verified by the port authority. Everything is shipped through the airport and needs to be inspected beforehand. You can check their records if you like."

"What if—"

"I'll save you some time, Sergeant. If we'd shipped them out any other way, there would be a paper trail for every mech we sent. We would need to be paid for them. More importantly, they would have been inspected on arrival too. We aren't authorized to handle weapons, you see, so any weapons would need to be deactivated as well. All mechs would have been reported on arrival."

The sergeant looked around the garage.

"If they found that any of the mechs have been imported without that kind of authorization," Taylor continued, "we would have been shut down a long time ago. So, Sergeant, we've more than cooperated with your investigation. Is there anything else you need to know?"

"Not at the moment." Creighton seemed frustrated now and scowled as most of his people began to leave the building. "We will have more questions for you, that much I can guarantee."

He nodded. "I'll be here. And I think you have my number already?"

"Of course. Don't leave town, and thank you for your cooperation, Mr. McFadden."

The entire police crew left the building, mounted up in their cars and vans, and drove away. They seemed like they didn't like being associated with any kind of failure to acquire data. Taylor could only imagine the kind of pressure they were under to find something—anything—that would give them a lead.

"What are you thinking?" Vickie whispered like she wasn't sure whether bugs had been left by the officers.

"I think it's time to give your cousin a call to see if she can tell us what's happening with local law enforcement."

"Shit, I had a bad feeling you would say something like that. I'll let you know if I can find her."

## CHAPTER EIGHTEEN

Niki sighed as her phone vibrated on the table. Her team had begun to wrap up yet another hunt and currently took all their devices apart to pack them and head back to base to report. There wasn't much she could do to stop them, but if she took the call instead of packing her own shit up, it meant she would inevitably be the last one out of this damn place.

The number wasn't on her registry, which meant there were only two people it could be. Jennie still wasn't talking to her after the whole episode in Vegas, which left only one.

She pressed the button to accept the call. "Good morning, Vickie. How can I help you?"

"How did you know it was me? This isn't my usual number."

The agent shrugged, mostly for her benefit than anything else. "Instinct, I guess. Not many people know how to do that. Then again, you're the only one I know who's still speaking to me so maybe merely an educated guess?"

"Very entertaining."

"Yeah, I am one hell of an entertainer. Now, what can I do for you? Sorry for the curtness but we're in the middle of a little something here, so if it's not an emergency, I'd appreciate it if you could contact me some other time."

"Well, I'm not sure if this qualifies as an emergency or not, but— Well, I have something I need to tell you but its…uh, kind of sensitive. You know, something that would be better said face to face and…and girl to girl, I guess. But I'm here and you're there and it can't really wait until our next fun get-together. By then, it might have grown too big to do anything about it, so we need to have this conversation now. I guess. So yeah, maybe it is an emergency."

Niki scowled as she tried to make sense of what her cousin had said. She immediately disregarded the obvious direction in which her startled brain had leapt—no, Vickie could absolutely, definitely, and kick-her-fucking-ass not be pregnant. With an inward sigh of relief, she focused on the most logical explanation for the girl's evasiveness —subterfuge.

"Give me a sec. Desk?"

"What do you need?" The AI sounded bored, which was even more irritating than her usual snarky sharpness.

"Can you pick this call up and route it through you?"

"I can…and it's done. It's a burner by the looks of it."

"Yeah. That makes sense. Okay, I need this secured—so tight it doesn't even squeak."

"Done—and I won't ask where you originally used that particular analogy."

Niki grinned. "Yeah. Best you don't. Vickie, relax. This line is now secured—and by the best, too. Even you couldn't come close to what she can do."

"Ugh. Whatever. Look, I'm using a burner here, and I'm as far away from the strip mall as I can get without being suspicious. Who the fuck ever thought I'd willingly volunteer to buy cleaning shit?"

"Okay, you said something about a possible emergency —which, if I throw in things like burner phones and suspicious, makes me a little nervous. Especially after a momentary panic about whether you were in the family way or not."

The hacker laughed. "It was the only thing I could think of to get the message across. Wait—you said panic. Don't tell me you believed that shit?"

"Like I said, momentary. Then I realized that it would involve— You know what, moving on. I need to get out of here and preferably sooner rather than later. What do you have that I should be nervous about?"

"I don't think you need to be nervous exactly—well, not yet— but there is an issue I thought you should be aware of."

"That you, Taylor, and Bobby took it upon yourselves to rob six million dollars from an armored truck in broad daylight? Yeah, it's kind of been hard to miss. You guys have trended online for the past few weeks. When I see something like that associated with the location, I have to assume it's something to do with you dumbasses."

"Honestly, it wasn't as bad as it looks. It was simply how Taylor got back at the people who have tried to kill us. He wanted to do something to put them on the back foot and make them think twice about trying to give us trouble again. I thought it was done ingeniously, actually. A ton of noise, very little actual damage, and the perfect distraction I needed to get into their files to take a good look at their operation."

"So, it was all a distraction, yeah?" Hopefully, Niki thought, she might find a perfectly reasonable explanation in all this that didn't include theft.

"Oh yes."

"Are you saying it had nothing to do with the six million dollars they picked up from the armored vehicle?" she pressed.

"Oh, well…that was mainly to get their attention and yeah, it's a nice little bonus, but the whole point of it was to get a real idea of where all the people who attacked us came from. We have a lock on the guy in charge but as of right now, I think our real problems are the police officers who seem to think we had something to do with the robbery."

"You did have something to do with it."

"Well, they're not supposed to know that."

"Come on, Vickie. When you're the only damn mech suit shop in the fucking city, they will absolutely knock on your door. You have to see that it's a little thing called making yourselves the only people who would be persons of interest in that kind of case. I don't know where the hell Taylor got the idea of robbing an armored truck."

"Well, we wanted to rob the casino but that was even more impossible,"

Niki rubbed her eyes. She would so have to take the last

flight out of there. Fucking Vickie. And fucking Taylor McFadden with all his not so bright ideas.

"Fine. What is it that you need me to look into?"

"Well, the cops arrived and searched the premises, scanned everything, and looked through everything. We cleaned up well enough, though. It wasn't a major issue and we anticipated that they would do a quick search so that was fine. Unfortunately, they have been on our asses and not only come in with more questions, but they also tried to get their hands on the mechs we're working on. They know they have nothing even remotely incriminating but for some reason, they still want to pin it on us. I hoped you would be able to pull a few strings and divert the investigation somewhere else."

The agent glanced quickly at her watch. "Did you happen to catch the name of the officer in charge of the investigation?"

"Detective Pembroke and Sergeant Creighton. Those are the only ones we've interacted with so far. Well, aside from the veritable army they have running in and out of here. Despite the fact that they copied everything they could find, they still insist that they have to run checks on our computers and stuff. It's forced us to play the nicest citizens of all time and honestly, it's not a good look on me. And Taylor has this whole thing lined up for next Friday..."

She tilted her head when Vickie's voice trailed off. "Oh? What the hell is Taylor having next Friday? Because my connections in the task force tell me that a group of his merc buddies is coming in on Friday. Something about a business meeting."

"I... Fuck, that wasn't... Is there any chance I can get you to forget I said that? Taylor will figuratively kill me if he finds out I told you about it."

"Well, maybe you could simply explain it to me. If Taylor's holding a business meeting, that shouldn't be something he'd hide from me, right?"

"You're not wrong, I guess. Yeah, it's a business meeting. He's invited some of our clients to have a quick look at the place to show them how we treat their mechs so they'll spread the word about what we can do. It'll be a huge bummer if a group of cops shows up while we're having this meet and greet."

"Yeah, I can see that and I'll see what I can do. I don't really have the kind of pull it would take to make them drop the investigation, but I do have some influence. Maybe I can show them that there are mechs that are distributed by companies in the country that have legal troubles and get them to shut some of the FBI's problems down along the way. I'll see what I can do. I'll talk to you soon."

"Sure. And please don't tell Taylor?"

"Promise."

---

He wasn't sure why he felt so nervous. Anxiety would be the death of him, but having people visit the business somehow made it all very real. He had worked hard to get his start-up running efficiently. It was his full-time job despite the work he put in for the FBI, and it was his dream to have everything working as a professional and successful company that he'd founded and made his own.

Oddly enough, it hadn't felt entirely real until this moment when he had people coming to see his work and what they were doing. It was his little piece of earth, and they would come to judge its worth. If they didn't think it had value, that would be the end of it, more or less.

"I simply need to focus and get the pitch right." Taylor felt a little silly talking to himself in the mirror, but it was a way to psyche himself into the right frame of mind. "Stay on target. You know these guys. They like working with you, so show them how good you are at it and walk away. Oh, yeah, there's that little point of getting that other pitch right too, but let's not focus on that."

He pulled his shirt on. It fit a little better now that he had begun to fill out again. As stupid as it sounded, he was able to wear his clothes instead of having them wear him. While he still had a way to go, he would continue to make progress because he'd set his mind to doing what was needed.

However he felt, though, he couldn't delay any longer. With a sigh, he stepped out of his room, descended the stairs, and headed to the garage where Tanya, Bobby, and Vickie all waited. None were in their traditional work garb and most of their tasks were done for the day anyway. Bobby looked dashing in a tweed jacket that somehow fit his form rather nicely. Tanya wore jeans, heels, and a snug-fitting tank top.

Vickie was the only one who hadn't changed her attire at all. She still wore her platform boots and black tights with a torn jean skirt and jacket over a black shirt, all of which complimented her short hair rather well, he thought. She also seemed more confident in her look than she had in the past, and he was all for that.

"Are we ready?" Taylor asked and gave the work area one final quick scrutiny.

"The caterers will arrive soon," Vickie told him. "They'll set up shop as soon as they get here. I still don't know why we don't take our clients out for a big dinner and a night on the town. It seems a little low-brow for the impression we want to make, right?"

"We'll take them out for a meal after. The caterers are only to provide food and drink for them to enjoy while they're still here. You guys don't need to hang around for the meal at the end, though."

"If you're paying for all that, do you really think I'll pass on having dinner with you guys? Where are you taking them, anyway? And don't say Il Fornaio."

"Why would I say that?"

"Because that's where you always go."

Taylor shook his head and smiled. "I'm still working on that, actually. I have a couple of reservations, but it depends on the kind of afternoon we have with them. Cars will bring them over, but you have to understand that these guys are salt of the earth. They are army folks like Bobby and myself and a little like Tanya too. Tough guys but mostly simple and not really into all the fancy shit."

"I don't see how you can say that and go to someplace called Il Fornaio for breakfast."

"What's wrong with breakfast?"

"Nothing is wrong, particularly, but it's still annoying

that you think of yourself as a simple guy with simple tastes."

"I am!"

"Bull-fucking-shit."

Taylor didn't bother to suppress a laugh and left Vickie to work on her computer as he wandered to where Bobby had obviously been unable to resist work. Despite his cleaner clothes, his hands had a couple of grease stains as he took pieces apart and showed them to Tanya. The two were getting along better than he'd expected, and their interaction revealed that she was more than capable of taking up a more profitable position as a mechanic.

Having her get a proper education in the field seemed like a better plan every day, but he hadn't made an effort to address it with her aside from the one time they'd discussed it in passing. They would deal with those kinds of details come the end of the next quarter. He would talk to her about it then.

For now, though, they had to deal with the issue of their clients visiting to inspect the business.

"I had a call from the airport. Our clients have arrived and are on their way," Bobby said, his focus still fixed on his work. "They have an ETA of about fifteen minutes, depending on traffic. There isn't much we can do around here until they arrive, so I thought it would be a good idea to get some work done while I waited."

"I don't think our clients will mind seeing you working and getting your hands dirty but you might want to take your jacket off, though. Washing grease off tweed will be one hell of a headache, even if you dry-clean it."

"It's nylon. It only looks like tweed."

"Is that because you're cheap, or—"

"It fits better. And it's cooler. It would be really stupid to walk around in tweed in the middle of the fucking desert."

"I'm sure every professor buried in a five-hundred-mile radius kind of rolled over in their graves. Or...urns, as appropriate, I guess. Anyway, washing grease off nylon will also be a pain."

Bobby nodded and paused for a moment to take his jacket off. Tanya helped him and eased the sleeves free so they wouldn't come in contact with the grease on his hands. He was the kind of worker who took pride in his craft and returned to it quickly to draw out the wiring he had attempted to remove from inside the mech suit. The way he worked deftly to clean and repair each connection revealed that it wouldn't take too long before he had it functional again.

A short while later, Taylor's phone vibrated to alert him that new arrivals had pulled into the back. The garage door began to open as the two town cars came to a stop and parked outside.

The first man to exit was taller than Taylor and much leaner. Freddie had many nicknames in the Zoo, but the most popular one was the Scarecrow. He didn't mind people calling him that but he did take offense to people singing the song from the *Wizard of Oz*. The last man to do so had been knocked out with a single punch.

Taylor recalled that vividly, having watched the fight in person. He had bet on his fellow corporal to win the fight and lost big time.

"Taylor!" the man shouted and crossed to where the tall redhead stood to shake his hand firmly. "Goddamn, it's good to see you again. You have no idea how boring the Zoo is without your ginger ass around."

"Well, what can I say? My luck of the Scottish did follow me here, at least in part." He needed a moment to shake a little feeling into his hand as the other two members of their group climbed out of the second car.

One was a shorter fellow and on the burly side with a thick beard. He was one of the Zoo locals, a Moroccan by birth who had served in the French Foreign Legion before he set out on his own. St Just was one of the true veterans of the Zoo and one of the first mercs to be employed by the commander of the US base to make runs into the jungle.

"It has been a long time, *mon'ami,* and Fredrick is right. The Zoo has not been the same without the lucky McFadden leading the charge."

"You guys still have me in the fight with you," he pointed. "Working with the suits we send back is something."

"Better than nothing, I'll admit."

The last man was a little slower to exit the town car and needed help from the driver to get to his feet. He had light brown hair cut to regulation length and the familiar lean, muscular build of the armed forces.

It hurt Taylor a little to see him favor his right leg and need a cane to walk across the tarmac toward him.

"Sergeant Matt Davis, it's a real pleasure to see you again," Taylor said and extended his hand in welcome.

Davis reached out and shook Taylor's hand firmly. "I

dare say it is a pleasure to see you again too, McFadden, though it's not sergeant anymore. It hasn't been for a little while now."

"Yeah, I heard. You have an in with some mega-corporation that's helping to run shit in the Zoo area. Was that before or after the...accident?"

David chuckled and patted his right leg where it separated into a prosthetic. "It all kind of happened at the same time, which means the military is still working out if they owe me any disability pay, but I'm not pushing for it. I was technically already a freelancer when this happened, so when the time came, the company I worked for elected to pull me out and give me a desk job with full benefits. I don't need to tell you that the benefits in the private sector are a league over what we'd get in the military anyway."

Taylor smirked, thumped the man on the shoulder, and nodded as the caterers began to set a table with food and drinks for the group. "Anyway, I appreciate you taking the time to come out here. It's not like we're employed by... what is it, Poseidon?"

"Pegasus."

"Right. I had the mythology right anyway. My point is, while we don't necessarily work with Pegasus, it would still be a boon to have someone like you come over and give our facility a once-over."

"Well, I did owe you that favor, so why the hell not."

Taylor laughed and suppressed a grimace as anxiety tightened his chest for a moment. He gestured for the three men to make their way inside the garage, where Bobby had begun to clean the grease from his hands with a cloth.

"I think you guys already know my head mechanic,

Robert Zhang." He motioned for the man to get up from his seat. "The dude fixed all of your mechs at least once—and more than once for you, Davis."

Bobby took a moment to greet all of them by name, careful to offer his forearm so he wouldn't stain their hands with grease. None took it and each understood that there were no cooties transferred when you shook a working man's hands.

"Here's our newest recruit, Tanya Novak." He introduced them to her. "And you all know the one and only Victoria Madison, also known as Vickie."

The hacker looked up from her computer and waved at the trio in front of her. "What's up, losers?"

Freddie laughed. "Holy shit, it's almost like meeting a celebrity at this point."

"Yeah, well, don't let that go to her head. She's already difficult enough to deal with as it is."

"It's a little late for that," Vickie pointed out and turned quickly to her computer.

Taylor thought she looked anxious and maybe even a little nervous about meeting new people. He kept the small group moving to the table that now offered a wide variety of snacks and drinks.

An ice-filled bowl was full of beers and a small drinks station was stocked with a handful of spirits and accouterments to make simple cocktails.

The platters were filled with small treats—mini quiches, sausage rolls, coconut shrimp, beer-battered shrimp, barbecue bacon sliders, beef samosas, and more. He had placed the catering order with a local company that had a package labeled *The Works* but hadn't expected quite this kind of feast. It was certainly more food than the group would eat, although it looked like the three intended to put that assumption to the test. Drinking and eating were something military men had a knack for during their downtime.

The brochure had mentioned there would be refills available should they be needed. A couple of workers from the catering company waited near the table in case there were any questions about the food regarding allergies or anything like that.

While St Just began to talk with the waitress about his dietary preferences and Davis was in conversation with Bobby, Taylor approached Freddie where the man piled his plate with enthusiasm.

"Are you enjoying the buffet?"

Freddie chuckled. "Are you kidding me? Do you know how difficult it is to get some of these deep-fried delicacies out there in the middle of the fucking desert? Who the hell am I kidding? Of course you do. But yeah, this shit is great. You sure as hell know how to keep your clients happy, I'll tell you something."

He smiled. "Well, make as liberal use of the buffet and the drinks as you like. I'm sure we'll have leftovers for days as it is, and we are going out for dinner later so maybe if you fill up on this, I'll have a smaller bill to pay later."

"In your dreams."

"Yeah, I didn't have high hopes for that one. If you don't mind talking a little business while you're eating…"

His voice trailed off and Freddie nodded in response as they moved a little farther from the rest of the group.

"You mentioned there was a little situation that you

wanted to talk to me about. I gathered it might be something that wasn't one hundred percent legal." Freddie seemed unperturbed as he chewed on some of the coconut shrimp.

"I actually avoided saying exactly how illegal it was. Now, though, I need to tell you that it's one hundred percent illegal."

"My man McFadden doesn't do anything half-heartedly, I get that."

"The situation is that I've come into cash I need to… launder as it were. I remember the restrictions on where cash comes from being much looser in the Zoo than they are around here."

"You're the ones who pulled that mech heist on the Strip," his friend responded in almost a whisper. "I fucking knew it!"

"I can neither confirm nor deny these allegations," Taylor asserted and kept his voice lowered. "But if there were a way for us to move the cash to you guys and charge you a little extra over the next few invoices based on that, what kind of a fee do you think you would feel comfortable charging for that kind of service?"

"Well, we could always say you do our actual work for free and only charge us to get your money back—maybe something like that would work."

"It would be a risky business so I wouldn't want to leave you in the lurch without any kind of a payday."

"Look, we make our profits on the work anyway. If we get this kind of deal, we don't want to be caught spending your money on anything but large-ticket items, which means if it goes into a bank, we'll move it out quickly. This way, we have space in our budget that the repairs used to fill—even at your lower prices, they still ain't cheap—and you get your money back clean. Everyone wins and the chances of being caught are at their lowest."

Taylor scratched his cheek idly. "I guess you've already put considerable thought into this."

"My man, from the moment you said you had a business proposition for me and I realized it was on the DL, I already assumed you were the ones involved in that heist and needed a way to move the money. Like I wouldn't recognize your mech. Give me some credit."

"Yeah, that's fair. I appreciate this, Freddie."

"Hey, I appreciate getting all my team's mechs repaired for free."

Taylor was about to discuss the details when a car pulled up next to the town cars. The black SUV was the kind he had seen before and was driven by only one person —the only person, in fact, who actually bothered to come to his strip mall for a visit.

"Is that something you need to take care of?" Freddie asked when he noted the shift in his attention.

"Yeah. We'll talk about this more, okay?"

The man nodded and moved toward the snacks while Niki climbed out of her SUV and stretched slowly the way she did after a long drive. Taylor wasn't the only one who watched her, of course, but when he walked out to greet her, most of the attention moved elsewhere.

The agent grinned as he approached. "Nice to see you again, Taylor. It looks like you guys are having a party."

"Yeah, and it looks like you knew a party was happening," he noted in response. "How did you—it was Vickie, wasn't it?"

"I promised her I wouldn't tell you."

He shook his head. "Well, it's not a big secret or anything, I suppose."

"So does that mean you won't slam the door in my face?"

"Well, you've approached us during regular business hours and aren't beating the door down with your monster hands, so yeah, I won't slam the door in your face. Imagine that."

She laughed. "Won't you invite me in, you red-headed Cro-Magnon with a small dick complex?"

Taylor narrowed his eyes. "What's the magic word?"

"Please won't you invite me in, you red-headed Cro-Magnon with a small dick complex?"

"There we go. We have drinks and food on the table there, and I'll take the guys out for dinner later. You know, to make sure the clients are happy about having to come all the way to Vegas to have a look at our little shop."

"If that's an invitation to go out to dinner with you—"

"Me and my Cro-Magnon friends with small dick complexes, or so your hearsay evidence states."

"Right. I might have to see what you're like in your natural habitat. And if you think all I have is hearsay evidence, I should remind you that no, that's not actually the case."

Taylor opened his mouth to reply but nothing came out as a sudden memory of her watching him in the shower came to mind. She grinned and walked past him toward the table where the rest of the group was already waiting to meet her.

"Huh," Taylor grunted, unsure of how exactly he should interpret her comment. He needed a second to recover from being poleaxed like that but managed to do so quickly and returned to the group.

CHAPTER NINETEEN

A long meal at one of the best steak houses in the city proved to be one of the most interesting nights of Taylor's life.

Well, his civilian life, anyway.

Niki did, in fact, join them for the evening—much to Vickie's chagrin—which made it an interesting evening for him to watch from a family's perspective.

Of course, Freddie, St Just, and Davis knew how to have a pre-party almost as much as they knew how to party. Taylor and Bobby knew that about them, at least, but for Vickie, Niki, and Tanya, the experience was altogether different. Most of the booze provided by the catering company was consumed or stashed away for later consumption. Taylor asked them to keep the food for later and let them clean up before they all headed out.

The steakhouse was nice enough and provided enough food and booze to keep the party going but, as Taylor had suspected, they were all in the mood for something a little less high-class. The establishment was the kind that had a wine menu like the one Jennie had chosen for them when they'd gone out.

He already felt a little under the influence when the others began to get into the groove for the party. Heading out into town didn't seem like a good idea, which meant it was only a matter of time before they ended up at Jackson's.

"I assumed we would come here," Vickie grumbled as the group climbed out of their town cars.

"What do you mean?" Niki asked and let Taylor, Bobby, Tanya, and the clients move ahead of them.

"Taylor has this... Well, I hesitate to say that she's his girlfriend, but she is someone he likes hanging out with—the kind of girl who's of a similar mind. She tends the bar here. Alexandra is her name. I won't lie, I took a minute to look her up when I heard she and Taylor were shacking up on the regular. I didn't think it was possible that a woman would agree to spend that much time with him without having something on her mind that wasn't sex."

The agent scowled at her and let the group step into the bar before she spoke in a hushed voice. "And why the hell are you telling me this?"

The hacker looked around quickly to make sure they were alone. "Well...you know."

"I don't know because the conversation to which that might be pertinent didn't happen after that conversation ended, right?"

"Come on, you don't expect me to act like it didn't happen when we're alone, right?"

"I do. I expect you to act like that."

"Well, I won't," Vickie stated firmly. "You're my cousin,

although you have been more like a mom or maybe an aunt than my cousin, and so I'll look out for you. Even if all I can do is warn you that you'll meet someone who could be one of Taylor's squeezes."

"Don't say it like that," Niki snapped, took her arm, and pulled her into the bar. "And keep it down. I'm fine and I don't need to know about Taylor's...squeezes."

Once they were inside, it looked like their group had already gathered around a couple of booths.

"I still can't believe you're a Pack man, Taylor." Davis groaned and shook his head as the TV screens around them showed replays of the weekend's games. "Honestly, you're a reasonable guy, so why would you choose to cheer for a team that's so...shit, so annoyingly bad?"

"They're rebuilding this year. You know that," Taylor replied and chuckled as their drinks—beers for all of them—arrived at the table. "There's a reason why it's called Titletown, you know. Besides, do you think your forty-niners are any less annoying with Jerry Rice admitting to using an illegal substance to catch all those passes from Joe Montana?"

"Blow it out your ass," St Just shouted. "You all have this hand-egg game that you watch so much but you can't abandon the real sport of football. You know, the one where you kick an actual ball with your actual foot?"

"And you're saying you can't enjoy two different sports with the same name?" Taylor asked, took a long sip of his beer, and glanced at Vickie and Niki who still stood over them. "What...what are you looking at? Are you waiting for an invitation or have you decided not to sit?"

"I..." Niki didn't finish her sentence and simply dropped

onto the seat beside him. She caught the attention of the young waitress who had delivered everyone else's drinks. "I'll have a beer too. The same as them."

"Coming right up."

Taylor leaned back and studied the woman as she settled into the booth.

"What about you, Miss Banks?" St Just interrupted and nudged her arm. "What kind of sporting events are you a fan of?"

"Well, I don't have much time to watch sports these days, but when I do, it's a little more relaxing to watch while you're doing something else. My dad is a huge White Sox fan, so I usually cheer along with him."

"Let's be honest, baseball is only popular these days because people are all caught up in the nostalgia of it," Taylor stated. "You should start talking to them about upgrading their rules and their equipment into the twenty-first century, but no, they want to maintain all the old records intact—like anyone will ever break any of Babe Ruth's records. Seal the record books and move on."

"Look, I can tell you're trying to get a rise out of me, but I don't care enough about the sport to tell you that you're either wrong or right. I don't even know enough about the sport to be able to fight back, so maybe try someone else."

"Ah, well, she's no fun," Freddie muttered. "How is it that you're with us anyway? Are you Taylor's girlfriend?"

"In his dreams, I might be—no, wait, not even then."

"So, you're single?"

"Not in your dreams either."

"So, you're not single?"

"I am, but to you, I'm unavailable."

Taylor was quick to come to her rescue. "Niki here is a friend of mine and she's the reason why I actually hired Vickie, who is her cousin. That's not to say that if Vickie had applied for the job she wouldn't have got it since she's more than talented enough. But the point is…what was the point again?"

"I think the point is that the celebrity has a cousin. And a hot cousin in that strong, powerful Eva Longoria sort of way."

"See, Taylor thought I looked like Eva Longoria too. Is it only because we're both Latinas?"

"Wait," Vickie interjected. "Are we thinking *Young and the Restless Eva* or more *Desperate Housewives?* Because I can see it when Eva was a little older."

"Fuck you, Vickie."

"Don't take it like that. Eva has matured and become better as an actress during her career. You have the same kind of mature look about you."

"Yeah, I know, and I still think you should go fuck yourself."

"Oh, wow. I guess Vickie's sass runs in the family," Freddie said.

Taylor could only imagine the sheer amount of drinks the man would make off this interaction between the two, provided the people in the Zoo believed what he said. It was always a hit or miss kind of situation when it came to telling stories like that. He wasn't sure what his friend had in mind when it came to telling the story. Either he'd run with the fact that Vickie was a punky character in person as well as over the phone and had a cousin who had the same kind of spunk, or maybe the sexy cousin story.

The drinks would flow with the former story. The second had a higher reward but a higher risk attached to it too.

He shook his head as the conversation continued while his mind began to wander. The other members of the group handled their booze far better than he did. Maybe all that time in the hospital had ruined his body's ability to process toxins.

*Speaking of which.*

"I need to hit the head—be right back," he said, stood, and squeezed out of the booth to move toward the bathroom. It had been a long day, but with the clients now settled for the most part and arrangements having been tentatively made to effectively launder the cash, he wasn't sure he had the energy to hang out with his old pals from the Zoo.

They talked like he was somehow still in the business with them—which he was, technically, but from afar. They acted like he was still in the trenches with them and that brought up a couple of uncomfortable memories.

He finished at the urinal and washed his hands before he returned to the booth again, ready for another rousing round of talks about how high Freddie's headcount was, or how much St Just made on each of his runs into the jungle. Maybe Davis would know a thing or two about how he felt, but the man showed no sign of it.

The conversation at the booth was still as loud as before and Vickie had taken center stage. She said something that made the others laugh and continued to talk in the way she did when they were on the phone. Her anxiety over meeting these guys in person instead of on the other side of an impersonal device had faded with a couple of drinks. She now acted in the way she did when she was a little more confident, and he liked to see that.

It was still a little too loud for him, though. For some reason, his mood had begun to get worse and worse and he wasn't sure why.

"Hey, come join me," said a voice from his left. Taylor turned to where Niki sat at one of the empty tables not far from the rowdy group.

"Do you feel a little out of your element?" he asked and slid into a seat across from her.

"I'm struggling with a realization that hit me like a ton of bricks." She slid his glass of beer across the table.

He picked it up and took a long sip. "And what realization is that?"

"That you're actually the best of your Cro-Magnon brothers. Seriously, is there something in the air there that makes you all a horde of vapid assholes?"

Taylor shrugged. "In the air. In the trees. In the water and the dirt. In the monsters that try to kill us and even in the trees that want to kill us too, if you can believe it."

"I'm not sure what you mean."

"It's like I've explained to you before." He took another sip from his beer before he continued. "When you're in a situation where people are almost constantly killed or maimed or otherwise injured, you kind of lose track of all of the old societal norms that used to hinder you before. You stop caring about hurting people's feelings or offending them. You are forged into someone who's a little vapid and something of an asshole because if you die tomorrow, why should the norms of society matter that much to you anyway? It's not like they'll stop a venom-fanged panther from tearing into your neck."

Niki sighed and shook her head. "I guess that makes sense, but still."

"It might also have something to do with the people you interact with. A kind of don't-give-a-shit crowd tends to flock to the military these days, and even those who weren't like that in the beginning end up with the sentiment rubbing off on them. It's not the best side effect that comes from running into an alien Zoo full of monsters but it's far from the worst, I'll tell you that much."

The agent couldn't help a laugh. "You have this weird way to rationalize your behavior in a way that almost makes it sound rational. Almost."

"I'll take that as a compliment."

She leaned across the table, her features more serious as she spoke in a whisper. "So, do you plan to tell me what the fuck you're up to here?"

"I…don't know what you're talking about."

"I know you don't think I'm an idiot, so don't treat me like one, Taylor. I know you were involved in that little heist that was on…oh, every fucking news station in the world. Seriously, I think they even reported that shit in North Korea."

"Well, with all the people who know we were involved in the robbery, you'd think I would be behind bars by now."

"Look, Taylor, I understand why you did it. Getting back at those sons of bitches who attacked your premises and your team was well done. I even understand why you didn't involve me in the heist, me being in law enforcement and all. And I appreciate the fact that you were careful enough to keep the cops off your trail, kind of. Obviously, you're still a person of interest, but they're pursuing other leads at the moment."

"And I guess we have you to thank for that?"

"Well, I get a little something out of it too so you don't need to worry about paying me back for it. The only thing I'm interested in is what you plan to do with the information you picked up off the hard drives."

"How did you—Vickie?"

"Vickie."

"Fuck. Is there anything she hasn't told you?"

"I'm your white knight in shining armor, Taylor. Do you really want to keep any secrets from me?"

He took another long sip from his beer and drained the glass. "Not really, no. I assume you know everything we do?"

"More or less. Vickie gave me the name of the big cheese who's the source of your trouble, and I looked him up. Castellano is a tough son of a bitch. How do you plan to deal with him?"

"Do you want the truth?"

Niki nodded.

"I don't have a plan. I have no fucking clue how to get all the way to fucking Italy to eliminate a guy with more pull than your average state governor."

"Awesome. I didn't want to step on any toes."

"Do you have a plan?"

"Yep."

"And do you intend to tell me the plan?"

She tilted her head and grinned. "Sure, but it's still in progress. I've heard from sources outside the country that they have monster issues in Sicily. That close to the Zoo, comparatively speaking, stories about creatures that go bump in the night is bound to start a panic. As a result, the locals have kept it quiet but also asked around for professional help. I've managed to get in touch with their *Polizia di Stato* and offered them the services of one of my best."

"I've been out of the game for a while now, but am I supposed to assume that means me?"

"Well, sure. For now. Like you said, you've been out of the game for a while, so I might need to reevaluate the situation. For the moment, though, I'm waiting to hear from them, but they seem very interested in having someone with your qualifications handling their problem as quietly as possible. I think we can turn that into an opportunity, don't you?"

Taylor nodded. "Agreed."

"I do have a condition, though," she told him as another two beers were brought for them and the patrons of the bar grew even louder.

"What kind?"

"I come with you."

"Do you honestly think you have it in you to kill someone like this? It's cold-blooded murder."

"This asshole tried to kill a member of my family, Taylor. If you think I'll let that slide, you'd better have another think coming, and fast. Besides, he wouldn't be the first person I've killed. So get used to it. You have all fucking night."

"Right. Well, I have a condition for your condition."

"What?"

Taylor leaned in a little closer. "I guess from the way you spoke that only the two of us will head out there?"

"Sure."

"Then you have to tell Bungees he's not coming."

"I...uh, I didn't think he'd want to come."

"Vickie's family to him too. He's raring for blood even if he doesn't show it."

"Fine, I'll tell him. So are we agreed on this?"

He raised his glass to tap hers. "I think we have ourselves a fucking deal."

# CHAPTER TWENTY

Something was happening around him and people were moving and talking. Taylor rolled over on his bed and tried to cover his head with a pillow, but it didn't do any good. It wasn't long until he was dragged fully from sleep and was able to hear what was said.

Vickie's voice was the first he recognized and he scowled and tried to focus on her words.

"Why are you cutting me out of this?"

Niki spoke next. "I didn't think you'd be interested in going all the way to Italy—"

"Who doesn't want to go to Italy?"

"To kill a dude. It's not like you would hang out and shop in Rome. We will go to Sicily to kill this guy." The agent sounded more tired than she usually did, which was significant.

"Do you think I don't know that? Do you honestly believe I didn't look into every fucking detail about this guy? Bobby and I were the ones caught in his crosshairs, so why the hell shouldn't we be involved in hunting and killing this asshole?"

"You will be involved. It'll merely be from a safe distance."

The hacker snorted. "That's bullshit right there. I should at least fly to Italy."

"I'll be able to mask Taylor's flight there, but if they ping both of you going as well, the jig will be up."

Speaking of jigs being up, Taylor had the feeling sleep was a ship that had sailed by this point. He groaned softly, turned again, and shoved the pillow aside impatiently.

The motion made him realize that his head pounded painfully. As if the headache wasn't enough, it tasted like a cat had crapped in his mouth, and the feeling came with a dry throat and an unsettled stomach.

In short, he had a hangover. He couldn't remember the last time he'd been hungover, which was telling—either of how long it had been since he had gone out to get drunk or of his body's ability to process large amounts of alcohol without leaving him under the effects.

He scowled at the two women in his room and tried not to open his eyes too wide since even the dim light that filtered through the shades of his windows seared his eyeballs like tuna steaks.

"Could you guys be a little quieter?" he rasped through his hoarse throat. "Just...like, lower the volume to maybe a private conversation."

Vickie approached and held a glass of water out. "We were having a private conversation while we waited for you to wake up. Come on. You need to hydrate."

Taylor took the glass from her hand and gulped the

liquid eagerly despite the fact that his mouth still tasted like crap. It didn't do much for the dryness of his throat but it would have to do for now. "Which brings me to my next question. Why the hell are you in my room?"

Niki stepped closer to answer him. "Well, we intended to wait in the garage, but you left the door to your apartment open so we thought we might as well wait in here. I won't lie. We hoped that talking loudly would wake you. We have business to attend to this morning after all."

She turned the volume up on the last ten words of her last sentence to the point where she practically shouted in his ear and grinned when she got the reaction she wanted. He winced and pulled away from her as he covered his ears slowly.

"Jesus Christ, woman. Inside voice. Inside voice or I'll kick you out of the damn strip mall and sleep for the rest of the day to spite you."

"Hah, you have to know I don't believe that for one second. You want this situation handled as much as I do and as quickly as I do."

Taylor winced again and glared at the woman. "Fine. But first things first. How are our friends from the Zoo doing?"

"Bobby made sure they were all ready to drive to the airport to catch their flights," Niki said. "Only one will go directly to the Zoo—the French guy."

"He's Moroccan but he's worked with the French Foreign Legion, hence the accent."

She shrugged. "Freddie said he would spend time with his family before he headed back, but he did ask for you to give him a call about your particular situation. I will go ahead and guess that I don't want to know what the hell he was talking about."

"I've brought him on board to launder the money we stole from the armored truck."

"Like I said, I don't want to know."

Taylor pushed from his bed. It was weird how he was able to hear the blood pumping in his head with each beat inside his chest.

"I thought you wanted to be in the know of all the details of the situation. That you were…what was the term you used? My white knight in shining armor?"

Vickie perked up. "Wait, she actually said that?"

He nodded. "Her exact words."

"I was drinking, and when I drink, I get all…philosophical." Niki didn't look happy about the revelation.

His smirk drew a scowl from her. "We'd better get started on business before you call my mother a hamster and talk about how my father smells of elderberries."

The agent scrunched her face. "Your what?"

"She's never watched Monty Python," Vickie interjected. "I've tried to get her to watch it but she never does."

"Still, that phrase has soaked into pop culture for years. It's not like only the people who have watched it will get the reference." He shook his head, his brow raised.

Niki flipped him off. "Well, I don't. So can we move right along?"

"Right. Did Davis happen to mention where he was going?" he asked.

The agent thought for a moment. "I think he said he was flying to Philly and mentioned something about how he even had a private plane waiting for him."

Taylor nodded. "Yeah. He's working for a multinational corporation now. The guy is one of the best so it would make sense that they would want to keep him on the team even after the incident."

"Incident?" she raised an eyebrow.

Taylor sighed. "Oh…something happened in the Zoo and he lost his leg. Didn't you see that he walked around with a limp and a cane?"

She looked surprised. "I did but I thought it was only an injury. The guy moves well for someone missing a leg."

He nodded. "Chalk that down to him having the body of an Olympian and the IQ of a chess grandmaster. You know, the kind of guy they usually have in the special forces."

"He didn't seem particularly intelligent last night."

"He's very good at hiding it, but yeah, the guy's a stone-cold genius," he told her. "He got me and mine out of the Zoo alive more times than I can count and if I'm honest, he deserves a fucking break at this point."

Niki rubbed her eyes for a moment. "Well, if you're done defending your man crush, can we move onto something that actually matters?"

"Like laundering our stolen money through merc companies in the Zoo?" Vickie asked.

Her cousin scowled. "No. Like I said, I want nothing to do with that. As long as you guys do it smartly and carefully so you won't have the IRS climbing up your ass—because believe me when I say that no matter how much pull I have, I won't be able to get you out of trouble with them."

Taylor walked to the minifridge in his room, refilled his

glass with cold water, and took another long drink. "Well, as chilling as that warning might sound, I think we have more pressing concerns to talk about. Is there any word from our friends in Italy?"

"The captain of the *Polizia di Stato* who's dealing with the monsters in the area messaged me this morning," Niki advised them. "He said he doesn't like to admit it but they're a little stumped when it comes to what to do with the reports of monsters in the area. This is their first time dealing with this kind of thing."

He grunted softly. "It makes sense. They have imported very little of the goop that's ferried out of the Zoo, which means they'll probably not have much access to what's causing these monsters to appear all over the place. China, India, and the US are the main buyers, so I'm reasonably sure they'll have all kinds of different types of monsters showing up, but they keep it on the down-low because they don't want any kind of panic."

"If that's true, why have they cropped up in Italy now?" Vickie asked.

"Who knows?" He shrugged. "Maybe Castellano imports it to keep himself young or something. The real problem, like you said, is that Italy is much closer to the Zoo than I would be comfortable with. If it starts to spread in that area, there won't be much we can do to stop it from somehow linking with the rest of the Zoo and facilitating its spread."

The hacker didn't look comforted. "Why...why are you talking about the Zoo spreading?"

His expression serious, he took another sip of his water before he answered. "Because while putting assholes like

Castellano in their place is important, it's even more important to make sure that the Zoo isn't able to spread beyond what happens in the jungle itself. Why do you think I've put this much effort into fighting the monsters outside the Zoo? Do you really think I only did it for the money?"

Niki tilted her head, her expression faintly challenging. "You can't say the money had nothing to do with it."

"Yeah, that's fair," he admitted. "But the point stands. We'll have to deal with the monsters they have there and hopefully, at the same time, deal with this mafia don. I… shit, I had something for this."

"Something for what?" the agent asked.

"Something like a Zoo's version of killing two birds with one stone. Idioms have never been my forte."

Vickie rolled her chair closer to the conversation. "Something like…killing two killerpillars with one rocket?"

"How…how did you know about that?" Taylor asked.

The young hacker grinned. "Oh, they talked about the kinds of creatures they hate the most last night. All three agreed that they hated the killerpillars the most and that they are incredibly difficult to kill. It can be done, though, with a single direct strike with a rocket."

"Yeah, but the critters are fast and hard to hit directly with a rocket, which means you need to shoot them at almost point-blank range," he explained. "And yeah, if you don't like creepy-crawlies—which almost no one does—you'll hate to see them up close. They are about the size of a small car. I bet even the most enthusiastic entomologist would be creeped-out by the fuckers."

"Back to the point," Niki snapped. "Do you want to

shoot the shit about the biggest creepy-crawlies the alien goop has to throw at us or will we discuss the Italian police captain? He wants to talk to you about bringing you to their country in secret to deal with the threat without alerting the general populace."

"Did he really want to talk to me?" He frowned, a little surprised.

"Well, why wouldn't he given that he'll effectively put his career and probably his life on the line to vouch for you?" she countered.

"Fair enough." He nodded. "Let me get coffee in me and we can give the guy a call."

The drive didn't take long at all but the inconvenience was enough to make Taylor vow to order a coffee machine online sometime in the next couple of days. Assuming, of course, that he wasn't traveling halfway across the world.

"In that case, I'll have to order it when I get back," he mumbled, slid out of the car with the tray of coffee, and hurried to his room where it appeared the two women were already setting up a conference call.

He shook his head and took a hasty sip. "You guys know you can do this in the room next door, right? There's a whole setup there for precisely this kind of situation."

"It's dirty and we didn't feel like cleaning it for one call, so we'll use your room," Vickie replied and looked at him with a small grin. "It's weird. Every time I come in here, I assume you're a sloppy kind of slob, but when we actually come into your little domain, you're very clean and neat."

Taylor narrowed his eyes at her. "I… That almost sounds like an insult coming from you."

"Always trust that instinct," she replied.

He laughed, settled into his seat, and sipped again as he looked enquiringly at them. "Well, while I sit here and you insult me for my cleaning skills, why don't we try to get hold of this captain of the police?"

Niki sat beside him and called up the sheet on the man in question. "His name is Captain Sergio Gallo. He's been with the police for almost twenty years. There have been some charges for corruption in the past and they've all disappeared without a trace."

"Does that mean what I think it means?"

"Probably," she said," but his ties were to the *Camora*, not the *Cosa Nostra*, so even if he does put the pieces together of what we're trying to do, he probably won't mind."

"Unless the *Cosa Nostra* decides they want to pay him back for whatever part he has in getting one of their dons killed," Taylor pointed out.

"Connection established," Vickie told them. "He's up late, I guess. We'll be able to talk to him over a video call in five seconds."

The screen came alive and filled with the image of a shorter, rotund man with a bald patch and a graying mustache. "Good evening, Mr. McFadden, Agent Banks. I am most pleased that you are able to speak to me on such short notice. As you may have heard, we have something of a situation in *Sicilia*, one that has gone well beyond my control. My hope is that you know how to handle it."

"Well, I've been on eighty-three missions into the Zoo itself," Taylor explained. "Plus...how many missions here?"

"He's been involved in ten operations on American soil dealing with monsters from the Zoo," Niki added. "I think I can safely say you won't find anyone more qualified for the position, Captain Gallo. He will need to bring his own suit and weaponry but there might be a need for support on the scene."

"We have soldiers available but they are hardly as well-trained or armed as your Mr. McFadden. I fear that if he takes this mission on, he will do so on his own in too many ways."

She nodded. "He won't necessarily be alone. I could go in with him if need be. I have some experience piloting a mech suit and fighting those monsters although not as much as he has."

The Italian smiled politely. "Well, I hope that you are right, Agent Banks. I have already issued a petition from my government to yours to authorize the international cooperation between our agencies. Given the urgency of the matter, I expect word of the authorization to come through by morning. I hope you will already be on the plane by then."

"We'll work on that," she assured him. "I'll keep you informed."

"I appreciate your help, Agent, Mr. McFadden. *Arrivederci!*"

## CHAPTER TWENTY-ONE

Taylor leaned back in his seat and tried to relax around the vibrations of the aircraft. It had been a while since he'd flown in a cargo plane. While he hadn't ever found it an uncomfortable experience, he'd never adjusted to it. There had been a time when he could simply set up a small hammock and sleep through the entire flight across no matter what the duration.

It had felt like time traveling. He could simply fall asleep and wake up however many hours later on a different continent.

He needed to be able to do it again. The fact was that he hated flying but being able to sleep through the whole damn thing had always been a bonus. He'd sometimes resorted to a little help from sleeping pills but still, he'd done it.

In his current situation, there wasn't much he could do but grasp the arms of his seat and think of better times.

Niki placed her hand over his. "You really hate flying, don't you?"

"I fucking hate it. But I have it under control. Just because I don't like it doesn't mean that I can't do it when I need to."

"You were in the military for years. How did you survive being shipped all around the world?"

"Sleeping pills, mostly," he admitted. "You take a little something before the flight and sleep all the way through it. I would always feel a little drowsy once the effects wore off, but it beat having an anxiety attack every fifteen minutes or whenever there was a little shudder or turbulence. In the end, that helped me get over it. I was able to rationalize that sleeping wouldn't change the flight path and while I had no power over the plane itself, I did have power over how I handled being without power."

"Mind over matter and all that. I like it. You like rationalizing your way through life so it makes sense that it would help you get over your fear of flying."

"I never really got over it and rather managed to gain control over the anxiety. It was my way to survive. I still get—"

The words cut abruptly when the plane shuddered. Turbulence outside made the aircraft jerk and bounce a few more times over the next couple of minutes. He gritted his teeth and clutched the arm of his seat until his knuckles turned white.

"Still get what?"

"Heart palpitations every time that happens. But I guess everyone gets those, right?"

Niki laughed and squeezed his hand. "Well, it's not a pleasant experience, I'll grant you that. I think we can pick up sleeping pills for the way back. We might have been able to find some before leaving but we were in a hurry."

Their departure had certainly been far swifter than they'd initially anticipated. They had received word that the authorization would be in place for them by the time they arrived and Niki had immediately initiated the paperwork and pushed it through. She had offered to bring one of her task force's mech suits in for Taylor's use, but he'd chosen to stick with his third suit. Fortunately, Bungees had long since completed any repairs he thought were necessary, so it was in working order.

The two and their equipment were loaded in the cargo plane that would fly all the way to Sicily and land on a nearby military base with a landing strip. Judging by the rushed process and the efficient but confidential way everything had been handled, it was very clear that the entire operation was intended to be covered up from the start.

The Italian government didn't want word to spread that there were monsters in the countryside, and Taylor could sympathize. Still, it worried him. Keeping it secret would be dangerous if people wandered into the area where the monsters apparently roamed.

A red light came on in the cabin and he buckled himself quickly into his seat. His ears popped by the time his seatbelt was fastened, which meant they were already making their descent.

"I've never been to Italy before," he said softly as Niki clicked her seatbelt in place. "I'm not sure I ever wanted to visit Europe. It doesn't hold much appeal for me, except maybe up north or in the Islands."

"As far away from the Zoo as possible? Keep talking like this and I'll think you have unresolved issues about that place."

He winced at that. "Unresolved issues is right."

She looked at her lap rather than at him and the silence between them continued for a while. "Sorry. I didn't mean to be that blunt about it."

"I know, you like to give me a hard time once in a while to keep me honest. I understand that much."

The agent laughed. "Well, yeah, but if I'd known you'd have that kind of an honest reaction to it, I wouldn't have given you a hard time about it. Making fun is all well and good but it's not appropriate to make light of trauma or anything like that. I like to think I'm not that particular brand of asshole."

Taylor shrugged. "I tend to be that particular kind of asshole, so I wouldn't hold it against you."

"Well, I guess that makes me a better person than you are."

Taylor smirked, but it vanished abruptly when the plane descended a little faster, buffeted by the turbulence as they dropped out of the sky.

That was what it felt like anyway. Almost a half-hour passed before he relaxed as the aircraft met the tarmac in the brusque kind of way cargo planes did.

"Know that I won't tease you about flying cross-country ever again," Niki told him while they unbuckled from their seats.

"Tease away but know that I'll continue to drive wherever I can and complain loudly every time I'm forced to fly where I can't drive."

The plane rumbled to a stop and the doors were pulled open. The men who manned the aircraft immediately began to offload the cargo inside and practically ignored the two passengers they had ferried across the Atlantic. They left the mech suit alone as well and also pointedly paid no attention to a small group of men in black suits who stood out of the way of the bustle and activity.

The greeting party moved forward as soon as they saw the two passengers exit. They had the look of cops but oddly, Taylor noted that they looked very much like the criminals he and Bobby had dealt with since they started the business together.

They clearly had no intention to wait for the plane to be fully unloaded and approached the two Americans with purposeful strides. He recognized one of the men as Captain Gallo from the thick mustache at least, but the other two were strangers.

"Agent Banks and Mr. McFadden. I hope your flight was at least somewhat pleasant. I can't say a cargo plane is the most comfortable way to travel, but I can say it was the only way we could arrange it without having you go through customs. Obviously, we needed to avoid it being advertised to all the wrong people that an FBI agent and a former Marine entered our country with the kind of weapons most countries can't afford."

"Well, there aren't many other ways to deal with monsters," Niki said firmly. "There is, after all, a reason why you called us in to handle the situation."

"Yes. The specialists we sent into the hills never returned. My bosses think the men took the half we paid them upfront and ran away, but I have it on good authority that none of them left the hillsides of Sicily. Or, at least, not in the form in which they arrived."

"They might have been shit by a bird into the ocean, though," Taylor mumbled under his breath but didn't really care if any of the people around him could hear.

"So, while we are a little...uh, cautious about having only one man head out into the area to deal with the situation, I was assured by those I spoke to that he is more than effective if his past efforts are any indication."

"While I'm glad you believe that I'm the right man for the job, I still don't have any idea what I'll have to hunt in those hills."

Gallo shook his head. "We actually have no idea what you will hunt either. The eyewitnesses have reported anything from a swarm of smaller beasts to one larger one, and everything in between."

"Do you have any pictures or film evidence?"

All three men shook their heads but seemed to expect the question from him. One of them replied quickly, "Nothing would stop people from heading up to see the monsters if there was any kind of visual evidence. Monster hunters have been a real problem all around the world since word of their appearance outside of the Zoo came out."

Taylor nodded. "It's better to have someone who can get the job done as quickly and as quietly as possible."

"Indeed. The FBI agreed to pay the fee you usually charge, which will be billed in turn to the *Polizia di Stato* for services rendered. You need not worry yourself about the details, I suppose, but the money will be paid."

"Well, I guess I should get started. Point me in the right

direction and I'll get you the first images you have of the beast or beasts. And send me what you might have about who the monsters may have killed or injured."

"That has already been sent, along with the authorization for you to operate within our borders. If you wish to start immediately, I shall arrange for the area to be cleared of any and all operations. It won't do, you see, for anyone to see someone in a mech suit running through the hills."

---

He needed a couple of hours to get the operation started. The mech itself was in decent enough condition, obviously, because Bungees had worked on it. While he trusted the mechanic's workmanship, Taylor didn't necessarily trust a suit he hadn't inspected himself. It was an old habit, but in the end, the fact that he was still alive after a long time of abiding by old habits meant he wouldn't drop any of them until it was proven that he could.

Still, the suit was in good condition, and after almost a full hour of tweaking and making adjustments to fit him personally, he was ready to climb into it. As his spare suit, none of this had been an issue before and he needed to be sure he'd be comfortable and would be able to manipulate it effectively. Niki busied herself setting up a small center of operations from where she would oversee his time and progress, as well as keep the operation insulated from anyone who might try to listen in.

"Taylor, can you read me?"

He tapped the side of his helmet as he moved through the underbrush that covered most of the hillside. "Yeah, I read you. Although I wish I could have my usual suits for this mission. Not to trash this one, but it was always intended as a spare. The other one is a better model and has more upgrades which I'm used to."

"Don't be facetious, Taylor. You know you couldn't bring yours because—"

"I know. There are pictures of it in every newspaper in the world. The point remains, though. I was able to make improvements on the comm system, but there aren't any live feed on the mech's HUD."

"I think that's for the best since the hillsides they would have covered in search of the monsters are about fifty klicks from where you'll go to find the villa of a certain Don Castellano. I don't think we want our Italian friends to find any sign of you surveilling the villa while you're supposed to be hunting those monsters."

"I guess, but it also means you'll be blind while you're covering for me."

"Well, in that case, I suggest you bring someone who can help you keep track of the surrounding area."

"Are you suggesting I carry someone on my back? These suits are big but not big enough for two pilots to ride around in."

"Well, the suggestion is that your helpful helper is already in the mech with you," Niki replied. "Well, not in the mech with you, but she's already been helping you with the software."

Taylor needed a moment to realize what—or rather— who she was talking about. "Desk, I should have known. How long has it been?"

"It is nice to hear from you again, Taylor." The familiar

feminine voice spoke smoothly through the suit's internal speakers and her presence was revealed on his HUD. "And it has been one hundred and thirteen days. Ever since the moment you decided to have that bomb dropped too close in order to kill all the monsters in Wyoming. I did fear for your life, although I guess my fear was misplaced."

"No, it wasn't," he admitted. "I'm simply more stubborn than most of the others who would have gone through that and even then, I was lucky to escape with my life. And your concern is definitely appreciated."

"Well, with that in mind, I think I should inform you that the motion sensors on your mech report movement about three hundred meters from your current position, to the east."

"And heading directly to the villa, I might add," Niki added.

He nodded. "They would hang out in that area given that it's the largest construction and would be the kind of thing to attract their attention. The smell of food and humans will draw them like the smell of a bleeding deer does a pack of wolves."

"And speaking of a pack, I should notify you that there is more than one source of movement to the east too," Desk added.

Taylor scowled. "Well, I guess it means the people who saw multiple creatures were right. Can I see those reports again?"

Desk called them up in the HUD as he made his way toward the movement. The monsters detected his presence early. Most of them had begun to pull back but not all of them. A few remained in place and climbed into the low-hanging trees, likely to catch a glimpse of whatever creature they thought was attacking them.

As he pushed forward, he was able to see that there were dozens of them. They were almost like a swarm. The closer he got, the less he needed to rely on the motion sensors to see what was happening around him.

He approached cautiously and it soon became obvious that they had begun to feel bolder. They had greater numbers and now that they saw him clearly, they were less afraid. He wasn't as fearful either. The mutants were about the size of large dogs and his growing proximity revealed that they were covered in soft, gray-green fur.

Their six legs seemed to enable them to climb the trees as delicately as insects. The branches didn't even sway under their weight. It seemed impossible, but he had long since ceased to wonder at the anatomy of what the Zoo created.

There were at least fifty of them by his rough count and maybe more hidden among thick bushes and tall grass. The ears and the tails made them look like cats or perhaps lynxes. He wasn't sure and while he'd never been much of a cat person, he knew enough about them to know that their restraint wouldn't last for very long.

"Do you see this?" Taylor asked.

"I don't see anything," Niki snapped in response.

"They look like cats—six-legged cats, with long, pointed ears."

"Lynxes?"

"Sure, six-legged lynxes. And there are…easily fifty of them, probably more."

"Will you start shooting them now? Maybe you could get a couple of bodies to show off for Gallo?"

He bit his bottom lip and retrieved one of the flares from his suit. Right now, he needed more time and maybe a distraction would be enough to buy him some.

The flare arced into the sky and even in the bright warmth of the midday sun, the creatures were clearly able to see the bright light. All heads traced the trajectory with alert gazes.

As it descended, he noticed that a couple of them followed it. It started as only a handful but a few more moved away until the group set off in pursuit of the flare in greater numbers.

It wasn't long until thoughts of Taylor and his suit were lost and all they could focus on was the falling flare.

His eyes were drawn to the villa walls in the distance and something cold and tense settled in the pit of his stomach as the thudding in his chest increased speed.

"No, I don't think I will shoot," he said in answer to Banks' earlier question.

"Do you have a plan?"

"Yeah."

"I won't like it, will I?"

He couldn't help a smile. "Actually, I think you'll really like this one."

# CHAPTER TWENTY-TWO

Having been moved from the outer edges of the villa certainly had its advantages. Flavio knew for a fact that staying out of sight meant staying out of mind at Don Castellano's villa. While that was what some of the men who had done the same thing for their entire lives craved, he wanted more.

The don's daughter had come and gone, along with her party guests, and as a result of the events that transpired, a couple of the guards were sent away. He had never found out why but it had apparently been enough to make sure they were never seen again—not in the towns nearby, not in their homes, and not by their families.

When the call had gone out for more people to join the guards in the villa, very few had jumped at the opportunity. He had and thus far, he didn't regret his decision.

There was only one way off this damn island, and that was to rise through the ranks. He intended to leave the island and live the good life while serving the family.

Everything started there, serving the family in Don

Castellano's villa, where the views were better, the pay was better, and the hours were much better. He wouldn't go anywhere from there but up.

But it wasn't all about the work. He looked at the other three men who took a break at the same time as him. They had the same look as he did and were all young, still in their twenties. One of them wore the tattoos that marked him as having served in the military, and the other two looked equally comfortable with the shotguns they carried.

They shared his desire to rise in the ranks. In the meantime, though, they checked their phones and lit cigarettes, and two of them played a game of poker.

"What are you playing for?" Flavio asked as he sat next to them.

"Different things," one of the gamblers told him and placed a fourth card on the table while he held onto two. "Mostly jobs or responsibilities. You know, cleaning, extra rounds, extra shifts, that kind of shit. And failing that, plain cash will do the trick."

"How much cash?"

"We're not rich, so every one of those bottle caps is worth five Euros. It's a little extra spending money on days off, really."

He leaned forward a little to show enthusiasm but not enough to come across as arrogant. "Is there any chance I can get a piece of this action?"

The other two eyed him closely and laughed. "What, do you think that you can walk in here on your first week and play cards with us like you've been here all your life?"

It seemed a reasonable question, so he thought about it for a second. "Well, yes, I think I do."

Both laughed again and began to place the cards on the table again. This time, they dealt two in front of him. "You need to lay something on the line. Either a job or five Euros."

A stack of papers with their duties written on them rested beside a pile of bottle caps he could play with.

"You know, I think this is bullshit anyway." He helped himself to a few of both and arranged them in front of him. "But if you think I'll let you guys take my money, you're in for a very big surprise."

"How big?"

He shrugged and placed one of the bottle caps in the center of the table as an ante. "I guess you'll have to play me and see, right?"

All three guards laughed and the two other players pushed their antes into the middle of the table as well. "You know, I think you'll be right at home here at the villa."

"And hopefully more," he muttered.

---

"This whole idea was all kinds of interesting in theory," Niki said over the radio. "But the more I think about it, the more it's...not. You'll get yourself killed out there. You're doing it all over again, and I'll be damned if I'll see you in the hospital for another three months. I don't think my reputation with the bureau could take that kind of damage."

Taylor shook his head. "It's not like I'm putting myself in the blast radius of a building-killing bomb here."

"No, you're making yourself bait for dozens of blood-hungry monsters."

"Please, those kitties?"

"You don't know what those kitties can do," she pointed out acidly. "All you saw them do was chase a ball of light in the sky. They could be able to tear through your armor, spit acid, and melt you into the kind of goop that goes in a fifty-gallon drum. They could be—"

"They could be a whole ton of shit but for now, the only thing that matters is the fact that they chase a nice little bright ball in the sky. That is exactly what this plan hinges on, so keep your eye out for what they might do out there and let me do my thing."

"Satellite imagery is giving me…well, not much. I have a fair number of heat signatures, but that's to be expected given that it was a scorcher of a day and not all the heat will have dissipated. How will you draw the creatures to your location?"

He shrugged. "How did I draw them out last time? They follow the bright little ball in the sky. That's literally the only thing I need to draw them on."

"And then you'll have a horde of crazed creatures on top of you. Again."

"Seriously, you need to chill the hell out. These things aren't nearly as deadly as those fuckers in Wyoming. They're actually kind of cute when it comes down to it. You know, if you tend to like your furry friends having six legs and shit."

"Goddamnit. Don't you even start with that."

"Wait, are you saying you have issues with people wanting to adopt Zoo critters?"

"Seriously, it's like you don't even know how the human race works. Are you serious? There are apps out there of people choosing the cutest monsters that have come out of the Zoo. We even deal with activists who think the mutants have rights and should be left to their habitat."

"People like that don't understand what's happening in that fucking jungle."

"Again, it's like you don't know what humans are like. Do you honestly think disinformation isn't something all these game companies and Zootubers make their bread and butter off? People think that either the Zoo is some kind of wild West where people can take their most sadistic impulses and act on them or a brand-new and beautiful world for them to explore. Do you think they'd believe that if they were actually in the Zoo? Are you telling me that's what you think it is like?"

He needed a moment to process all that verbiage. "How long have you held that in?"

"Sorry, I didn't mean to take it out on you. I'm dealing with a group of idiot politicians about our budget issues. While they raised the budget, it means more strings attached all over the damn place, so I have even more people to answer to these days. Getting you out here caused a veritable shitstorm of people asking questions."

"Fair enough." Taylor grunted and retrieved a flare from its section in his suit. He'd taken the time to get a couple more in case they were needed. There was no way to tell if the monsters would require extra incentive to get into the mood to fight.

He aimed it at the sky and fired. It was considerably brighter in the late afternoon than it had been at midday.

The sun had already begun to set and painted the Sicilian sky with a smattering of reds, oranges, purples, and pinks. It was a fantastic view, especially from the hillside overlooking the Mediterranean.

"It seems almost like a sin to do what we're doing here," he murmured.

"Where would you rather it happened?"

"I don't know. It seems like the kind of thing that would happen in a post-apocalyptic wasteland or maybe in an abandoned urban area."

"We're not looking for shooting locations for a movie."

"We could make a movie out of this and paint me as a serial killer who murders people by siccing Zoo monsters on them. That's a franchise tag right there."

She laughed over the radio. "Your mind really does go to weird places when you're about to get your fight on."

Taylor nodded and focused on his motion sensors when they alerted him to the approaching creatures. The flare had begun its downward trajectory and drew the mutants to a location about three hundred yards from where he stood. They were distracted but once the flare burned out, they would turn all their attention to him.

"I still think this plan is one of my best," he commented. "Seriously."

"I can believe it's the best idea you've ever had. The problem is that the bar isn't exactly set very high."

"Fuck you."

"Yeah, that's what we like to hear."

He pulled his assault rifle from its holster on his back although he didn't want to shoot yet. Gunfire would alert the folks in the villa that someone was approaching more readily than the flares did.

"Desk, is there any sign from our friends in the Villa that they see the flares?"

"Not yet, but I would be more concerned with the approaching monsters if I were you."

"Yeah, I have my eye on them. You make sure no alarms have gone off yet."

---

"Son of a bitch!"

Flavio couldn't help a small smile as the river card came up. He didn't have the best hand—only a high pair—but from the look of the man to his left who slapped his cards on the table, he at least had better cards than one of the players.

He looked at the man on his right, who had a considerably better poker face than his partner. "Are you still in?"

The guard shrugged and tapped his knuckle on the table. "Sure, why not? It's not that rich a round anyway."

While he'd never been much of a card player, his father had taught him how to play poker. It wasn't that difficult. The rules were simple and playing the players was more important than playing the cards.

"Well, let's make it a little richer," he said and pushed a couple of bottle caps into the middle of the table. "And I've been meaning to ask—what happened to the guys I replaced?"

"They didn't tell you about it?"

"All I know is that the don's daughter had a party and the next thing, they were looking for replacements."

"Not that it should be any of your business as to why the don does what he does," the man who wasn't playing cards said, cutting into the conversation. "But if you really want to know…"

Flavio shrugged. "Well, it's good to know what not to do, right?"

The man sighed. "Well, that's actually a good point. Anyway, it's not like this is news to anyone working on this property, but the don doesn't take kindly to his employees putting their hands on his daughter. He's a stickler for professionalism like that, even though it was obvious that she was the one who put her hands on them first. To cut a long story short, the old man walked in on his precious *figlia* with all three of them. It wasn't a pretty sight for the man, so they were all fired. Without benefits."

"I guess the moral of the story is—"

"Don't fuck the boss' daughter. Even if she makes you."

"My guess would be that they knew not to fuck her but she threatened to say they had anyway if they didn't," he commented. He had met the girl a couple of times and they were enough for him to know that she was the worst kind of a spoiled brat.

"That's possible. But they still should have known better and trusted the don to know that they didn't do anything inappropriate. The man knows what his daughter's like, after all."

Flavio was suddenly in the mood to change the subject of the conversation. "It seems like it was still one hell of a party, right?"

"You're damn right. It lasted three days with all the booze you could drink and all kinds of delicious views, if you know what I mean."

"As long as it's not the boss' daughter, right?"

"*Figlio di puttana,* will you play the fucking game or not?" the man to his right snapped.

"Oh, right." He grunted and shoved the right amount of chips into the growing betting pool.

"Wait." The guard who wasn't playing bolted out of his seat and stared into the landscape that stretched in front of them. The villa itself was massive but there wasn't much else but hillside beyond it. Castellano had put considerable money and influence into making sure he didn't have to worry about neighbors.

With that said, it was an oddity to see what looked like a flare arc into the sky. It cast a wide burst of light across the entire hillside as it began to descend slowly into the distance.

"What the fuck is going on?" the man to Flavio's left asked. He was out of the game anyway and therefore had no reason to remain for the show of hands.

"I think someone's calling for help or…something."

"Should we let someone inside know? Maybe to check it out?"

Flavio showed his cards and revealed his pair but the other man smirked and put his down to reveal a flush.

"Better luck next time."

"I hope so."

"There's another one—look!" the other guard shouted.

This time, there was no mistaking it and no debate about whether to investigate it further. It had been fired at a lower arc and aimed directly at the villa. While it still descended slowly, it did so inside the walls.

"Shit, we need to investigate." The fourth guard and ranking leader of the group had already snatched his shotgun up and now rushed in the direction of the descending flare. "If that thing sets anything on fire out here, you know there'll be hell to pay."

All four of them raced to where it had come down. Even with the reduced temperature when it flickered out, there were still signs of a blaze starting on the grass around it. They retrieved the nearby fire extinguishers to put the flames and the flare itself out.

"There'll be fucking hell to pay," Flavio echoed once the small blaze was out.

"Sure, but not as much as if we were caught with the don's daughter, right?"

He opened his mouth to reply but movement caught out of the corner of his eye distracted him. A little confused, he shook his head and narrowed his focus as the motion seemed to increase.

A faint light came from the house as the sun caught something and was reflected at them. Dozens of what appeared to be little spotlights stared at the group of four men where they stood in something close to amazement. Within moments, the lights were identifiable as eyes in creatures the size of larger dogs and which were already past the wall and coming closer.

A low hiss, like a large cat's, was heard and picked up by dozens of the animals.

"Son of a—"

# CHAPTER TWENTY-THREE

It was a relief to have the villa to himself again. After his daughter's birthday party and the distasteful issues that had resulted, it had felt like he would never regain the peace and quiet of his home.

He loved the young woman more than his own life but simply being around her could be exhausting and he was more than thankful that she preferred to spend most of her time with her mother in Monaco. At least she and the woman were two peas in a pod when it came to being the rabid kind of socialite.

Having to get rid of three of his guards after he'd found them with her had been the last straw, and he'd kicked all her party friends out a few hours later. She had remained for a few days to assuage what she saw as his hurt feelings, but she quickly grew bored and returned to her mother's.

Thankfully, everything had settled once again into his orderly and thoroughly satisfying routine. He'd shared a comfortable dinner beside the pool with his wonderful lady friends, followed by a quick swim and his daily quota of the medicine his people had gone through great effort to smuggle into the country. It was tiresome that Italy had put a ban on all Zoo-related products but like most things for someone in his position, money always found a way around such hindrances. All he had to worry about was to plan his meal for the next day.

His chefs had arranged for him to tell them on an online message board what he wanted to eat. It was simpler that way and gave them time to prepare the food to his exacting requirements.

Castellano sighed softly, put his tablet down, and took a sip of the brandy that had been poured for him once he settled into his comfortable seat.

Yes, it was pleasant to have his home all to himself again. He would need to talk about ground rules for whenever his baby girl came to visit again to avoid the same kind of mess that had disrupted his life so dramatically.

"Oh, who am I kidding?" he muttered. "She'll waltz in here and bat her eyelashes and as always, I'll give her whatever she wants."

His two partners looked up from where they stretched on the couches, but they knew him well enough to know he talked to himself. It wasn't sufficient for concern. He wasn't going insane and hadn't shown any signs of dementia yet but it was good, sometimes, to get those ideas out in the open and hear them himself.

He could even argue that it was healthy.

"That's how it's always been, yes," he continued and picked the tablet up again. "I tell myself constantly that I'll be sterner with her when she visits and every time, I'm a puddle of useless nothing when it comes to denying her what she wants."

"Until you found her with your bodyguards," one of the young women reminded him.

Other members of the family would take offense at being talked to like that by their arm candy. They were proud assholes who couldn't stand to be told what to do by those whom they considered inferior, the kind of men who couldn't endure the perceived blow to their fragile egos.

Of course, he had his rules and no one dared to break them. People had to believe he was like all the other dons, which meant they needed to act like the kind of arm candy his contemporaries flaunted as symbols of their power and virility. His women of choice had learned to remain silent around other people and only spoke their mind when they were in a private location.

All that aside, he saw no reason to be angry with them for speaking their mind. Intelligence was sexy in its own way, and a guy like him grew to appreciate that.

Castellano took another sip from his brandy and relished the burn of it all the way down his esophagus. "Even then, I didn't punish her for it. I took my annoyance out on the guards she probably threatened into having relations with her. While I don't necessarily deny her anything, I do know my daughter. Despite that, all she had to deal with was the fact that her friends were removed from the villa and having to sulk around the property while she pretended to be sorry. And I bought it, of course."

"You love her," the second woman pointed out. "You'll never be able to see anything she does objectively, which was why you elected to let her stay with her mother and only visit occasionally. That was your decision, and you made it with the intention of helping yourself to remain objective like this. It keeps you sane."

She wasn't wrong, when he thought about it, although he hadn't realized the truth of it. His precious daughter was exactly like his ex-wife. Both were capable of driving him crazy and knew all the buttons to press to do it. Keeping them far away while still close enough for him to protect them was the best option for all involved.

He sighed deeply, finished his brandy, and placed the glass on the ornate mahogany table beside his easy chair. One of the women stood, picked up the bottle next to her, and refilled his glass. The two had been with him for the past couple of years and had learned how to act around him.

His head snapped around. Memories of the old days when he had run drugs through the streets of Rome—and when he still pulled triggers himself—flashed through his mind. It had been a long time since then but the old memories and instincts surged to the front of his mind at the sound of shotguns being fired.

Old habits died hard, and when people began to shoot in an area around him, he didn't want to be left without any kind of protection. Some of the other dons didn't like to do their own killing and Castellano had learned to dislike it himself. But there were few more inspiring feelings than the cold steel of a weapon in his hands.

He slid his hand to the side of his easy chair and pressed the button that opened a secret compartment he had checked every week. His staff cleaned and maintained the

.45 1911 he kept in there. It was a weapon from the old days and his favorite.

Both women pushed to their feet as well and were armed too. They weren't merely retained for their sharp wits and luscious forms. Those attributes were only perks, although they were ones he took full advantage of. They were trained and experienced killers, the kind who had been with the family for generations, and both carried shotguns with comfortable familiarity.

"What's happening?" one of them asked into the only radio that was allowed to be close to him at this time of day.

No one replied for a few long seconds and all that could be heard was more gunfire at the edge of the property. The muzzle flashes were bright and vivid through the window. He counted four of them at first, then three. Two vanished at the same time and the last man began to run while he continued to shoot at something that approached rapidly from behind. There wasn't much Castellano detested more than cowards, a fact all his employees were very familiar with. It meant that none of the men in his employ would flee from a fight they thought they could win.

If the man had chosen to run, there was a good reason for it. Given that three of his comrades were already down, it was a logical guess that the reason was a violent one.

He picked his brandy up from the table and downed it all like it was a shot, and it burned down his throat like fire.

"What the fuck is happening down there?" his body-guard shouted into the radio as she moved to the door to make sure it was secure before she returned to stand closer to him.

"We've…there are… What the fuck?"

"That's what I'm asking, goddammit!"

Additional gunfire and screams erupted as his security teams moved into action. The defense seemed to rally effectively but it wasn't long before more weapons fell silent—enough to trigger definite alarm. The remaining guards regrouped and retreated to a position beside the house. They were armed to the teeth and maintained their formation with clear determination. Castellano had a moment's pride before he looked beyond them and finally saw what had attacked them.

He had seen all kinds of shit in his time—more than most people ever did, even in the movies—but he'd never seen anything like this.

Monsters was the term that came to mind—real monsters like those they made movies about and that came from an alien jungle he liked to pretend was much farther away than it was. They looked like cats at first glance, but there was something off about them. Long, tufted ears flicked constantly as if they could discern sound beyond the barrage that greeted them. A couple fell when the shotguns fired and they sprayed the marble around his pool with bright red liquid. The rest darted away, where they hissed and growled from a safe distance before they launched into another assault.

"They have six legs," Castellano said and thumped his empty glass down with no intention to have it refilled. "Like motherfucking insects, they have six legs."

The fifteen men who stood between the monsters and

the mansion were swarmed from the darkness. The creatures vaulted almost five meters high and attacked his guards from above like they had climbed trees and jumped from there. It seemed impossible but his greater concern was their numbers. He estimated dozens of them but there could have been hundreds, hidden in the darkness as they were.

Another concerted fusillade erupted from his teams as more of his men arrived from the outer edges of the villa. The remaining guards were still alive and seemed determined to present a violent defense, but they wouldn't last.

"Come, we have to get to the panic room," one of the women said.

He nodded. That was a good idea. He'd built one into the villa when it had first been constructed and made sure it was secure enough to survive a nuclear war. That had been something of a worry back then, and while those worries had mostly dissipated, it would still be too tough for the monsters they now faced to tear through.

They made their way to his bedroom and his bodyguards collected a couple more guns while he punched in the ten-digit code that would let them in. The door hissed open and allowed them to step through the thirty centimeters of reinforced steel he believed would keep the creatures out.

A couple of beds and an easy chair stood near a small yet well-stocked bar, and enough food was stored to last them for weeks if they chose to remain there. The computers and screens were already on and provided him with views from all the cameras on his property as well as a few outside that monitored the walls.

There were enough of them carefully placed to reveal exactly what was happening in full HD, and even in night vision. The invaders were everywhere. His men were simply slaughtered and torn to pieces. It was no longer possible to even estimate how many of the attackers were on the property. The creatures moved constantly and quickly as they savaged a path through the defensive ranks. Here and there, some paused momentarily to feed before they resumed the onslaught and ultimately overwhelmed the guards until there none were left to fight back.

"Don, something is happening on the outside wall."

His gaze followed to where one of the women pointed to a screen with a feed from one of the cameras. Something wasn't happening to the outside wall, he registered immediately. It had already happened.

He scowled as he narrowed his eyes to focus on the obvious hole in it. None of the creatures had done that. They could jump or climb over it without too much effort and so had no need to destroy the structure itself. Something far larger had broken a hole through it like the fifty centimeters of steel-reinforced concrete were nothing.

"It's a person," she told him and her finger followed the cameras when they caught the intruder in the middle of a march through the property. A shiver of alarm traced through him as he recognized one of the mech suits of armor that clearly indicated someone far more dangerous than the average home invader. Not only that, but the figure headed across the grounds and toward the mansion with a definite sense of purpose.

Thankfully, it appeared that the monsters weren't ignoring him. It seemed like a him, although Castellano had no idea if it was a man or a woman in the suit. His gut simply told him a man was in there.

For the first time since the mutants had arrived on his property and begun to kill his men, the don hoped they would win. His mind focused on the odd connection between the creatures that had suddenly appeared and the man who materialized at the moment when they had eliminated his men. Instinct warned him that it was no coincidence.

The animals initiated a slow advance but the figure in the mech suit surged into the attack as he yanked the assault rifle from the holster on his back. The weapon was larger than three of the shotguns his men had been armed with. Something flashed brightly under the barrel and launched into the horde.

It had cost him almost twenty thousand Euros to establish his perfect lawn, and it was destroyed in a blaze of light, churned and gouged along with five of the creatures that were shredded on impact.

The muzzle flash was larger than any he'd previously seen but the weapon barely kicked in the suit's hands as the rounds pounded through the mass of mutants. A dozen of them fell before he needed to reload, and the creatures rallied as if they sensed that he was vulnerable.

The gunmen drew another weapon shaped like a pistol but the size of a shotgun and muzzle flashes followed immediately. The brightness disrupted the night vision and made it difficult to see exactly what was happening.

The results, however, weren't difficult to identify. Bloody bodies of monsters were left strewn across his villa. Another grenade launched from under the barrel and streaked through the million dollars he'd spent on making his villa a home he could enjoy and be proud of at the same time.

"I have half a mind to bill this asshole," Castellano commented when the marble fountain he'd imported from Greece shattered under the onslaught of rounds. The assault powered through the creatures that had savaged his men not minutes before.

The don had been shocked by the multitude of them but only a couple were left. These continued their relentless attacks as if to avenge their fallen comrades.

The intruder didn't use the gun on them now. The huge fists simply crushed them and flung them aside. In moments, the last of the monsters were dead and his property had been cleared.

Except, of course, for the man who probably wanted him dead. There was only one person he knew of who had access to mechs like that and the will to come all the way to Italy.

It could only be McFadden. It had to be. While Castellano had made any number of enemies over the years, they had all died conveniently a long time before he'd ever ascended to his current position.

McFadden had been his kind of creature—the kind of killer who brought all kinds of interesting propositions to mind. He had even considered inviting the man into the family.

But no, that was not an option. He had arrived at the villa and made short work of the mutants that had annihilated the guards.

There had been enough security to satisfy even the

paranoid—something he had never been. Still, he'd always believed in leaving nothing to chance and had hired extra men to allow for the unexpected.

It seemed utterly impossible that there were only two left, both of them women.

"He's coming to the panic room," one of his bodyguards stated. She didn't appear to feel the panic that tightened his chest. He could almost feel the weight of the three-and-a-half-ton suit as it marched through the halls, ruined the expensive floors, and mounted the stairs to where they waited.

"He won't come in," she added, although he couldn't be sure if it was for his benefit or hers. "There's no way he can get through the door."

She was right. No mech suit in the world would be able to rip through the walls of his panic room.

The cold feeling in the pit of his stomach lingered, however. It insisted ominously that something was wrong. The man knew where the panic room was, he realized when he gave it a moment's thought. He had put planning and effort into using the monsters to remove his men and simply eliminated them expediently thereafter. Everything appeared to have been perfectly planned. Was there any real reason to think that the panic room might prove any different?

As if the same question had occurred to his guards, their gazes followed his to the door. From what they could see on the feed, the invader stood in front of the barrier and after a moment, a soft snick seemed unnaturally loud in the silence.

After another muted click, the screens went dead and

all the electronics inside followed. The air pump, the water, and the lights deactivated at the same time that the door swung open.

The two women hefted their shotguns and stood in front of him. They were his bodyguards and assumed their responsibilities without flinching. He had to admire them for that, given that it seemed obvious that it wouldn't be for long.

The mech stood motionless and took the full weight of four rounds of buckshot fired at him without even the slightest reaction to the impact. The invader moved forward through the door. He had holstered his assault rifle so his hands were free to snatch the women's weapons and break them in half. A quick twist of the hydraulics in the suit flung both girls against the wall with a solid crunch that removed them effectively from the equation.

Castellano steeled himself and aimed his weapon at the suit that now stood in front of him. Eight feet of solid steel stared at him without a damn sound except for the soft whirring of the suit from the fusion reactor on its back.

The don shook his head and dropped the weapon. It clattered loudly on the floor and he winced at the sound.

"What are you here for, McFadden?" he asked in English and focused his stare on the suit's faceless helmet. If there was ever a way to go, this was it—crushed by the overwhelming weight of modern warfare technology.

"Your head."

He nodded. "You do know that if you kill me, there will be hell to pay."

"No one knows I killed you. Your people will wait for orders—and wait forever, I might add."

Stupidly, he realized that was exactly what he'd thought McFadden would sound like. Even the mechanical echo of his voice through the suit's speakers seemed character appropriate.

"Is there any chance I could ask you to spare me? Money? Power?"

The suit's head shook in an exaggerated motion. "Nah. But you can have fun trying, though."

"I will not beg for my life."

Another exaggerated movement followed, this time a shrug. "Suit yourself."

The sidearm raised, the weapon the size of a fucking shotgun. Castellano refused to close his eyes, even when the muzzle flashed.

# CHAPTER TWENTY-FOUR

Niki sat quietly beside him.

There wasn't much left to talk about between the two of them, and Taylor merely stripped the armor off and examined it. Blood was splattered all over it like a new red coat of paint they would need to wash off before they transported it and themselves to Vegas.

"How did it go?" she asked finally.

He looked up from his work. While his hands didn't stop, there was a hint of hesitation as he began to take the pieces apart by feel and muscle memory alone.

"I've had worse days."

She smirked. "I won't lie, your idea was a damn good one. I'm not a fan of you putting yourself in unnecessary danger but in the end, you made the effort to keep yourself safe and performed the mission admirably. Both missions, of course, and with all kinds of desperate shenanigans between them. You made the monsters savage the guards and let the men eliminate a few of them at the same time. Finally, you came in to wipe up the mess they left behind."

"That was the idea."

"How will they know you didn't kill Don Castellano, though?"

"A couple of bodies cleverly maneuvered and a little gross abuse of a corpse were all I needed to have three bodies in the panic room that apparently hadn't closed—thanks to Desk's work—and who were killed by monsters before I could save them. "

"I guess she was able to wipe the security feeds to make it very clear that there was no ill-intent on your part?"

"Yeah, she did. I also retrieved the remnants of the flares, so there's no evidence there."

He returned his attention to taking the suit apart and set each piece out for him to clean it.

"You should have told me about her."

Niki tilted her head to regard him firmly. He simply remained focused on his work.

"How was I supposed to tell you about Desk? Think about that."

He pursed his lips and shook his head. "Simple. You tell me the truth and I handle it. Keeping secrets is not a good way to go about this kind of relationship, especially when it comes to Desk, who has supported me since I first worked with you."

She relaxed against her seat and sucked in a deep breath. The air was still warm despite night having fallen hours before. It was one of the reasons why she hated being in the hotter areas of the world.

Somewhat inconsequentially, she supposed it wasn't annoying to Taylor as the man had spent years in the Sahara Desert.

"Okay, I should have told you about it. I'm sorry."

He nodded. "Apology accepted and we can move on. See how I'm handling this so well? You had nothing to worry about."

Niki laughed softly. "Yeah, I guess."

More long few hours stretched ahead of them as they headed directly to Nellis Air Force Base. They expected to land there, thanks to the use of the military cargo plane they boarded, and Taylor settled himself in for another flight home.

Cars waited for them once they landed, and he was partnered with an unusually quiet FBI agent the whole drive back. Niki had always been willing to engage in banter with him, and it seemed she inevitably found a way to pick at his many flaws while she knew he could do the same to her and wouldn't.

But on this occasion, she completely surprised him with her lack of response. None of his attempts to engage her seemed to bear any fruit and they drove in silence into Vegas as the sun painted the sky above them when it set.

The city began to cool off and the nightlife gradually gained momentum. It made the trip a little slower, but they finally reached the strip mall and drove into the garage. They both clambered out of the black SUV Niki always seemed to have on hand when Vickie marched down the stairs to greet them.

"Well, well, well!" the hacker called. "I didn't think I would see the two of you so soon."

"Why the hell not?" Taylor rolled his shoulders and grimaced. He still felt a few aches and bruises from where he had been hit with a few shotgun blasts.

"I expected something to go terribly wrong that left you laid up in the hospital for another couple of months. That said, I'm really glad you're not making a habit of getting yourself hurt."

"Hurt badly, anyway," he corrected her and pulled his shirt up to show her where his skin had turned a dark purple. "Four shotgun blasts to the midsection tend to leave a memento or two. I didn't feel it at first but sure as hell did afterward."

She moved closer to inspect the injury before she hugged him gently. "I thought the suits were supposed to keep this sort of shit from happening."

"The newer suits are better at distributing the energy of a shot but since I was stuck with the older spare that hasn't had any upgrades, I still get injured when I get shot."

"Well, who's fault is it that you couldn't use one of your suits?" Niki asked.

Taylor regarded her with an unperturbed expression. "Fair enough, but we wouldn't have known where to strike if we hadn't gone through with the heist."

The other woman stiffened visibly and gestured her hand across her throat. "Ixnay on the eist-hey!"

"Come on, Vickie. Your memory's slipping. Taylor's already told me—even though I made it clear I didn't want the details. As I recall, you both had snark about Monty Python which I chose to ignore. Besides, even if he hadn't told me, it's already painfully obvious that you were all involved in it. I merely pretend not to know in case I need to have plausible deniability if the cops catch you because you fucked something up."

"Come on. I was the one who covered for us."

"And what happened the last time you tried to do something illegal?" the agent reminded her with a smirk.

"I was learning all the ways I would get caught and how to avoid them in the future. The hard way, but still."

"Well, don't assume you won't get caught simply because you're careful. Sometimes, people get lucky, and that counts for the good officers of the Las Vegas Police Department too."

"Well, now that we've established that everyone knows about everything," Taylor interjected, "I'm in the mood for a nice long drink with good company. Has Bobby already left for the evening?"

"Oh… This is a little awkward." Vickie's gaze shifted quickly before it met his. "Okay, maybe not awkward since everyone involved is a consenting adult and no one is doing anything illegal— I hope, anyway."

"Sure, hope away. And if you could get to the point sometime today, I'd take that as a kindness."

"Well, my point—when you're not busy interrupting me —is that Bobby is out on a date."

"Oh, well, where's Tanya—"

"See? It's a little awkward."

"Bobby and Tanya are the consenting adults in question going on this date." Taylor nodded slowly. "Hmm. Well, there's nothing awkward about that. Like you said, consenting adults and all. I don't suppose either of you would like to go out for a quick drink to celebrate a job well done?"

The hacker shrugged. "Sure, I'm down for a drink. How about you, Niki?"

Her cousin sighed. "I guess I have time to kill before I leave town tomorrow."

"I'll let Freddie and St Just know that you'll join us," Vickie told him cheerfully.

"Say what?" he asked.

"Oh, they missed their flights. Or flew back in. They didn't quite get around to a real explanation, but they're both in town for a couple more days and they invited me out for drinks too."

Taylor looked at Niki. "Do you feel like drinking with your cousin and three Cro-Magnons?"

"It's better than drinking alone, I guess. Barely."

They climbed into the SUV and drove to Jacksons, where the other two were already waiting for them. Taylor had thought he had seen the last of the assholes, but he was in a better mood than he had been before. For one thing, he wasn't pressured to impress upon them how much they needed to be his clients. Now that was over with, he was only drinking with a couple of friends.

And Niki, apparently.

The thought made him smile as he was greeted with bear hugs from the two men.

"Well, if you guys are simply going to laze around here in Vegas instead of heading back to work, I'll tell you right now that I won't pay any more bills."

"Don't you worry about that," Freddie assured him. "You've more than catered to our every need already, but since both of us had a fair amount of back pay to spend and wouldn't be able to do it on the base, we thought we'd extend our time here. It makes sense to spend time in the casinos, take in the sights, make more money, and then head back when we're broke and probably carrying a new kind of VD the doctors have never seen before."

"That was a little more graphic than I needed," Taylor said and tried not to wince. "But anyway, it is nice to be able to spend some time with you while not having to kiss your asses. Come on, let's get a drink—and you guys can buy the first round."

The five moved into the bar, where he greeted the bouncer. It wasn't the one he knew but apparently, word that he was one of their regulars had already spread among the employees. It wasn't long before they tucked themselves in a quiet booth in the back of the bar.

"Where's Zhang?" Freddie asked as he brought their first round of drinks to the table. "I thought you two were inseparable, working together and all."

"Well, for one thing, we're not inseparable. We're in business together and are good friends, but we each have our own separate lives. In his case, he's actually on a date tonight."

"And where's the other woman you're in business with? Tanya Novak?"

"She's the one Bungees is on a date with."

"Oh. Well, yeah, actually. I can see the two of them together. Anyway, can we assume they won't join us for the rest of the evening?"

"They're coming here after dinner for drinks and..." Vickie trailed off when she realized everyone was looking at her. "Bobby asked me about where he should take a certain someone for a date, and I helped him to plan it. If all goes as it should and he doesn't end up getting slapped or something, they should be here in an hour, maybe an hour and a half."

Taylor nodded. Bobby and Tanya had gotten along well while working together. The woman had a mind for the job, and he intended to evaluate whether he needed to promote her to a full mechanic at the end of the quarter. It would increase her salary and they would broach the subject of providing her with extra studying time.

In the meantime, if they did become romantic with each other, it was like Freddie said. He could see the two of them together.

"I'll pick up the next round," he said when he noticed that most of the glasses were already empty. Obviously, they would need refills before too much time passed.

He was surprised and happy to see Alex behind the bar when he arrived at the counter.

"It's nice to see you again, Taylor." She was already filling the glasses she knew he would order and bit her bottom lip gently. "It's been a while since I've seen you."

"Well, I was here a couple of days ago but you weren't working."

"And you know that isn't what I was talking about."

He smirked as he retrieved his wallet. "Fair enough. There were…issues. I've been in the hospital for the last few months."

"Bobby told me. You should know there are issues on my end too," she told him and placed the full mugs on the counter in front of him. "I've been seeing a guy over the past couple of weeks. I didn't tell him that I was seeing you but things have become more serious."

Taylor nodded and stretched to the other side of the bar to retrieve two shot glasses and a bottle of bourbon. "Well, here's to you and this mystery gentleman. He's one hell of a lucky guy."

She took the toast and tapped her glass to his. "I hope you find a lucky gal of your own."

He downed the shot quickly and winced at the burn down his throat.

"I don't know." His gaze drifted to the table. "I think I might have already."

CHAPTER TWENTY-FIVE

Taylor hadn't been out long enough to close a bar for what seemed like forever. It honestly felt like he had been the paragon of responsibility for a good long while. Or, at least, the kind of person who didn't stay up until the early hours of the morning and make trouble for waiters and bartenders alike.

The drinking proceeded with far less intensity than it had during their previous party night at Jackson's. The beer still flowed, though, and it wasn't long before they all reminisced about everything that happened while they were in the Zoo. Bobby and Tanya did arrive later in the evening but only joined them for one beer, which they finished fairly quickly.

Vickie explained that they had various other plans for the rest of the evening, and the group merely shrugged and continued their drinking with only five members.

An hour or so later, Freddie and St Just headed out as well. They were in Vegas for a night on the town, not to simply sit and reminisce about a jungle they would return to in a couple of days.

Vickie called it an early night as well. She had a class in the morning that she couldn't miss, although Taylor doubted that reasoning almost by instinct.

"Maybe she is getting serious about her studies," he said and took a long sip of his beer.

"Well, if anyone could get that girl to focus on her studies and get her life in order, it would be you." Niki was the only one at the booth with him, and Jackson's had now begun to wind down in its later hours. They were open all night, of course, but most of the regulars had already left. The hard drinkers seemed to realize they were going too far by this point, and the night shift had already taken over.

It wasn't a bad environment to be in, of course. With fewer customers, the wait staff had fewer people to look after. Now that it was only Taylor and Niki, he wasn't sure how long the FBI agent would last.

Despite his misgivings. she held her liquor, and from the lack of any slurring in her voice, he had a feeling she held hers better than he did his.

And she showed no sign of stopping either.

"Well, it's only the two of us now." He knew he was stating the obvious but it seemed enough to start a conversation from. If she had any way to explain how they had ended up alone at a bar together at around midnight, he was open to hearing it. No matter what, though, he was sure it wouldn't make sense, but they were both deep in their cups so it wouldn't matter.

"Imagine that. Me out late at night with a Cro-Magnon. My parents will be so disappointed in me."

"I think your parents wouldn't mind. You, on the other hand, are probably disappointed and trying to pass it off as how your parents would feel."

Niki leaned back in her seat across from him in the booth and rubbed her chin idly. "You know, you might be right about that. I think it might be that I should feel disappointed and maybe a little scared and annoyed by you, but amazingly, I do not feel any of that. It's nice to be out with you. Is that how you get all those girls to sleep with you? By making them feel warm and comfortable before you put the moves on them?"

"If I were trying to get you in bed, I would have put the moves on you already." He didn't know why he was still talking, but she was right—it did feel comfortable.

"What kind of moves would I expect?" she asked.

Taylor shrugged. "They're different for every person. In your case, I think we would be about three shots into a never have I ever kind of game. The important thing is to learn as much as possible about you, and in sharing personal details, there's a certain vulnerability that many people think is sexy."

"Well, you and I will never play never have I ever, and certainly not over shots."

"I know." Taylor nodded without rancor. "I'm not your type and you're not mine. And the fact that we know there's not a single chance in hell that we'll end up in the same bed come the morning is maybe why we feel so comfortable together."

She couldn't help a small smile. "Well, I don't want to write anything off, but yeah. There is no chance that we'll end up in the same bed—tomorrow morning, anyway."

He tilted his head and leaned closer but quickly pulled away and took a long sip of his drink. "You know, lately, you've said shit that's broken from our usual and very enjoyable banter. Not in a bad way but in a way that has me very confused. Honestly, I don't know how to reply. I don't want to make you uncomfortable."

"Have I made you uncomfortable?"

"I…maybe. I don't know. I'm not often confused about interactions."

"You think that human interactions should remain the same for the entirety of the relationship?"

"It only seems like boundaries set should be adhered to. Respected, you know?"

She leaned closer. "Did you place any boundaries on what our relationship was supposed to be?"

"Yes. Right about the time you did."

"But I think that relationships and boundaries can change over time."

Taylor nodded. "See, this is one of those times when I'm not sure if you're serious or not. But okay, for fun… How do you think our relationship should change?"

She opened her mouth to speak but she focused on something over his shoulder and looked as confused as he felt.

He turned and his gaze settled on a young man dressed in a suit and tie. It looked expensive but the wearer did not. He looked uncomfortable in the clothes—like he wasn't used to wearing something quite so expensive and that fit so well.

"Mr. McFadden?" he asked.

"That's my name. Don't wear it out."

Niki groaned. "God, do people still use that line?"

"Of course. Assuming you think of me as people, anyway."

The stranger shifted on his feet. "I'm sorry, you are Mr. Taylor McFadden, right?"

"Yeah, that is my name. Who are you? Do we know each other?"

"No, but I was entrusted with a package that was meant to be delivered to you on your arrival in Vegas. He said you would know the name—that you've never met but that you have financial elements in common."

"Financial elements in com…" Taylor started but let his voice trail off as he scowled at the package the young man held in his hands. "Would you mind opening it for me?"

"Sorry?"

"Don't be. Just open the package for me."

"Why?"

"Because if someone wanted me to have that, they could have simply sent it in the mail. Now open it, please."

He looked at them a little strangely but shrugged and began to peel back the wrapping paper to reveal a box with a bottle inside.

"Do you want me to take the bottle out too?" he asked.

"Sure."

It was removed slowly and placed on the table and Niki picked it up. "Thirty-five-year-old Macallan Scotch—are you kidding me? Who is this from?"

"There's a note with it as well. I'm sorry. Can I put the box down?"

"Only if you don't take all day."

The kid placed it on the table and handed him the note.

Taylor retrieved his wallet and withdrew a hundred-dollar bill, which he handed to the messenger.

"What is that for?"

He smirked. "For risking your neck."

The boy nodded and walked away.

"Well, the fact that I don't even know how expensive this scotch is means it's very expensive," the agent said and continued to inspect the bottle. "Seriously—single-malt, aged for thirty-five years? It has to be about ten grand at the very, very least."

"Now, who the hell would send me a ten-grand bottle of scotch?" he muttered, picked up the note that accompanied it, and inspected it closely.

"And why did you ask the kid to unwrap the package?"

"Because I have a feeling I know who it's from. Financial elements in common sounds suspiciously like someone I recently stole six million dollars from. I couldn't be sure this wasn't his attempt at vengeance, and given that he is a mafioso, sending me a bomb does sound right up his alley."

"Oh. I guess that makes sense. Kind of. But if you think I'll be the first one to open this bottle, you're fucking crazy."

"Well, we've established that." Taylor pulled the note out of its envelope. "Ah, well, it looks like I guessed right. The note says it's from a certain Mr. Rod Marino."

"And what does he have to say?"

He narrowed his eyes. Things had become vaguely fuzzy in his eyes about two beers ago, and he needed to focus to see the lettering so he could read it aloud.

"Dear Mr. Taylor McFadden. My name is Rod Marino and I'm the proprietor of the Stardust Resort and Casino.

You may already be aware that I am also an affiliate of the Sicilian Family known locally as the *Cosa Nostra*. It should probably interest you to know that I have elected not to pursue any further hostilities with someone like you, and you might even consider this bottle of scotch to be an olive branch of sorts. On that note, you should know that not only will no further hostilities be pursued, but should anyone give you any trouble—even the police—I would be honored if you alerted me. Simply advise me of your difficulty, and I will handle it for you. They will not give you any trouble regarding the money you charged us either. You may consider your emphatic message received loud and clear. With the kindest regards, Rod Marino."

Niki snatched the note out of his hand to make sure she had heard him right. "Well, he sounds scared. I guess the message he received also has to do with our little excursion to Sicily."

"If that's the case, I wouldn't expect them to hold to that message of peace for too long. I had hoped the responsibility would remain directly on the monsters."

"Apparently not."

"And if they happen to have a change of heart, they know where to find us."

"And if they do?"

"They know we'll be ready for them."

She nodded. "Well, with that in mind, I suggest we find out exactly what a thirty-five-year-old bottle of single-malt scotch tastes like."

"I assume it's like any other scotch, only more so."

Taylor asked for a couple of glasses from the waitress and poured three fingers for each of them.

"What are we drinking to?" he asked and raised his glass.

"Maybe we can drink to fighting the *Cosa Nostra* to a standstill?" Niki suggested. "Or maybe...to changing boundaries?"

He laughed, shook his head, and tapped his glass to hers. "Maybe the next drink will be to you explaining what exactly that means."

"Or maybe the drink after that."

Have you read *The BOHICA Chronicles* from C.J. Fawcett and Jonathan Brazee? A complete series box set is available now from Amazon and through Kindle Unlimited.

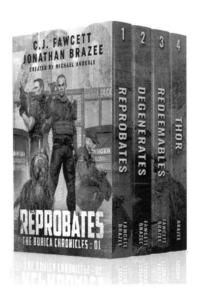

**Kicked out of the military for brawling, what can three friends from different countries do to make some needed money?**

Grab your copy of the entire BOHICA Chronicles at a discount today!

**Reprobates:**

With nothing in their future, Former US Marine Charles, ex-SAS Booker, and ex-Australian Army Roo decide to give the Zoo a shot.

Without the contacts, without backing, without knowing what they are getting into, they scramble to get their foot in the door to even make rent in one of the most dangerous areas in the world.

*With high rewards comes high risk. Can they learn on the job, where failure means death?*

**Relying on their training, they will scratch, claw, and take the most dangerous jobs to prove themselves, but will it be enough? Can they fight the establishment and the Zoo at the same time?**

*And what the heck's up with that puppy they found?*

**Degenerates:**

**What happens when you come back from vacation to find out your dog ate the dog-sitter?**

*And your dog isn't a dog?*

The BOHICA Warriors have had some success in the Zoo, but they need to expand and become more professional to make it into the big time.

**Each member goes home to recruit more members to join the team.**

*Definitely bigger, hopefully badder, they return ready to kick some ZOO ass.*

With a dead dog-sitter on their hands and more dangerous missions inside the Zoo, the six team members have to bond and learn to work together, even if they are sometimes at odds with each other.

*Succeed, and riches will follow.*

**Fail, and the Zoo will extract its revenge in its own permanent fashion.**

## Redeemables:

### NOTHING KEEPS A MAN AND HIS 'DOG' APART...

*But what if the dog is a man-killing beast made up of alien genetics?*

Thor is with his own kind as they range the Zoo, but something is missing for him. Charles is with his own kind as they work both inside and outside the walls of the ZOO.

**Once connected, the two of them are now split apart by events that overcame each.**

*Or are they?*

Follow the BOHICA Warriors as they continue to make a name for themselves as the most professional of the MERC Zoo teams. So much so that people on the outside have heard of them.

Follow Thor as he asserts himself in his pack.

**Around the Zoo, nothing remains static, and some things** *might converge yet again if death doesn't get in the way.*

## Thor:

**The ZOO wants to kill THOR. Humans would want that as well, but they don't know what he is.**

*What is Charles going to do?*

Charles brings Thor to Benin, where he can safely hide out until things calm down. Unfortunately for both of them, that takes them out of the frying pan and into the fire.

The Pendjari National Park isn't the Zoo, but lions, elephants, and rhinos are not pushovers.

**When human militias invade the park, Thor and park ranger Achille Amadou are trapped between the proverbial rock and a hard place. How do you protect the park and THOR Achille has to hide just***what* **Thor is...**

Can he hide what Thor is when Thor makes that hard to accomplish?

*Will the militias figure out what that creature is that attacks them?*

Available now from Amazon and through Kindle Unlimited.

## AUTHOR NOTES

FEBRUARY 13, 2020

THANK YOU for reading this story! We now have a 7 of the Cryptid Assassin books planned, but we don't know if we should continue writing and publishing without your input. Options include leaving a review, reaching out on Facebook to let us know, and smoke signals.

Frankly, smoke signals might get misconstrued as low hanging clouds, so you might want to nix that idea...

### LIVING LA VIDA LONDON

Well, it's not exactly living life in London, it's more like trying to LEAVE London.

Judith and I were in London last week when President Trump announced he was shutting down the United States to flights coming back from the EU in forty-eight hours. This would be about thirty-six hours before our plane was set to leave London.

Judith and I were both suffering from jet lag, so we were awake when the alert came across our iPhone and iPad about 2:30 AM in the morning as we laid in bed.

Neither of us felt we needed to stay for the weekend and not really sure we felt the government in the US wouldn't change their mind and block the UK as well.

Thank goodness American Airlines was able to move us to Friday's flight (same time), and we arrived in Las Vegas about 8:30PM.

We stayed in line a total of maybe fifteen minutes (most of that was a faulty machine that wasn't registering Judith's fingerprints.) The next day (Saturday), we see photos of six-hour lines.

Maybe it was that we came into Las Vegas Internationally? Not too many people visiting Las Vegas last weekend, trust me.

Las Vegas is SHUT DOWN.

I would never have imagined that ALL of the casinos in Nevada would be off-limits, but it has happened.

I live near the Aria, and when I come out of the batcave (our parking for my condo is underground), I saw that Aria had blocked entry into the Aria parking garage. MGM (who owns the Aria) was not messing around when they said they were shutting down the casino and hotel.

So, I went shopping on Monday morning (hungry – that is an important note.) I went to Smith's, but there was a line outside the grocery store.

Pfft, I'm not waiting in line.

I found a Von's store about two miles from Smith's with no wait. I found out later Smith's wasn't full inside, they had merely set up a prudent limitation to something like twenty-five or fifty people.

So, I grab a basket and go inside. Sure enough, no toilet paper, but I did find a couple rolls of paper towels. No meat (a bit of a surprise), but I strolled right on over to the deli, which had plenty of meat on display.

The problem, it seems, is I so rarely order meat from the deli that I do not understand just HOW MUCH a pound of sliced deli meat is. Since Judith does not eat meat (well, she likes seafood), I came home with five packages of deli-meat, all a pound or slightly more.

HO@Y @#IT! How the HELL am I going to eat all of that before it spoils?

I dumped some extra cheese into the freezer, and I have eaten more sandwiches in the last seventy-two hours than I have the last seventy-two days.

This roasted chicken deli meat is delicious. The spicy seasoning not so much.

The only problem for me is, I'm anxious that the meat is going to go rancid. I'm expecting any moment for pounds and pounds of meat to all start smelling.

I think I might need to go check it again. I'll see you next week!

Ad Aeternitatem,

Michael

CONNECT WITH THE AUTHORS

**Michael Anderle Social**
**Website:**
**http://lmbpn.com**

**Email List:**
**http://lmbpn.com/email/**

**Facebook Here:**
https://www.facebook.com/OriceranUniverse/

https://www.facebook.com/TheKurtherianGambitBooks/

https://www.facebook.com/groups/320172985053521/
(Protected by the Damned Facebook Group)

One Crazy Set Of Stories (12)

## SOLDIERS OF FAME AND FORTUNE

Nobody's Fool (1)

Nobody Lives Forever (2)

Nobody Drinks That Much (3)

Nobody Remembers But Us (4)

Ghost Walking (5)

Ghost Talking (6)

Ghost Brawling (7)

Ghost Stalking (8)

Ghost Resurrection (9)

Ghost Adaptation (10)

Ghost Redemption (11)

Ghost Revolution (12)

## THE BOHICA CHRONICLES

Reprobates (1)

Degenerates (2)

Redeemables (3)

Thor (4)

Printed in Poland
by Amazon Fulfillment
Poland Sp. z o.o., Wrocław

58457530R00190